Small Town
BIG CITY

WHEN TIME STOOD STILL

Small Town
BIG CITY

WHEN TIME STOOD STILL

JEFF A. LOPEZ

CITIOFBOOKS, INC.
3736 Eubank NE Suite A1
Albuquerque, NM 87111-3579
www.citiofbooks.com

Hotline: 1 (877) 389-2759
Fax: 1 (505) 930-7244

Ordering Information:
Quantity sales. Special discounts are available on quantity purchases by corporations, associations, and others. For details, contact the publisher at the address above.

Printed in the United States of America.

ISBN-13: Hardcover 978-1-962366-57-1

Library of Congress Control Number: 2023919094

SMALL TOWN BIG CITY

When Time Stood Still
(By: Jeff A. Lopez)

The year was 1963, and the times were changing.The music, the culture and the attitude of the folks who lived in the times. The youngsters were being taught that they are the future of America, the new future business leaders, the new government. The small town folks seemed to be behind in the times, as the pace was by all means a slower environment then the fast pace city lights and city life, of the Big City.

Girls, music, cars and money seem to be the priorities of the teenage boys, and boys, boys and more boys were the driving forces of the teenage girls. The Rock & Roll Revue show is headed to the Big City and it's a chance for the Small Town boys to score some serious points taking their steady girlfriends and a chance for a good date with some new ones, not to mention to score some serious points.

There's just one problem, the parents are 50/50 on the idea of the kids going to the Big City for the Rock & Roll Revue because of an altercation that took place 21 years ago when the small town (South County) guys went to a musical event in the Big City (Midland). You might say it was a clash of cultures that ended in a tragic event. The question is, do next generations hold grudges? Let's just say time never forgets, hopefully people do.

Although the town is small, but the stories within the story are ever so interesting and will keep you fascinated in the overall story. With all the different characters and their story lines you'll be amazed at the situations and drama that can captivate and never be lost in a Small Town.

Cast Members:

Nick Pagani - 21 yr. old ex- tough guy who is an excellent mechanic like his father was (Dominic), and knows everything about cars, trucks, and diesel trucks and tractors and knows his way around them. Nick is cool, somewhat quiet. He is dating his longtime girlfriend of over 3 years Josephine Colletti and one day has plans on marrying her. Nicks father died 10 years ago and his mother (Virginia) lives in New Mexico with her sister and is very ill, being treated for alcoholism. Nick had an older brother (Mark) who mysteriously died at the age of 5 when Nick was 2 years old.

Tommy McCall - The star & stud football quarterback and 3 sport letterman athlete who is on his way to a big time college on a scholarship to play football. He is all around cool and is devoted to his high school sweetheart Maryann Swenson who is a cheerleader and in her junior year. Both come from successful families. Bill McCall (Father) Philys McCall (Mother)

Clendon Flannigan (Moose) Stands 6'3 weighing 260 lbs. is a senior, football stud, but doesn't have the grades for a big college, so he will have to attend a JC temporarily and he is a leather jacket wearing tough guy, who looks like a bully but is the total opposite. The popular smoking tough guy who is everybody's friend, in secret he is referred to as Aly Oop as he refers to many with a nick name as well. He is infatuated with the senior class slutty labeled girl Cindy Allison, but is afraid to make his move because of her reputation, but that is all it is, reputation, but Moose is well liked by Laura, who is waiting on Moose. Moose's mother is single and has 2 younger daughters that are Moose's 12 and 11 year old little sisters. They are a very close family.

Stewart Combs (Stew) The Sophomore class clown that every one picks on but he is o.k. with it as long as he is excepted by the most important and popular group of the high school students and others. Has a tenancy of falling in love with a different girl every week. He's not an athlete, nor a tough guy but is actually a straight A student and very talented, make no mistake about it, outside of his humor the boy can dance and has ambition to become famous one day. Stew's parents (Bob and Susan) are young parents in their mid 30's trying to get financially established. Stew is an only child.

Jimmy Tolan (Red or Red Bird) A bushy red headed friend of Stewart and his co-prankster partner, but very quiet, bright and overall nice kid. Somehow some way knows everything as far news and information on every one and is very close friends with Stew. Jimmy is politically driven by family to one day hold a city or government job. His parents are successful in politics.

Paul and Andrew Styles - Paul a senior and Andrew a junior, both brothers play football, Paul being somewhat of a hot head loud mouth, but people like Moose keep him in check because of a past altercation years earlier and his mouth kind of cooled off.

Andrew more calm, and outgoing also a star baseball player for the high school, with desires to be a DJ like Wolfman Jack only calm and cool and not so rowdy. Their parents are newly self employed business owners struggling to make ends meet. Paul Sr. and his wife Deborah.

Josephine Colletti - 21 years old, the longtime girlfriend of Nick Pagani. Parents are well to do (Joe and Gina). She is in her 3rd year of Law School in college away at the Big City and stays at the dorm to study. Her parents, mainly her mother has been against her dating Nick since their senior year in HS. Her father is somewhat o.k. with it but keeps his opinion to himself and doesn't defend his daughter to not aggravate the wife. Josephine rebels against the mom in defense of Nick and tries to make amends for the relationship. Josephine is an only child to the stay home mom and her local bank president father.

Maryann Swenson - The high spirited junior cheerleader, who is the girlfriend of the high schools top star Tommy McCall. She has big plans on marrying him and he is o.k. with it. Her father (Todd) owns a very successful trucking co. and has big plans for his daughter. Philys (Mother) Maureen 13 year old sister, Tim brother Laura Snyder - Just a plane Jane senior school girl with good grades, who is really infatuated with big Moose. She is always very nice to him, she is a little chunky, not much, but would like to wear the jacket of the big guy.

Although his mind is on the girl with the reputation, she is bold with a goal to land Moose. Very open personality with goals to be a successful business women one day.

Julie Bennett - The new girl in town, well, sort of, her and her mom just moved back into town after being away for the past 15 years. They moved out right after Julie was born and 4 years after her mother's boyfriend and father of her first baby she was carrying (Joann) was tragically killed (Steve). They moved back because Julie's mom (Terry) went through a divorce and moved back to South County to go back to work as a secretary at the elementary school. Julie is very pretty, with a great sense of humor and very respectful, because she was well taught.

Cindy Allison - Her reputation exceeds her, she is a free talking girl, bubble gum chewing boy crazy, but well in control of everything. Rumor has it that she loves to be with different boys and is willing to do anything for them. She doesn't want to be tied down unless it's to a bed post, that's the rumor now. But in reality, she likes to keep the boys dreaming of her.

Mr. Ron Tompkins - A local farmer, who's youngest son would have graduated 2 years ago but was killed in a car accident 3 years ago after getting jumped in the city after a girl set him up. Raymond was a good kid, athlete and popular, but had been drinking that night. After getting jumped, he made his way back to a party in South County and asked Sergio Perez who worked for Tomkins Farms for a ride home because his head was hurting. To this day Sergio feels bad for the death of Raymond Tompkins somewhat feels partially responsible and having trouble dealing with his death.

Old man Celetti - Sal Celitti is the local gas station owner and garage and has been in business for ever, fixing everything for everyone. He has no kids and is married to his wife Sofia for 55 years and ready to retire. He has Jorge an immigrant part time mechanic who pumps gas and fixes flat tires and such, and also employs Nick Pagani. He also emplooyed Nicks dad prior to him dying of liver decease due to being an alcoholic.

Sheriff John Coleman – Long time sheriff of South County area, originally from the Big City Police Department and from the Midland area. He is a tough but law abiding law man with laurels and passion for his job.

Juan Ramirez - 1 year out of school, son of immigrant workers, his father works on Mr. Tompkins farm as a tractor loader and labor, his mother cleans houses and washes & irons clothes for others. Juan has a younger brother a junior in HS, who is very free spirited, named Jesse. It's only Juan that keeps him under control. Below average grades in trouble quite a bit and also a star running back for the high school football team.

Tony Melendez 19, a dropout from high school, had decent grades, good athlete but didn't like taking orders from anyone. He works at Tompkins Farms as a loader and shipping control supervisor. He had a stricked up bringing, but could explode on a dime, his young wife is Marianna Santana 17. Loyal quiet and loves Tony and loves to dance to any type of music.

Arturo Nunez - 1 year out of school, works at the local grocery store, as an all around, bagger, janitor, stocker, has high hopes of going to college when he saves enough money.

Enrique Alvarado (Ricky) a junior, high school running back, very kind, very polite, very liked, also a star baseball players. The other Mexican guys like him they just think he tries to hard to fit in with the white people. Although short in stature, always big in good spirit. Pays no mind to what others think of him.

Alberto Perez, The 22 year older brother of Sergio Perez, very tough, grumpy, thinks the world is out to get him. Likes work but his attitude doesn't get along with anyone.

Mrs. Jean Garrett - The sweet little elder woman who is ever so generous, and bakes pie's.

Rev. Al Williams – Has been the town Reverend, Pastor and Chaplain for 25 years assigned to the South County Community Church. He is well liked and respected by everybody.

Molly Anderson – Is a college graduate and daughter the longtime local financial business owner Don Anderson. Molly has taken over for her father after his death. Molly is a notary public, insurance agent, book keeper and accountant and financial planner for many of the local business owners.

Main Local Establishments:

Howies Burgers

The Malt Shop

Perry's Grocery Market

Maxwell's Pharmacy

Sal's Gas & Garage

Tina's Diner's

Cal County Bank

Goldman's Jewelers

Tompkins Farms

Andersons Financial Services

South County Feed Store

Opening Seen:

At night looking out from the hill top known as Hill Top Point, onto the towns lights, where couples go to make out, 'Oh What A Night' from The Dells is playing on the car radio, and Tommy and Maryann are kissing in Tommy's 1955 Chevy Convertible.

Maryann - I can stay here forever in your arms'... It's such a beautiful night.

Tommy - And I can hold you and kiss you forever, night or day, rain or shine.

Maryann - Can you? (pauses) I mean forever, until we are old and gray?

Tommy - You better believe it. But for now, (Looks at his watch) I gotta get you home so I don't break my streak and disappoint your papa. (Takes his times as finishes some last kisses)

Maryann - Oh come on, we can be 10 or 15 minutes late, it won't kill him...be a rebel, for me.

Tommy - Hey, in 2 years I've never disappointed your folks and I ain't about to start now, I'm going to keep my streak alive and strong.

(Tommy starts the car and checks his watch in the moonlight, as Maryann finds her panties and slips them back on)

Maryann - Well are we going tomorrow or what? I want to go so bad and you don't seem to want to give me an answer.

Tommy - Look, everyone seems to want to go but no one wants to commit unless plenty of us go, you know the safety in numbers thing, so I will have an answer for you in the morning so you'll have plenty of time to get ready.

Maryann – Well I'll have the phone in my room incase you here anything tonight... Oh my goodness I want to go so bad!

Tommy – O.k. I'll call you if I do here anything, you know that.

(As they pull out of the make out area with just his parking lamps on, very slowly)

Maryann – Well what changes from now til morning?

Tommy – I'm going to talk to some guys and see if we can get organized to make this happen or not.

Maryann – What's the big deal anyway? I mean it seems all the parents are more concerned than us, what gives?

Tommy – Oh, I don't know something in the past that seems to haunt the old folks I guess, that incident that happen a life time ago.

Tommy pulls out of Hill Top Point, and the view focus's looking over the city lights zeroing slowly on a home in the country where there is a party going on at the Styles residence, as if the camera were as a set of eyes slowly entering the house, the music plays

'Come On Baby Let The Good Times Roll (Shirley & Lee) - As the eyes walk through the front door, seeing all the talking, singing , dancing and things taking place at this lively party - Andrew Styles talks with 2 girls, looking over records as per their requests – The eyes continues to walk to the kitchen area and stops a few seconds focuses on Paul Styles on the phone, who signals to the person behind the set of eyes to stop a moment, while he finishes up on the phone call.

Paul – (On the phone and tells Stew and Jimmy), 'Hey hold on a second it's for you! ' (*As Stew and Jimmy stop and pay attention, Paul hangs up the phone)* ' It was both your moms, they said it's 3 hours past your bed time, and you guys really need to get home because your fathers are on their way here with the belt!' (*Paul begins to laugh losing his breath and leaning unto the counter, as some girls giggle at Stew and Jimmy)*

Stew - Yea, that's creative and real funny Paul, how come you don't get that creative to bring your grades up from an F- to an F you dip.

Paul - Don't sweat it dork's, I'm just pulling your leg man. (Continues to laugh)

Stew – Yea, yea if you're gonna pull anything it should be your head out of your butt, moron.

Paul – Oh, Oh, come now, I'm sorry boys, I hurt your feelings, cut it out, go ahead, enjoy the party, the kids nursery things are in the garage. (breaks out laughing again)

Stew and Jimmy begin to make their way to the backyard.

Stew - Man I wish I had the nerve to punch that snap case right in the face.

Jimmy - Yea well, it'll take a lot more than nerve believe me.

Stew - Yea I know, (they spot Moose in the backyard) but not for big Moose.

As they made their way to the backyard and see Moose talking to a group of guys - they pause just outside the back door.

Jimmy - Moose won't beat up Paul for us, or for you, for no reason.

Stew - Hey he did it once, kicked his can all up and down the street... remember?

Jimmy - Yea he did, but it wasn't for you. it was because ... Stew - I know, it was because Paul tried capping on Moose and making fun of his name in front of some chicks, I know the whole story man, but you never see that thick head mouthing off any more do ya? No you don't.

Jimmy - So what are you thinking?

Stew - Lets you and I convince Moose that Paul is inside and lip flapping about Moose and we'll watch Moose destroy Paul at his own house, huh?

Jimmy - O.K. so picture this, Moose asks others who saw or heard Paul and no one backs us, and then they tell Moose that Paul played a major prank on us in front of them, and Moose turns loose on us and we spend the weekend in the hospital... no thanks.

Stew - Ahh, you're right, again, I probably would have had many broken bones if I not had you for a friend, (puts his arm around Jimmy) you know that?

Jimmy - Ah, you wouldn't have a friend if you didn't have me period.

Stew – (Stew takes his arm off Jimmy and gives him a slight shove) Oh o.k. another

Red Skelton here, how bout I tell Moose you were mocking his name huh? Yea, wise crack.

Moose - Oh it's Suzy Q and Peggy Sue, What are you girls arguing about now... come on... come on lets kiss and make up (Moose grabs each one by their heads and tries to make them kiss), come on now, this is a party, no fighting especially chick fights. (Moose rubs both Stew's and Jimmy's hair)

Stew - Cut it out Moose, I was just telling Red, that you're not as ugly like he said you are, but you're a handsome fella and you're not dumb either like Red said you are.

Moose - You said that about me Red Bird?

Jimmy begins to back up ready to run.

Jimmy – Not true.

Stew – I'm just jiving you man . . . come on Moose stop man!

As Moose punches Stew on the arm.

Stew - Hey are you going to the City for the Rock & Roll show or what?

Moose - Or what.

Stew - Come on Moose.

Moose - You asked if I was going to the City for the rock & roll show or what, and I said, or what!

Stew - So does that mean you're not going?
Moose - Or what. (shrugs his shoulders)

Stew - Come on Red, let's go, It's obvious Moose didn't get a date either so he's probably gonna stay home and watch Lawrence Welk again.

Moose - Hey! I don't have a problem getting a date you moron, I just can't afford hurting any of the girl's feelings, know what I mean, so I just stay ah unbiased, that's all... Lawrence Welk, that's a good one pin head.

Jimmy - Is that true, are you serious?
Moose - Sure.

Stew - Come on Red, he's clowning, he wishes he can take sin Cindy sin, (Stew runs a short distance as Moose goes to punch his arm again) Oooooh, struck a nerve line huh.

Moose - You know what, you better be glad your fast, cause if I catch you, your gonna pay for that, I promise you.

Jimmy - Hey no disrespect Moose but you been diggin on Cindy for a while now, why don't you ask her to the show?

Moose - Well for one thing I aint got no wheels right now, cause my calaboose is down again, and she's probably got a date already.

Stew – (*From a distance of 20' or so)* - Probably 3 or 4 dates, (laughs) There is always Chunky bottom baby... or perhaps Peggy Sue or Mabeline I heard she ain't doing nothin either tomorrow night.

Jimmy – Nah, that's not what I heard.

Moose – What do ya mean? Come on let's have secret agent man.

As they stare towards the back door as Cindy, Laura and a couple of girls enter the backyard area talking and smoking cigarettes.

Jimmy – Ya, I was talking to her earlier in town and she ask me if I was going, and I said more than likely not... and I asked her if she was going, (pauses)

Moose – Come on what she say?

Stew - (walks back to Moose and Jimmy) - Chee whiz Moose give em a chance to say it.

Jimmy - She just said she wanted to go but she didn't have a ride or a date, but she said she wanted to go real bad that's all.

Moose - Oh wow, wow!

Stew - Now's your chance Moose, hit her up man. Jimmy - Perfect timing Moose, this is fate man.

Moose - Wowsie wow wow!

Stew - Hey what about that new chick, is she coming tonight ? You said she might... Is she coming?

Jimmy - I thought I saw her here. but I...
Stew - Where?

Moose - Oh you're talking about Julie, the new chick per se. Stew - What do you mean new chick per se?

Moose - Yea she use to live here when she was a kid, born but not raised, know what I mean, they moved away.

Jimmy - Yea I heard her mom took a job for the school in the office, so they moved back to town.

Stew - What about the dad, what is he like a professional wrestler or something?

Moose - No he died like before Julie was even born, that's what I heard a long time ago.

Jimmy – No I don't think her dad died, I think it was her older sister's dad who died, he was from here.

Stew - Wow, no dad, I could be her dadio man, Iiiii like it! (spins around and snaps his fingers)

Moose - Sure, but her mom is 6'4" and weighs 280lbs. and is a part time wrestler on the side.

Stew – On the side of what?

Jimmy – Apparently on the side of anything she wants (they alllaugh)

Stew – Hey I want to make my way out front I heard Nick is here and he's got Josephine with him, woo woo woo wooooo! I just love that Josephine... slick chick man.

Moose – Yea he's out front, waiting on Tommy, I had a beer with him a while ago, and yea lean mean Josephine is with him, looking good as usual.

Jimmy – Mean? What do you mean, mean?

Moose – Ahh you know tough looking, you know sharp.

Stew – Ohh man, that chick is hot dadio, Nick is one lucky dude that's all I know.

Jimmy – Ya well Nick is like the coolest of the cool, and those type always get the chicks.

Moose – Hey Jimmy crack corn what about me, ain't I cool?

Stew – No you're...

Moose – Watch it hair brain, you don't want to run into Julie with a fat lip do ya?

Stew – Hey maybe she's in the garage, let's go check!

Moose – Ah you guys go... I'm gonna hang here for a bit.

Jimmy – Come on Moose, what do you got gas again? maybe you'll dance with Cindy Lou and get lucky too.

Stew – Get lucky? He'll get lucky if he even talks to her.

Moose – (As they start to make their way up front) You know I can see that fat lip on you already, I just know it's coming so don't say I didn't warn you.

As they make their way towards the front of the house, Nick and Josephine sitting outside of Nicks 1950 chopped top Mercury, looks black at night, but is deep plum during the day, a real beauty.

Josephine – You know, we could be at your place right now.

Nick – I know, I told the guys I'd stop by for a beer, and some of the girls asked for you earlier this week at the shop and I kinda told them you'd be home this weekend and they said if I could drop by so they could say hi, so we both have a reason to just stop by, right?

Josephine – So why aren't we going in?

Nick - I said we'd stop by, and this is stopping by, not going inside to a high school party, even I have my limitations and standards believe it or not.

Josephine leaning face to face with Nick

Josephine – That's my baby, always thinking of others (kisses him) trying to keep everyone happy (kisses him again)

Tommy pulls up and approaches Nick and Josephine.

Tommy - Hi Josephine (Tommy hugs her) how are you?, good to see you.

Josephine - Hi Tommy, thank you - Where's Maryann?

Tommy – (Points at his watch) Curfew, she was here earlier...

Josephine – Ahh... I missed her.

Tommy – Hey Nick.

Nick – What's shakin Tommy boy?

Tommy - Thanks for waiting, Hey I wanted to talk to you about tomorrow night, you know the Rock & Roll Revue show?

Nick - Yea, yea what about it?

Tommy - You guys going?

Josephine - I want to ...

Nick - I don't know man, you know, it's ah, ah I don't ah

Just then about 5 girls come running out to greet Josephine, hugging her - saying 'You came!, oh my God, how are you? - heywe want to show you something... 'Hi Nick, can we barrow her for a few, please?'

Nick - Yea sure why not ... So long as you bring her back in one piece (*They walk Josephine back to the house, as Josephine looksback at Nick smiling)*

Tommy - I was talking to my dad and ...

Nick - Yea and your dad was talking to Mr. Tomkins and Mr. Tomkins was talking to some of the other dads and they talked to the town counsel and Ron came over earlier today to talk to me.

Tommy - O.K. about?

Nick – (*Nick rubs his stressed neck and sighs)* About this Rock & Roll show.

Tommy - Really! why is Mr. Tomkins going?

(Tommy laughs)

Nick - No, I guess some of the dads have been talking and somehow think it be a good idea for Nick the town mechanic to go with the Rock & Rollers to the rock & roll show in case they need a referee or a nurse or something, I don't know.

Tommy - You mean like a chaperone or baby sitter?

Nick - Nah, I didn't mean sarcastically man, I just, you know, I guess they think I can fix everything man, I don't know (shrugs his shoulders)

Tommy - Me and some of the guys were talking too, but we figured, we'd like to go enjoy the dance & music and stuff but it's not a real comfort knowing if those clowns from the city are ...

Nick - Look man, that was a long time ago, probably half those cats are dead and gone now and life moves on man, it really does, that's what I told old man Celetti & Tomkins, you know.

Tommy - So what was the outcome of the conversation?

Nick - Ahh - I told them I'd talk to Tommy boy & Moose and see if we get this program together, in order, coordinated and planned out militarily, so the parents could feel their babies are safe.

Tommy – O.K.

Nick – It just seems to me that some old timers just keep this fued or whatever you want to call it, alive and just don't let it stop breathing, you know? Just let it die man, leave it go already...

Tommy - So were on ?

Nick - (Sighs and pauses) Yea I guess Tommy boy, were on, o.k.?

Tommy - O.k. Nick my man! how do we do it?

Nick - Look, we're all gonna hook up (looks at his watch) by 6:30pm, right?

Tommy - Right.

Nick - At the shop, gas'ed up, every car checked out well before 6:30, understand?

Tommy – Understood!

Nick - Every car has to be gas'd up Tommy boy, tires checked, radiators full, do you understand? We don't need anybody breaking down or running out of gas man.

Tommy - Yea Yea, I hear ya.

Nick - We line up in order, in a straight line, no one passes, no one up, we get to the city, we do not park in the parking lot, understood?

Tommy - Understood, no parking lot... why not?

Nick - We park on a street together, right? we park on a street lined up facing towards our town, get it? All together.

Tommy - Got it.

Nick - We go together, travel together, we park together, no one separated, everyone parks lined up facing our towns direction, we stay together inside, keep an eye on one another no one leaves out of sight without having someone else with them, when we leave we leave together, get in our cars, make sure everyone's cars start, make sure every car is running and we all leave together following each other the way we left, is the way we come back, Understood Tommy boy?

Tommy - Yea man I sure do, (pauses) hey it sounds like you gave this a lot of thought man?

Nick - Nah, I just thought this is the way it has to be so I don't have to answer to nobody's parents, that's all.

Tommy - Right Nick, you're a good man...

Nick – Ahhh, Remember, you tomorrow get on the phone you and Moose and whoever is going has to be ready to roll by 6:30 in line and on time, it's up to you and Moose to tell everyone, you guys are my sergeant's, you here?, I aint gonna be out there telling no one what to do, I'm telling you and you and Moose spread the jam on the bread, comprende?

Tommy – You're our general done, big Nicky (Tommy runs towards the backyard as Josephine heads back to Nick) I'll see you in the morning at the station

Nick – Yea, yea . . . Hey baby did everything go o.k. in there?

Josephine – Wow, he's happy... Oh yea, just girl stuff you know, bringing back memories, it kind of feels good reminiscing about high school, all the fun, seemed so easy, (pauses) now it's all studying and reading, research and tests and all that legal mumbo jumbo law talk, ughhh (Nicks holds her in his arms)

Nick - Hey, it'll all pay off when you have your degree and license to come back home, to bail me, Tommy, Moose, Stew, Red bird, and probably Los Muchachos all out jail and then represent us as our counsel in court. (Laughs)

Josephine - (Hits Nick on the arm jesting) - Where we going baby? (as Nick holds her)

Nick - To see Los Muchachos, before I get you home. (The seen in the garage captivates their attention as they slowly wonder towards the garage) What's going on now? Let's go say goodbye.

They approach the garage, as Moose, Stew and Jimmy make their way into the garage where the music is hopping. Cindy asks Stew a question.

Cindy - Hey Cool, can you do us a favor and do a number for us?

Before he could answer several of the fellow students, more girls start to shout encouragements to Stew, and applaud him.

(Stew is a little embarrassed)

Stew - What dance? Ah no, no, no,no, no thank you...

Cindy - (Chewing and popping her bubble gum tries to sweet talk him, while Moose looks a little envious) ' Oh come baby, not even for me? (blow's a bubble in his face)

Stew - I didn't even bring my dancin shoes man, I can't dance without my shoes!

Cindy - Pretty please. (blows into his ear)

Stew - No, I can't, I won't... there's nothing you can say or do to convince me otherwise.

Cindy - Pretty, pretty please with a cherry on top?

As Moose and Jimmy look on, Moose a little jealous look on his face

Stew - (Pauses) O.K. but only if you do something for me.

Cindy - I'll do anything for you, (looks around) Well almost anything (Smiles)

Stew - Set me up with the new girl to go to the Rock & Roll show tomorrow night.

Cindy - With Julie… sure no problem, she's been checking you out this past week anyway.

Stew – Really?

Cindy - Yea, cause she's kind of like you and all, cause of her sense of humor and stuff, that's why she digs you dadio.

Stew – You're kidding? - Oh my goodness gracious (Holds his head in disbelief) I can't believe this… me?

Cindy - O.K. dance time. (grab's him leading him towards the center of the garage)

Stew - Wait one more thing . . .

Cindy - Now what?

Stew - (Looks at Moose, as they make eye to eye contact , Stews and Moose's eyes enlarge, back and forth 3 times and gets closer each shot, Moose is breaking out in a sweat)

Moose - (yells out) It's gotta be a superfast song. (Moose looks at Stew and whispers something to him, Stew looks blank, he was going to set Moose up with Cindy)

Cindy - O.K. ,, Listen up, Hey ! listen up, (everything becomes quiet as the music stops) Stewart is gonna cut the rug for us, come Stewie baby, and I bet if we really cheer them on, since they are all here, maybe The Four Stars will do their award winning act for us too!

All party goers yell with their approval. Stew, Jimmy Moose and Andrew look at each other kind of surprised

Andrew - A fast song? O.K. Fred Astaire here we go, Listen to the voice, it's the DJ's choice, Take your stance, here's your chance, hold on to your pants... Dance! (Rockin Robin start's from Bobby Day) Stew dances and tears it up.

After the dance everyone shakes Stews hands and applauds him - Nick and Josephine start to head to Nick's car

Josephine - Man that guy can dance, can't he?

Nick - Yea, that he can, do you wish I could dance like that?

Josephine - I just wish you can dance period. (laughs) wait what's happening now?

Nick – Looks like those guys are gonna do that routine that won them the high school talent contest.

Josephine – I want to see this!

The Four Stars get introduced by Andrew

Andrew – O.K. ladies and gentlemen, boys and girls, live from the Cedar Rd. Auditorium from South County California, The one and only FOUR STARS! – (Lip-sync – Blue Moon from The Marcels/1961)

Josephine – So amazing, that those guys are so talented, I would have never thought of anything like that, it's so cool, right?

Nick - Well that kid is special, no doubt.

Josephine - What do you mean?

Nick - Yea well Stewie Stew Stewart, he gets good grades, I'm talking about Stew, he helps a bunch of other kids with their school work, He's funny, a good sense of humor and he's kinda of a fun guy to have around and he's a great dancer, Don't tell em that I said that cause I don't need him hanging around, you know? (they both laugh) he's the one that put that whole thing together.

Josephine - Well that's awfully nice of you to say that about him.

Nick - Yea, like i said don't tell anybody that I said that, especially him, he'll be like a tick on a hound dog.

Josephine - And you're the hound dog I presume (laughs)

As the Merc drifts off into the night – Back at the party Tommy, Moose, Paul, Andrew, Cindy, Laura, and a handful of boys and girls are listening to Tommy giving the instructions that Nick had told Tommy

Tommy - So again, call who ever isn't here tonight, tomorrow morning, and tell them about the meeting place & time, and have their cars fueled up, tires checked, radiators etc. . . O.k.?

The handful of others separate as the party comes to a slow end

Moose - Man so Nick planned it all out in a flash huh.

Tommy - Yea man, he thought of everything like in a flash, the guy is brilliant.

Laura - So Tommy do you know if anyone needs a ride?

Tommy - Well I think Abbott and Costello over there do. (referring to Stew & Jimmy talking in the garage)

Moose - Yea they been asking everyone for a ride.

Cindy - Well I'm expecting a phone call in the morning from an out of town guy, I'm hoping he can get off work to take me, I hate waiting, but he's so cute he's worth it. (As she's all giggly)

Moose looks disappointed

Laura - How about you Big Guy, need a ride?

As Cindy, Paul and Andrew all walk away

Moose - Well, sure, I was ah gonna see if a Nick could look at my car, but he's been so busy, it's like take a number guy, and you know.

Laura - Hey that's what friends are for, don't you know (As she grabs hold of his arm and walks back to the house)

Stew - Well I guess they all had a meeting and said Make sure no one gives a ride to Stewart or Jimmy huh, that would be uncool.

Jimmy - Ah come on fancy dancer, stop being a baby.

Stew - Yea so Cindy gonna tell what's her name in the morning if she would go with me to the show and what am I gonna do borrow your bike and give her a ride on the handle bars?

I mean I probably would be one of the best dancers there, but no, I'll be the one sittin at home watching Lawrence Welk, what else, with my mom and dad, Oh gosh (grabs his head), I don't believe this.

Jimmy - How cool would it be if we went with Nick and Josephine?

Stew – (Turns around in disbelief) Oh my heavens, have you been drinking?

Jimmy - No, I've been thinking not drinking.

Stew - He'd probably punch us in the face just for thinking of asking him, more less asking him.

Nick gets off his car and walks up towards Juan's garage, where the scene is kind of dark and Ray Charles plays on record player. Juan and his

clique and their girlfriends enjoying the music, some drinks and the calmness of the night, the way their use to

Nick - Amigo's! What's shakin my friends?

The Muchachos – What's up vato - Whats up Nicholas - Hey ese

Juan - Nick, what's up?

Nick - Just in the neighborhood thought I'd stop by and say hello to my amigo's that's all.

Juan - Oh, that's all huh?

Nick - Well ese, actually...

Juan - Oh now the real story, here we go... orale lets here it.

Nick - Actually I come to ask a favor, from my brothers.

Juan - You mean you come calling on the favor I owe you, yes?

Nick - I don't keep score man, do you?

Juan - It all depends ese, who's playing?

Arturo - What you mean, what favor?

Juan - About a month ago, I was over in the City buying some paint for my papa, and a couple of maricons gave me a hard time, so I squared with one of the pendejos, well turns out I guess I was the pendejo and I got jumped from behind by those find folks.

Tony - So what happen?

Juan - Well before things really got carried away, the Lone Ranger here saved the day.

Jesse - Yea, Like the cabarierro on the white horse Nick pulled in and jumped in the rumble and the 2 small towners kicked butt ese.

Sergio - So why we just hearing about this now Holmes?

Juan - Because I asked Nick to keep it under rap, that's why.

Tony - So you mean you didn't want us to know cause you're embarrassed? you didn't think we would go back to mariconville and take care of business and straighten things out or what?

Juan - Nah ese, I knew you would, and that's why I didn't tell you vato's cause I knew you would go against my wishes anyway and start a big pedo over a misunderstanding.

Sergio - A misunderstanding?

Arturo - The misunderstanding? feels like a slap in face holmes.

Juan - Look man, sooner or later we got to realize that we're not kids anymore ese, we don't have to prove the size of our hevos every time we get confronted by someone or some gringo, sabes?

Nick - Look man, it wasn't no big deal, I pulled in just in time and seen that there was 3 against 1, then I realized it was Juan, so I jumped in, and Juan jumped to his feet and we cleaned house, it was over in 30 seconds (Nick shakes Juans hand)

Juan - Orale, that's it, over, no smoke, no fire and we're all here enjoying the evening, right?

The Muchachos all agree, Orale, simon ese, that's right . . .

Juan - Now then how can we help with the favor?

Nick - The Rock & Roll show tomorrow night, you guys going?

Tony - We're thinking about it, why?

Nick - Well some of the parents are concerned over the kids going, you know, some paying too much attention, some saying it's not a big deal anymore and you know...

Juan - So where does Nick fit in and where do we fit in?

Nick - Mr. Tomkins asked me if I would go just to keep an eye out on things, and to make sure we don't let nothing get out of hand, so I ...

Sergio - Yea, he asked me today at work this morning, what I thought about him asking you to go along with the kids, you know, I told him that he should, only because, he tries to be big and tough you know but he's always caring about the kids and people of this town even before Ray died, but it seems like he got more concerned or something after Ray died, you know he's alright in my book.

Nick – Yea Raymond and Ron Jr. are his everything you know, That's cool, I told him I'd get together with Tommy and Moose so they can get the troops in one accord, all together follow the plan you know, But deep down ... I'd feel a hell of alot better knowing the real strength behind this small town was behind me and with us... what you say?

Tony - What do you say baby, wanna go to the dance?

Tony's girl Marianna - You know I'd love it chulo (she backs up)

Tony - You wanna dance? Dance mama.

Marianna dances - Josephine gets out the car and walks up next to Nick, as they watch Marianna tear it up to Ray Charles, I Got A Woman'. Those watching shout encouragement.

Josephine - (When she finishes) Beautiful girl ! (Everyone claps)

Nicks - Looks like you're ready - *said Nick to Tony and shakes hishand*

Tony - So are we taking a vote or just saying yea, cause either way, (kisses Marianna) I'm in ese.

Juan – We're there Nick, I'll come to the shop in the morning to fuel up and we'll talk.

Nick - Right on my home boy (they shake hands and turns and leaves)

Jesse - Hey Josephine?

Josephine - Yea

Jesse - Are you becoming a criminal attorney? cause if you are we have a lot of business for you in the future (Everyone laughs)

Josephine - O.K. good (laughs)

Sergio - Callete hombre, then she's gonna label us ese

Arturo - Orale holmes, we're already labeled like a can of corn ese, (Pause as they watch Nick drive away) We didn't even ask how there snow white party was.

Juan - Are you kidding, Nick wouldn't go to a high school party ese, not with his old lady coming home for the weekend, shoot, I'm surprised he even came up for air... (They all laugh) Who wants another beer?

Orale, right here, I'll have one too ese, hey save one for me, Ima leakit out

Back in Nick's car the radio plays Send Me Some Lovin (Little Richard)

Josephine - Wow, wouldn't that be a sight to see?

Nick – What's that?

Josephine - Stew and Marianna on the dance floor, wouldn't that be neat to see, I mean those are the best 2 dancers I've ever seen.

Nick - Yea you're right that would be something, buy Tony, I ahh, I don't know... (Nicks stomach roars)

Josephine - Was that your stomach? (laughs)

Nick – Yea (grabs his stomach)

Josephine - Oh my God, you haven't eaten huh?

Nick - Yea I had some ...

Josephine - What crackers 2 days ago? You are coming off at my house and I going to fix you a sandwich.

Nick - No that's o.k. I can grab a bite at home.

Josephine – Yea... of what? rotten cheese and molded bread? No you're coming in if I have to scream to wake people up, I will not take no for an answer, and that's all there is too it!

Nick - Ok. Ok... I don't know what's worse, your bite or your mom's bark... either way, it's stressful.

Nick and Josephine arrive at Josephine's house and they sneak in and go to the kitchen to the back of the house

Josephine - (In a whispering voice) Sit down there I'm going to go wash my hands, I'll be right back.

Nick - O.K. are you sure your folks are asleep?

Josephine - Yea they're knock out cold, sit.

(About 15 seconds pass – Josephine's mom walks up to the kitchen entrance with a robe and curlers on)

Nick looks startled

Mrs. Coletti - Huh, did you break in? or...

Nick - No Josephine's washing her hands.

Mrs. Coletti - I don't blame her.

Nick - uhhh O.K. I'll just be on my way.

Josephine walks back in

Josephine - You sit down you're not going anywhere til you eat and you mother you or your sarcasm aren't welcome (Josephine turns on the radio to the song, Mother In-Law)

Nick – Wow, how appropriate, (pause, while he holds his head) bad omen or what (he says to himself)

Mrs. Coletti - Make sure you clean up and throw out the mess (as she looks at Nick)

Josephine - Don't I always?

Mrs. Coletti - Apparently not always. Josephine - Mother please go to bed.

Nick - I don't know if I'm gonna be able to hold that sandwich down after that.

Josephine - You know what's amazing to me? Nick – What's that?

Josephine - You're supposed to be this leather wearing jacket tough guy who everybody respects and likes cause you're nice yet tough and you fight with the best cause you are the best, and yet my mother intimidates you like... a cat to a mouse.

Nick – More like the devil to a little kid (they both laugh as Nick bites into his sandwhich)

And the Friday night comes to an end

Saturday morning starts out with the rising sun early in the morning with most still sleeping. A couple of vehicles travel the roads. The Garage door opens up as Nick prepares to get things started at work. He walks up to the radio and turns it on too Ya Ya / Lee Dorsey. He starts up a car in the garage and backs it out to the open area, when Mrs. Garett pulls in to the front area of the garage

Mrs. Garett - Good morning Nick ... How are you this early morning?

Nick - Hey, good morning to you Mrs. Garett, I'm doing good how about you?

Mrs. Garett - I knew you'd be here so I thought I'd bring this tractor down here early before Mr. Garett gets up.

Nick - Oh did he give a tune up again? (laughs)

Mrs. Garett - Yes he did... it was running good and I guess he felt it was time to make run bad, I guess.

Nick – O.k. let me pop the hood here and we'll see just how bad things are... hit the gas Mrs. Garett ... (vroom vroom) O.K. that's good, shut her off for a minute. O.k. let me take this off (removes carburetor cover) O.K. let me put this here and this one over here and tighten this up a little - (pause 5 sec) O.K. Mrs. Garett fire her up, O.k. hold it (adjusts the carburetor and puts the cover back on) - O.k. rev it up (vroom vroom) There you go as good as new.

Mrs. Garett - Oh dear, you're just as good as your daddy only more handsome. Here sweetie, what do I owe you?

Nick - Oh no, Mrs. Garett you don't owe me anything, I can't charge you for 1 minute worth of work, it's no big deal, really.

Mrs. - Oh Nicky, you're exactly like your father, always giving and doing things for others.

Nick - Yea I hear that quite often Mrs. Garett and I still appreciate it... and things like this, gives a good reason for you to come see me.

Mrs. Garett - I'll tell you what, I have some fresh apple pie's baking right now, I'm going to bring you one as soon as their done and cooled off.

Nick - O.K. now that I'm going to hold you too (points at her with a big smile)

Mrs. Garett - Thank you so much Nicky, I'll be bye a little later.

Nick - O.K. Mrs. Garett, you have yourself a great day, (as she drives off he say's) and don't tell Mr. Garett you came here.

While Mrs. Garett drives off and waves bye to Nick and hi to Juan, as Juan pulled up to the gas pump. Nick walks towards Juan

Juan – Is that your date for tonight?

Nick – You know it, she makes a mean apple pie.

Juan – Yea, what about cherry pie? That's my favorite ese.

Nick – I would imagine she can bake and cook anything great.

Juan – You know when I was about 12, her old man busted me breaking into his daughters car.

Nick – Oh yea?

Juan – Yea, ese and you know what?, he asked me why I was trying to break in the car.

Nick – (Laugh's)And what did you tell him?

Juan – I told him I wanted to buy lunch at school this coming week, because they were going to have hamburgers and hotdogs all week long.

Nick – What did he do when you told him that?

Juan – He said he wouldn't tell my parents if I did some work around his yard for 1 hour.

Nick – Really? And did you?

Juan – Yea man, my butt couldn't afford for my dad to find out.

Nick – So did you work the whole hour?

Juan – Yea man, I picked apples and peaches and berries, I filled up 5 baskets of fruit aye, and she send me home with 2 pies and Mr. Garett gave me a dollar for lunch for the next 2 weeks man.

Nick – Wow, that is super cool Juan, they are really good people.

Juan – Yea, (pauses) so anyway Nick what time again are you guys leaving?

Nick – We blast off at 6:30, where there by 7, parked, paid and ready to rock & roll, I guess.

Juan – O.K. ese, fill'er up with 2 dollars holmes.

Nick – Is that American money?

Juan – No man it's peso's from home aye (They both laugh)

Tina's Diner where some of the men are having breakfast and coffee

Mr. Tomkins - Thank you Connie, (Connie, one of Tina's daughters, just pours Mr. Tomkins a cup of coffee) So it looks like a go huh? For the kid's?

Mr. McCall (Bill, Tommy's father) – I believe it's a go, yea.

Todd Swenson (Todd, Maryann's father) – I know Maryann is all jumping for Joy, last night about midnight, Tommy called her with how Nick said their going to do this and boy oh boy was she in 7th heaven.

Bill - Wow... I'd say she's looking forward to it.

Mr. Ron Tomkins – Yea well, I still have my reservations on it but, I feel a lot more relaxed knowing Nick is going with them.

Bill – Sure, even Tommy was reluctant about going without Nick, I guess because of his reputation in both places, I would imagine.

Sheriff John Coleman – (Steps and pays for his coffee to Connie) Couldn't help over hearing you fellows.

All 3 say 'Good morning John, Morning Sheriff, Good morning

Sheriff Coleman - Good morning guys, you know Nick was involved in a little altercation a few weeks back in the City with a few rough housers, are you guys aware of that?

Todd – No we weren't aware of that!

Ron – I heard something about a little squabble over Juan I believe, right John?

Sheriff – Yea, Juan Ramirez.

Bill – Well what happen?

Ron – From what Sal told me, I guess Nick had gone to pick up some paint for some cars and ah, he pulls in the parking lot at Millers Hardware and sees a fight going on, where 3 guys are putting the boots to one guy and that guy was Juan, so Nicky got off and jumped in and I guess Juan was playing possum and jumped to his feet and both him and Nick really put it to those 3 guys.

Sheriff – Yea that's about what I heard also, except I got a call from Capt. Billings and he said that Juan started name callin and somewhat instigated the altercation, and I guess one of the boys suffered a severe broken nose when all was said and done.

Todd – Well there is going to be a lot of kids there, I guess the question would be, do you think they'll be noticed?

Sheriff – Well I know Nick and our boys will blend in.

Ron – And Juan and the Muchachos will be noticed, right?

Sheriff – (Turns hands upwards) Are they even going?

Bill – I don't know, I wouldn't think so, is that even their type of music?

Ron – Their young people Bill, what do you think, they love that rock & roll stuff… but I haven't heard anything about them going.

Sheriff – Well you guys a have a good one (Sheriff leaves)

Todd – Hey John? Why would Juan instigate a fight with 3 other guys?, it doesn't make sense, the odds weren't in his favor (sip's his coffee)

Sheriff – That's the question I raised to Billings… you know after talking to Nick it was actually Sal that was going to go and at the last minute he sent Nick, I bet Juan appreciated that (shrugs his shoulders and leaves)

Ron – Lucky for Juan it wasn't Sal huh?

Just then the Reverend Al Williams passes to pay his bill

Rev. Williams – Good morning gentlemen!

All – Good morning Reverend, How are you?

Rev. – I'm just dandy… did you have a nice breakfast this morning?

Ron – We sure did, I imagine, just like the other 800 breakfasts we've had here, we're all still alive.

Rev – Well that alone gives us all a reason to be grateful right? You gentleman have yourself a wonderful day now (as he pays Tina for his breakfast and leaves) Thank you dear, it was wonderful as always.

Tina – Thank you Reverend Williams, we'll see you after church tomorrow... bye bye!

Ron – Tina... (raises his cup) one more sweetheart, that ought to get it going and hopefully keep it going.

Tina – Well I certainly hope you're talking about your heart Ron (they all brake out laughing)

Back at the gas station

Nick is working inside the engine compartment of a car when he notices Mr. & Mrs. Sal Celetti pulling in (The Owners of the service station)

Nick – (Approaches the Celetti's, greets Mrs. With a hug) Hello Mrs. Celetti, If I knew you were coming, I would have made some coffee.

Mrs. Celetti – Oh Nicky, you don't have to trouble yourself for me.

Nick – Trouble, no trouble, you might have trouble swallowing the coffee, that be the only trouble. (laugh's)

Sal – Ahh, Nick gotta a minute, the Mrs. and I would like to talk to you.

Nick – Sure thing Mr. Celetti, let me shut this off. (shuts radio off, looks concerned) Well, you guys look pretty serious.

They all sit down in the office area

Sal – (pauses a bit) Look Nick, I ah, I've made a decision Nick to call it (Pauses to hold back tears)

Mrs. Celetti – What he's is trying to say Nick, is that Sal is gonna retire, we've both decided it's time.

Nick – Hey that's great, right, I mean this is what you worked for all your life right, to finally toss in all the marbles and cash in and take it easy right?

Sal – Yea son, that about boils it down, but you'll see yourself when you're use to the same routine every day, day in and day out for the last 52 years it's kind of hard to just wake up one morning and do something different, you'll see one of these days.

Nick – Hey Mr. C that's great, so do you want me to run things around here for you, I could do it.

Mrs. Celetti – No Nicky, he's retiring and pulling out completely, no more, the only time he'll or we'll come here is to get gas or our car worked on as customers.

Nick – So what are you going to do with the station & shop?

Mrs. Celetti – We're going to sell it Nick.

Sal – Yea I think you know the person I'm selling it to.

Nick – Who's that?

Mrs. Celetti – We want to sell it to you Nick.

Nick – Me? I don't know any...

Sal – Now hold Nick, I've been waiting for this day for the last 3 years, look, you are the best mechanic undoubtedly for a hundred mile radius, and everyone knows that, you've boughten used cars and have fixed them up from bumper to bumper, haven't you?, and you paid your mama's house off with the profits, right? Now you're here 20 hours a day it seems, you come in on weekends to keep the cars coming in and out and everyone appreciates you son like you don't really realize. So I couldn't think of anyone better to sell it to.

Nick – That's great and all and I appreciate the consideration and offer and all really I do, but ah, I don't have the money or means to buy this place off of you Mr. & Mrs C, but appre...

Mrs. Celetti – You know Nick, so many of the men from this town told Mr. Celetti that they would c0-sign for a loan for you and even Todd Swenson said he would give you a private loan for the value of the business and property.

Nick – Yea but, He did?, wow ...

Sal – Look even Josephine's dad Joe Coletti said he would approve a loan down at the bank for you because he knows how valuable you are to this community, it wouldn't be a problem at all.

Nick – I only got like $100.00 in the bank. $116.52 to be exact and about $60.00 at home, what would you be selling the place for?

Mrs. Celetti – Sal wanted to sell it to you for 5 and I told him no way, are you crazy?

Nick - $5000.00?

Mrs. Celetti – No $5.00, but he's pazzesco (crazy), looney, bonkers...

Sal - O.K. Sofie I think he gets your drift.

Mrs. Celetti – We want to sell you the business for $1.00

Nick - $1.00? $1.00 dollar?

Sal – Yea but if you want the property it's gonna cost another $1.00

Nick $1.00 more for the property?

Sal – And you know how I've been telling you that the County has been after me to sell them...

Nick – The lot next door, yea...

Sal – Well, I'm going to sell that to you also, so you can put your used car lot there and sell the best used cars in the state Nicky, also for another $1.00

Nick – I feel like I'm dreaming, I really do...

Mrs. Celetti – You know Nicky, we talked about this same deal with your father, but we never got the chance to present it to him, and we didn't want to lose you to a big company, so we thought, it looks like everything has fallen into place.

Nick – What about Jorge?

Sal – Hey that's your employee now, not mine.

Nick – Wow, Mr. and Mrs. C I don't know what to say, this is the biggest day of my life.

Mrs. Celetti – So far, and they'll only get bigger, your wedding, your children being born, and stuff like that.

Nick – So when does this all happen?

Just then Mr. Tomkins pulls in to gas up

Sal – Hey Ron, can you gas up yourself?

Mr. Tomkins – Sure thing Sal.

Sal – I'm having all the papers drawn up right now through my lawyer, and we'll have him here Monday a long with Molly here to notarize everything.

Nick – O.K. I still can't believe this is all happening, wow!

Sal – You know Nicky, I've had Molly for the last 3 years keeping my books and in the last 3 years I have never been so organized, I swear that girl knows her stuff especially taxes and write offs, I recommend you stay with her, as a matter of fact she'll be here in a bit to get some personal information from you for the paper work.

Mrs. Oh Nicky, I'm so happy for you, you are going to grow this business bigger than ever and you're going to be so successful and really impress those other Italians (she places her finger over her lips, Shhhh)

Sal – That's right, Son, you'll be making dollars per dollars if not more, than that attorney wife of yours when you guys marry (winks at him) Order your new sign... Nicks Gas & Garage!

Nick – No way Mr. C, it stay's Sals Gas & Garage.

Sal – I appreciate it son (As he walks out to greet Mr. Tompins at the pump, Nick walks Mrs. C to their car) Hello Ron!

Mr. Tomkins – Sal... so did you break the news to him?

Sal – Sure did, thought I was going to have to call an ambulance (they both laugh)

Tomkins – Well I'm sure happy for him, that boy deserves it.

Sal – That he does.

Moose picking up Laura's car, to fuel up and check out the rest of the car for the trip to the Big City. Moose is already in and sitting behind the wheel

Laura – O.k. big guy, I think you're all set, you're going to put $3.00 dollars of regular, and the ...

Moose – The water, the air in the tires and all the lights to make sure there in working order.

At that point Laura gets brave and leans on the driver's side window with some cleavage showing

Laura – Are you going to look under the hood? (smiles)

Moose – (Moose's eyes about to pop out of his eye sockets) If you want, I mean yea sure, I'll look, I mean I'll check, sure thing.

Laura – O.k. big guy, I didn't mean to startle you, but if you're good I'll have you check under my hood too.

Moose – I'll be back, (starts to back out and puts it in drive and stops) Hey Laura...

Laura – Yea

Moose – And I'll be good too (smiles and so does she and he drives away)

At the garage, Stew and Jimmy are standing quietly as Nick is busy inside the engine compartment of a car

Nick – (With his head inside working on the car) I know you guys are standing there, and I know you've been there for the last 3 minutes.

Stew – How did you know that? The car is running, the radio is on and we never even made a sound.

Nick – (Nick pulls up out of the car) Hand me the rag will ya?

Jimmy – Sure, here you go.

Stew – How did you know Nick?

Nick – How did I know? You wanna know how I knew you guys were standing there?

Stew – Yea, I really do, we really do.

Nick – Because all day long I smell gas, oil, air from the air compressor, car's overheating, engines burning and exhaust systems blowing black smoke and then a couple of time a month my baby comes home from school and I hold her a smell her outrageous perfume that drives me crazy... mmm.

Stew – So that doesn't answer my question.

Nick – Then you jokers walk in here with that cheap cologne that could start on fire at any minute and you ask how I know it was you, because you are the only 2 guys that don't think that pee mix doesn't smell bad man.

Jimmy – I told you it stunk.

Stew – Hey my grandfather gave me this just before he died.

Nick – Yea well, I bet that's why he died... just saying man.

Stew – Hey look Nick (As nick leans back into the engine area) ahh, Jimmy here wants to ask you something.

(Jimmy looks scared and shocked)

Jimmy – You said you were gonna ask him.

Nick – What's up Red?

Stew – Ah Nick...

Nick – Yea. Who's asking you or Red?

Stew – Ah, I guess I am... ah, hey we were wondering if ah, if ah, we were, ah if you and Josephine were going to the Rock & Roll show tonight?

Nick – Yea, I kind of got, ah, you can say I ah... Yea why?

Stew – Well Jimmy and I were wondering if ah, if ah, we ah ...*Nick pop's back up out of the engine area*

Nick – No, (curious) no, no way, are you guys gonna ask me if you can go with us?, like to the show, are you guys asking for a ride?

Stew – (With a big smile) Yea, you got it (Jimmy half smiling)

Nick – Come on guys, you can't be serious man, I…

Jimmy – Come on Stew, let's go, tell him we were just joking.

Nick – Yea tell me you were, please!

Stew – Oh come on Nick, you are like the coolest guy man, everybody knows that, and who are we?, man we are the laughing stock of the school, of the town, of the County and heck by tonight or tomorrow morning we'll be the laughing stock of the state, come on, what do you say Nick, please, this here would make our life, up to this point…come on Nick…please!

Nick – I don't believe this… no one else asked you guys?

Jimmy – We asked everybody but our parents and grandparents, and no one even asked us, they like already had their cars full yet nobody even new they were going actually til this morning really.

Nick – (Walks around by the car) O.k. look man… I can't even believe I'm even considering this but …

Stew – Do you have any idea how cool we would look, huh? if we rode with you

Nick, uh, do ya?, We would look so cool as well, just because we're with you and Josephine, man, they would start treating us like normal human beings man, I mean we would be excepted like part of the in crowd man.

Nick – Look man, I ain't promising nothin, you hear? nothing am I promising... I will ask Josephine, I will tell her that you guys need a ride, and if she says yes, it's yes, and if she's says no, than it's no, got it? comprende, comprende muy beuno?

Stew and Jimmy agree, and start to thank Nick for even considering taking them, they run out of the gas station area towards town

Moose pulls into the station in Laura's car to gas up

Nick – (Nick approaches the car) Well, look it here.

Moose – Hey Nick.

Nick – A new car for you?

Moose – No... no this is Laura's, remember chunky bottom?

Nick – Yea sure, I thought it was hers.

Moose – Well I discovered something else to just now.

Nick – What's that?

Moose – She's also got a chunky top... man oh man!

Nick – Yea well she's just like her big sister, and I do mean big sister, remember Lily?

Moose – Oh yea, what ever happened to her anyway?

Nick – Ah she went away to school and met some rich dude, and married him and from what I hear, she's doing quite well and has a couple of kids.

Moose – Wow, really? She was older than you right?

Nick – Yea a couple years, but wow what a looker, as a matter of fact, she was best friends with Molly, you know Molly Anderson?

Moose – Oh heck yea, man, sometimes I drive by her office just to get a glance of her through the window, man what a doll, huh?

Nick – Yea she is too, but those 2 use to drive all the guys in this town bananas, man, as matter of fact, Molly is supposed to be here later today to pick up some information from me.

Moose – Really, chee wiz Nick I might have to stick around for a while to make sure things go o.k. for you buddy (laughs)

Nick – O.k. Moose sure thing... So what's up with the ride?

Moose – Gasing up for the this evening.

Nick – Oh O.k. you want me to check under the hood?

Moose – No it's cool Nick, I'll gas it and I'll check it out, you can go back to whatever it was you're doing man, I got it.

Nick – O.k. you just want to reminisce when you use to work here huh?

Moose – Yea, Saturdays and after school 3 days a week, those were the day's... I always use tell myself... one of these day's I'm going to own this fine establishment.

Nick – Really, I never knew that, maybe I'll sell it to you one of these day's (they both laugh)

Tommy's house, as he rolls up the water hose and puts some tools away, his father arrives at home and see's that Tommy just mowed and cleaned up the yard and finishes washing his car

Bill McCall – Hey son!

Tommy – Hi dad!

Todd – Well thank you for the nice job son...

Tommy – Your welcome.

Bill – Getting her all cleaned up for tonight?

Tommy – Yep, I don't why, with the dusty roads going to the city, It'll be all dirty before we even get there.

Bill - Yea it's been like that forever and a day son, (pauses a bit) I ah, would imagine you guys have a safe plan for tonight, right?

Tommy – We sure do, man Nick just ran it down to me and he said it was militarily, you know like the military, a commander or something, but it is a pretty solid and well organized plan.

Bill – Yea well that's good, Nick is very intelligent young man, both street smart and school smart, he's done well considering he pretty much raised himself.

Tommy – Yea dad, he is a special guy, to everyone it seems, speaking of which, I need to go and fuel up and get the final detail from my general (salutes his father) May I be excused sir?

Bill – (laughs) You may private (salutes back)

Sheriff John Coleman cruises by the Big City police department in his personal car, observing the scene for his personal purpose. He spots a police officer talking to Capt. Billings out back of the station. The back lot is a parking lot for police cars and vehicles that had been towed in for violations. On the back line are the bigger vehicles like flatbed trucks and farming trucks etc... He see's another gentleman showing some teenagers those bigger trucks on the back line

Officer – All set Captain, all the security is set for tonight.

Capt. Billings – Good Mike, that's great, it's been a long time.

Officer Mike – That it has sir… that it has.

Laura's house, Laura is on the phone with Cindy

Laura - Oh sure, no problem girl, you are more than welcome, as long as you keep your hands off of the big guy, or I'll have to handcuff you in the back seat.

Laura - Oh that's nothing new, you've been there before huh? (laughs) Yea I can pick you up, is Julie going?

Laura - Yea that's no problem have her there at your place and I'll be there about 6… o.k. see you then.

Out front of Tomkins Farms warehouse loading docks where Juan and Tony are talking

Juan – Yea I gas'd up already.

Tony – Well I'm getting off in about an hour, I been here since 6 ese, The old man's son Junior called me at 5 this morning and asked me if I can come in at 6 to help with a big load for Tomkins going out of town tomorrow, he should of just said, hey menso come in and unload this truck all by yourself, and then load up the same one for Tomkins all by yourself.

Juan – Relax ese, one of these day's you're gonna own this place and then you just hire nothing but gringo's to labor, orale.

Tony – Shoot I'll go broke holmes, I'm going to the border to get my labor and quadruple this business (they shake hands)

Juan – Simon ese (When they notice a new corvette drive by and rev the engine as the 2 riders look at Juan and Tony)

Tony – Who the...

Juan – That looks like one the guys who jumped me last month.

Tony – Lets go get em!

Juan – Shoot ese we'd need a rocket to catch that ranfla.

Tony – So we riding out with Nick's army? Or que?

Juan – Ahh first I gonna talk to the old man, he called me this morning and asked me to come down, hopefully he's gonna give me a raise or something, ahhh

Tony – Te va dar un raise alright... the middle finger ese... O.k. let me know, I still have to wash my car ese... hey pongase trucha ese, Old man Tomkins has his business face on, he's already here aye esta in his office.

Juan – Later holmes... we'll talk.

The Malt Shop where Stew and Jimmy are sitting in a booth talking, as they wait for Nick's answer

Jimmy – (As they drink a soda in a glass of ice) So let's play the what if game...

Stew – O.K. play!

Jimmy – What if Nick tells us that queen Josephine said no...

Stew – Then I guess it's all about Lawrence Welk right?

Jimmy – What if Nick says, yes we can go with them and Cindy sets you up with...

Stew – What's her name? do you mean what's her name? I forgot all about that, Oh man I hope to goodness that she too forgot about that.

Just then someone walks up to the Juke Box and put's on a song and at the same time Julie walks in and Jimmy tells Stew turn around – The song 'What's Your Name' starts, as Julie and Stew make eye contact in slow motion for about 15 seconds

Stew – Oh my, heavens and everything there is good.

Jimmy – Put your tongue back in Stew.

Stew – Oh no, do you realize what is about to take place?

Jimmy – Yea, she's going to come over here and thank you for inviting her to the Rock & Roll Revue show.

Stew – No, I mean before that...

Jimmy – What?

Stew – I'm gonna pee my pants, in a state of shock because I have no feeling below the waste.

Jimmy – Well grab your shock because here she comes.

Julie slides in the booth right next to Stew

Julie – Hi guys, how are you? (with a big happy smile)

Jimmy – Hi Julie...

Stew – Ha, hillo, ah hello (takes a big swallow)

Julie – Hey Cindy called me this morning and told me I won a date with the best dancer in the County, for tonight for the Rock & Roll show and that I would find him here at the Malt Shop (As she looks around) Cindy said he's a fine looking cat, and I should recognize him real easy!

Stew – Oh I don't see anybody in here that dances good.

Julie – You don't think Cindy would have lied to me do ya?

Jimmy – Oh, no, not Cindy.

Julie – Stewie, do think she'd lie to me?, I really want to go tonight.

Stew – Well, I've known Cindy since I was 5 years old, and yes I have known her to bend, stretch and even twist the truth from time to time.

Julie – Wow, bend, stretch and twist, that sounds like a new dance to me.

Jimmy – Huh huh, that's funny!

Julie – Stew, being that I can't find this so called best dancer guy, will you take me to the show tonight in the Big City?

Stew – Julie, what a beautiful name by the way, it fit's you perfectly, I asked Cindy last night at the party to ask if you'd go with me to the show tonight, if I danced at the party to Rockin Robin…

Julie – So it was you?, you're the one who everybody said danced your butt off for me (looked upset, but playing it)

Stew – I didn't want to dance, and they wanted me too and Cindy trying to be all sexy said she would do anything for me, so I sad set me up with the new girl and she agreed, so I danced!

Julie – And so here I am, your reward in the flesh!

Stew – So you knew it was me?

Julie – Sure silly, Cindy told me, and I was thrilled! (she hugs Stew's arm with excitement yet gentleness)

Jimmy gives Stew the thumbs up – Scene moves outside the Malt Shop as Stew, Julie and Jimmy all walk out

Julie – O.K. so if Nick and Josephine is it?,

Stew – Yea

Julie – So if they say no, we all cram in Laura's car, If they say yes, then you guy's ride there with them and I'll go with Laura anyway.

Jimmy – O.k!

Stew – Wow, you are really smart on top of beautiful, huh huh

Julie – Silly.

Just as they finish their conversation another newer model vehicle drives by slow with 4 guys and all wave as 1 guy yells out, 'Hi girls' and all in the car begin to laugh'

Nick's garage, where Molly Anderson is finishing up some information from Nick. Moose, Tommy and Nick are inside the office area staring at Molly as she writes and Paul and Andrew are putting gas in their car while 2 others wait. As Molly is writing down information, she has her legs crossed, wearing skin tight pants, and dangling her shoe, and Moose's eyes are glued to her, when Nick signals with his eyes

to Tommy to look at Moose and Tommy gently back hands Moose on the chest to wake him

Molly – And again, that's 518 Pioneer Dr. right?

Nick – Yes mam.

Molly – (*Molly looks up at Nick)* Hey, don't call me mam, that makes me feel old (smiles)

Nick – Oh, sorry.

Molly – I'm only 3 years older than you... do you feel old?

Nick – It all depends what day of the week you ask me.

Molly – (Laughs) yea, you got that right.

Moose – How old are you Molly?

Tommy – Hey Moose, you never ask a woman that, unless their young.

Nick - Ohh, Tommy!

Molly – (laughs) Hey what are you trying to say?

Tommy – No I didn't mean like that...

Nick – Hey Tommy, why don't you and Moose go into the garage and give each other a tune-up… boy, not scoring well my friends.

Moose – How do you compliment an older lady?

Molly – Ooohhh, my goodness I better leave while I still have some confidence left (continues to laugh)

Nick – Aye, you guys have done enough damage already to this beautiful young vibrant and obvious intelligent business owner, who just so happens to be my accountant and tax person, So…

Molly – Nah, that's o.k. it's all in fun guys!

Nick – Excuse me for being so unhospitable, would you like a piece of pie?

Molly – Ohh it looks good but, I'm watching my waist line.

Moose – I'll bet a lot of guys are too.

Tommy – Yea you're one of them.

Nick – O.K. kids let's not…

Molly – Is that one of Mrs. Garett's pies?

Nick – Sure is!

Molly – Well ah, I'll take a piece for later if you don't mind?

Nick – Oh heck no, I don't mind.

Moose – You know what they say where it goes right?

Tommy – Ahh Moose let me show you something out here (*pushes Moose outside towards Paul and Andrew)*

Nick – Now that's much better, I'm sorry about these 2 guys, you know...

Molly – Hey no need to apologize Nick, they're just trying to establish themselves, we were there once.

Nick – Yea well hey, I appreciate all you're doing and I...

Molly – Let's just look forward to a long lasting business relationship, huh? We're the new generation of this town, in a few years we'll be the force, the new business people making all the decisions... right?

Nick – Heck yea, you got it!

Molly – Mr. Celitti told me about some of the idea's you have for the station and the garage, but he didn't want you to implement them until you took over, and he asked me if I would help with my marketing degree as well, and I said sure, no problem, but it would be Nicks call right, and he agreed.

Nick – He told you some of my ideas?

Molly – Yea why?, were they top secret?

Nick – No, no what I mean is, that I thought he thought they were dumb and useless and here he...

Molly – He's anxious for you to take over to put those ideas to work and grow this business plus your used car's as well, and who knows, about that idea of opening up something in the City, huh? We'll do it, I'm here for you Nick!

Nick – Well O.K. then, I'm here too, here's your pie.

Nick and Molly laugh and hug to begin their new business relationship

Molly – See you Monday morn (Good Golly Miss Molly starts to play by Little Richard)

Nick – I'll be here bright and early!

Molly walks to her car parked on the side of the garage as Moose, Tommy, Paul and Andrew watch her shake that thing, Moose bites his palm, Tommy and Paul looked turned on and Andrew looks like he is in a trans, Nick starring at them shaking his head with a smile

Molly pulls out of the gas station and travels through the city, passes by the Malt Shop where kids enjoy their drinks and food, passes by the grocery store, pharmacy, Howie's Burgers, passes through some of the neighborhood's showing guy's washing their car's, back to the city passes by the feed store and packing and loading dock where Mr. Tomkins is chatting with Alberto, shows truck leaving out with loads and follows Molly into the jewelry store to pick up a watch she had engraved for Nick, as the song 'Good Golly Miss Molly' comes to an end, back to the Gas station where Nick is closing up about 4 p.m.

Stew's house, he is asking permission to go to the Rock & Roll show tonight

Stew – (Comes in the back door into the kitchen where mom is cleaning) Hey mom what's cookin good lookin?

Stews mom (Susan) – And where have you been, my little friend? You see I to can make a rhyme from time to time.

Stew – Yea maybe, but it ain't cool when it comes from an old person mom.

Susan – Hey you watch your mouth young man, I'm not old I'm in my perfect years at this stage of my life, you remember when you're 36 and you'll see, you'll still be feeling good and filled with energy!

Stew – (Looks through the door way into the living room where his father is asleep on the couch with his t-shirt raised up, his glasses falling off his nose and a newspaper on his chest) Yea like dad over here filled with energy...

Susan – Your father works hard all week long, he deserves to relax for all his valuable efforts, you remember that too, you'll see one day.

Stew – Hey mom did you and dad ever go out on dates back in the dinosaur days?

Susan – Sure we... hey there you go again with the old folk jokes (throws a kitchen towel at Stew)

Stew – I'm just playing, it was perfect timing that's all… but did you guys?

Susan – Yea we would go to dance recitals and dances, we would go to the movies and picnics… why?

Stew – Well I don't know if you know this or not but all the young people are going to the Rock & Roll show tonight in the big city and I want to go mom, everybody is going and I don't want to stay behind… can I go?

Susan – Well I don't know Stewie, that's going to cost money and gas to get there and…

Stew – No mom, don't worry about the gas, I'm hitchin a ride that's already taking care of, I might need a few smacks to get in and buy a soda but can I go,please?

Susan – Well it's o.k. with me, but you're going to have to clear it with your father over there.

Stew – Thanks mom, I'll check with Mr. Energy over here (Stew quietly tip toes by his father, sits on the coffee table right across from him) Pops, Pops… (father continues to snore a bit) Ohh pops? Pops! (shakes him awake, he's startled) Sorry Pops…

Stews dad (Bob) – Oh hey son…

Stew – Are you awake?

Bob – Yea sure, thanks (as he lays there with his eyes closed)

Stew – Pops can I go to the Rock & Roll show tonight in the Big City?

Bob – Yea sure son (with his eyes closed)

Stew – Thanks pops! (starts to walk away and stops to ask another question) Oh by the way… can I have a few dollars for some sodas for me and my date?

Stews dad – (still with his eyes closed as he lays on the couch) Sure son, no problem.

Stew – (Turns to walk away but instead turns back again to ask another question) Pops?

Stews dad – (groggy) yea son,,,

Stew – Can I barrow the car?

Stews dad – Sure son, no problem.

Stew – (With a loud voice) Aww man pops, you haven't heard a word I've said have you?

Bob – Uhhh, what happen? (As he sits up wiping his eyes) Whats going on son?

Stew – Oh nothing, I've been here wasting my time talking to a half dead man, that's all!

Bob – Look, Stewie I've heard everything you said (yawns and scratches his head) and no you can't barrow the car, and yes you can go and yes you can have a couple of bucks for some soda's for you and your date, how's that for listening?

Stew – Chee dad, and here I was beginning to think you were in a coma, but thanks pops (turns to walk away)

Bob– Ah ah ah! Not so fast young man...

Stew – What?

Bob – First of all, what date? Who is your date?

Stew – Oh her name is Julie, Julie Bennett, she's a new girl... sort of, can you believe it?

Bob – No I can't ... Honey?

Susan – Yea!

Bob – Can you come in here please?

Susan – Yea what's up?

Bob – Did you know our son has a date... with a girl?

Susan – Really? No I didn't know, how come you didn't tell me that?

Stew – Come on mom, that's something us men talk about, that's something guys talk to about with their dads, not their moms.

Susan – Who said? Why can't you talk about it with your mom?

Bob – Ah, honey, ask him who is date is with...dear.

Susan – And who is this lucky girl Stewart?

Stew – (takes a deep breath and looks at his dad) Her name is Julie Bennett, what's the big deal?

Susan - Julie Bennett? You mean Julie Bennett, Terry's girl?

Bob – Yea, I would imagine

Stew – You guys know her mom?

Susan – Yea we were friends in high school... and...

Bob – And that was a long time ago and that's all... Yea ah Mr. Stew, you got some chores I believe you need to do before you go.

Stew – Chores! Like what? (the song Yakity Yak from the Coasters comes on, from beginning to end – Shows Stew taking out the trash, shows him cleaning his room, sweeping, smashing down the garbage can outside and feeding the dog, giving the father as he sleeps a dirty look, then flops on his bed because he is exhausted from his chores, as the song comes to an end)

Stews mom and dad talk in the kitchen over lunch as Stews is in the shower

Bob – (Takes a bite out of his sandwhich0) uhm, should we tell him?

Susan – I think so, but not now. Bob – Well if not now... when?

Susan – Let him have his fun, I mean let's let him have fun for his first date, then we'll break the news to him when the time is more appropriate.

Stews dad – O.K., I agree ... Did you ever think this day would come, that our son is going to a rock and roll show and taking a date, a girl?

Stews mom – Of course, he's a handsome young man just like his daddy, it was only a matter of time.

Bob – Yea I guess your right . . . who would of thunk it though, Terry and Davids kid? Wow, didn't see that one coming

Susan – I heard she had moved back to town, I guess Becky Reynolds got her a job over at the school district office.

Bob Sooner or later you're gonna run into her, you know that don't you?

Megan – Yea I know, it's all good though … I hope.

Scene moves to Josephine's house, where she is getting ready for this evening

Mrs. Coletti (Gina)– Josephine, can I ask you a question?

Josephine – Yes, mama, but please don't make things complicated.

Gina – You mean to tell me that after 2 years plus of being away at law school, you haven't met another young man that sparked interest in you?

Josephine – I asked you not to make it complicated mother.

Gina – I don't understand what is...

Josephine – You don't understand because it's not you that's in a relationship with Nick, and your opinion of him is based on his past and upbringing and not what he has accomplished along with his short and long term goals are.

Mr. Coletti (Joe) – (Walks in) Hey what's all the fussing and hooplah?

Josephine – Ohh...ughhh!

Gina – I'm just wanting to understand that's all, with all the other guy's at law school, why hasn't she found someone more suitable for herself, someone with a future, someone with realistic goals rather than some grease monkey headed nowhere. Don't you want something better for our daughter?

Joe – I want what she wants.

Josephine – You see mother, that's a supportive parent.

Gina – He comes from a dis functional family and background, you don't think that could rub off on you or if you were to marry him, it could rub off on your children?

Josephine - Mother!

Joe– Josephine! Maybe I shouldn't say this, it's probably not my place to do so,(pauses and sits on the bed) but Sal is retiring and is going to sell the station and garage.

Gina - Oh great, nothing worse than an unemployed grease monkey!

Joe– Gina! Sal and Sofie are going to sell the business, the property it sits on and the lot next to the station, to Nick for $3.00 total!

Gina– Are you serious?

Josephine - Papa, where did you here this at?, Nick hasn't told me anything.

Joe - Well apparently he didn't know anything until this morning, because Sal and Sofie where going down to the station to break the news to Nick.

Josephine - Oh my, Nick is going to be so happy (she claps with joy)

Gina – And you're sure about this Joe?

Joe – Oh yea I'm sure, I shouldn't have said nothing because Nick would have wanted it to be a surprise to Josephine, but I had to stop the fire here this morning.

Gina – Huh, does he even have the $3.00 or is he going to have to barrow it?

Joe – You'll be surprised to know Gina, that when Sal broke the news to everyone at the lodge last month, plenty of people offered to co-sign a loan for Nick to buy the business if they had too, because of his value to this community and all the farmers,

Nick is the best at what he does.

Josephine – Oh papa, I love you (hugs her dad) you see the positive in him don't you papa?

Gina– Well good luck to him, if you were to marry him Josephine you guys are going to need each other with each other's trade.

Joe - Would you please stop already, the boy paid his mother's house off in 2 years after she left, by selling cars on the side of Sal's station, now he's going to open up a nice used car lot next to the station. The boy's got big plans Gina, the least we can do is support him with good wishes and thoughts.

Gina – Uhuh! (Looks disappointed)

Maryann's house, as she sits under a drier with a head full of curlers, having a conversation with her mother Philys

Philys Swenson – So I go to answer the door and it's your father rather than Sam, and he has a bouquet of flowers in his hand, and I said, Hi Todd where's Sam, and he said, He said, Hi Philys, Sam got to scared at the last minute, and I didn't want to have you been stood up and your feelings hurt so I took a chance ! (they both laugh) And the rest is history

Maryann – 3 Kid's, a house and a successful business later!

Philys – Unbelievable huh?

Maryann – And where is Sam today?

Philys – You know after that altercation at the city 21 years ago, his parents chose to move from here and he hasn't been heard of since.

Maryann – So did you go mom, to the dance that night?

Philys – Oh yes, I was there.

Maryann – What happen, did anything happen to you and where was dad, cause you guys were together by then weren't you?

Philys – Well your fathers family were out of town do to his grandmother's funeral, but he gave me his blessings to go ahead and go so I went with some friends, but we left about 5 minutes before everyone who were involved in the fight, so we didn't hear about it until the next morning.

Maryann – Wow, what did you say or feel about that whole ordeal?

Philys – Quite fortunate, I'll tell you (pauses) I just pray everything goes well tonight for you, well for all of you guys. It's one thing to worry but it's probably worse to hold you guys back from living and having your fun, plus that was a long time ago.

Maryann – Yea it was, I just want to make my memories with Tommy mom, I mean it's bad enough that we're in different grades, he'll be away next year playing football and maybe baseball, they'll be new friends, new girls coming into his life, and I just want to make him happy with me, you know? Making memories, and building towards spending the rest of our lives together.

Philys – I know, it's important to you, but Tommy to me is a very sincere young man, (pauses) not like Sam (they both laugh)

Stews bedroom where he is looking at himself in the mirror, turns the radio up and practices some dance moves to Lonely Tear Drops from Jackie Wilson, spins a move and confidently says "Yea, I'm ready!"

Sergio and Alberto's house. Alberto's is in his room packaging some cigarettes, Sergio knocks on the door and opens it up

Alberto – What's up?

Sergio – What's up with you carnal? I thought you went to work?

(Alberto shrugs his shoulders)

Alberto – I am working ese.

Sergio – Are you going with us? I thought we all said we'd help Nick out?

Alberto – Just because I'm not going with you, doesn't mean I'm not helping Nick ese.

Sergio – Well I guess I gotta catch a ride with another homeboy then.

Alberto – I guess your right... You better call Juan, he wants to talk to you.

(Sergio walks to the telephone to make the call)

Juan and Jesse's house, both are getting ready between the bathroom and their bedroom

Jesse – Hey, how come you ain't taking Gloria? And how come all the rest aren't taking their old ladies?

Juan – Don't worry about it carnal, you just keep those wondering questions to yourself... you hear me?

Jesse – So what are you guy's up to Juan, you guys on the prowl for some new play, or what?

Juan – Mira, don't be stupid ese, don't even think about talking trash like that, sabes? You keep your mouth shut and mind your business and do as your told, got it (*As Juan is up in Jesse's face in their bedroom)*

You're riding up with Tony and Marianna, got it? You don't be asking no questions and you don't be talking to no one about anybody... comprendes? You got a date or you flying solo?

Jesse – Yea I'm gonna meet Katie there?

Juan – Katie, Katie who?

Jesse – You know Connie? Paul's old lady.

Juan – Yea

Jesse – Her sister, Katie and Andrew's old lady Kathy...

Juan – Oh la gringita?

Jesse – Simon...

Juan – Why don't you have her ride up with you in Tony's car?

Jesse – Are you kidding, her Dad will scalp her and me if he sees her with us in the same car ese.

Juan – Just pull over loco, right outside of town, that way you guys can make out on the way there (*Juan grabs Jesse simulating kisses, and laughs)* and a little touchy touchy sabes?

Jesse – Knock it off cabron (runs into the bathroom laughing)

Juan – Yea, always trying to blend in with the gringos, don't forget to put some B.O. juice on ese.

Tony's house, Tony is outside wiping his car down and cleaning the windows and Marianna confronts him as a car drives away and Tony closes his trunk door

Marianna – Who was that?

Tony – He was just passing bye., Ron Jr. he was looking for directions to Chatos house.

Marianna – Hey baby, how come Nick wants all of you guys to go to the dance with them anyways, what's the real reason?

Tony – Ah, you know, just for some support you know... Him and Juan got in that fight with those 3 punks from the city, and I guess that plato that took place a thousand years ago still haunt's the town people, I don't know, but Juan asked us and we all need to back each other's concerns I guess, so we go and we dance and we have fun, right? (they hug and Tony spins her around)

Marianna – I've been wanting to see that chavalo dance.

Tony – What chavalo?

Marianna – You know that crazy kid with the black hair and he hangs around with the bushy red hair guy?

Tony – Oh yea, Stew and Jimmy, they call him Red or Red bird.

Marianna – Red Bird?

Tony – Yea, por que se parese un pajaro, looks like a bird...

Marianna – Well it's the black hair one, Stewie that's the good dancer I hear.

Tony – Do you wanna dance with him?

Mirianna – No, I wanna dance with you.

(Tony and Marianna kiss)

Tony – You can dance with him, as long as you dance and notouch.

Marianna – I won't touch him.

Tony – No, he don't touch you... that's what I mean.

Marianna – I'm gonna go get dressed.

Tony – I'll be in a minute... Vamos bailar la bamba...vamos bailar la bamba... tu tu tu una poca de gracias... una poca de gracias

(Marianna walks inside and Tony pops his trunk and checks under the spare tire, there tucked away is a small caliber handgun and in the center lies a light brown small sized suitcase, he closes the trunk door)

Nicks house, as Nick finishes combing his hair, he puts his wallet, change and knife in his pockets grabs his keys and shuts his radio off (Lonely Tear Drops), and stops a brief moment to view a picture of his parents in a family picture with Nick and an older brother which Nick never new, Mark. He stairs for a few seconds and kisses the picture and says 'You always said I was gonna be somebody mama... thank you, (kisses it again) thank you dad (kisses it again) I love you Mark.

Nicks Gas Station, cars are lined up with a few more arriving. Tommy and Moose check in with everyone to make sure they are fueled up and ready to roll, while Nick and Josephine hand in

hand are over at the empty lot next to the gas station, as Nick shares his plans with her

Nick - So that back corner will be the office and the other corner will be a carport cover for the detailing the cars.

Josephine - How many cars do you think you can put out here?

Nick – I figure about 20 easy, maybe 25... then a few out in that corner.

Josephine – Oh Nick, I am so happy for you baby, I'm so proud of you too.

Nick – (As Nick holds Josephine close) You know, if I never get the chance to tell you again, I'm going to tell you now... You're the reason for my turnaround you know that... right?

Josephine – Huh, what do you mean?

Nick – Yea, 3 and half years ago when my mom left to live with my aunt, I had nothing left in life but bad memories, but then you showed me some attention and affection and you gave me a new outlook on life, this is for you baby, this is all for you.

Josephine – Oh Nick you're going to make me cry and my make- up is going to run all over my face.

Nick – Let it run, I'll catch it (they both laugh)

Josephine – (They start to walk back to Nicks car) What are you going to name the businesses?

Nick – I told Mr. C that I was gonna keep his name still for the staion and he teared up, so I'm glad of that... The car lot will be J&N's Used Cars.

Josephine – J&N, who's J&N

Nick – Oh, well it sure as heck isn't John and Nancy's.

Josephine – Josephine and Nick's? Oh my goodness, Nick!

Tommy and Moose meet Nick and Josephine back at Nick's car as Josephine heads over to say hi to Maryann in Tommy's car

Josephine – Hey you!

Maryann – (Jumps out of the car to hug and say hi to Josephine) Hi Josephine! (Laura honks and waves at Josephine & Josephine waves back)

Back at Nicks car

Nick – All checked in?

Tommy – I think that's about it...we got 4,5,6,7 and they're all packed.

Moose – (Looks at his watch) We got about 2 minutes *Suddenly, Tony's car goes passing by headed to the Big City*

Moose – So much for following orders.

Nick – Yea well, outside of the work place they really don't take or follow orders to well (looks at Tommy and Moose)

Tommy – (Raises his hands) No comment.

Josephine comes back and Nick opens her door

Nick – Let's roll boys ('No Particular Place To Go/Chuck Berry Starts to play)

Tommy – Hey Nick?

Moose jogs to Laura's car

Nick – (Starts to get in and stop's) Yea?

Tommy – Thanks a lot man, this means a lot to bunch of people.

Nick – We'll see Tommy boy, we'll see.

All cars start up, as the sun begins to set, the excitement builds, the radio's playing in unison as they laugh, sing and anticipation fills the air. Nick leads the way in his 50 Mercury, followed by Tommy's 55 Bel Air convertible, Laura's 54 Ford, Paul's 57 Chevy and 3 others behind them

Josephine – Juan and the guys must have gone ahead too, right?

Nick – I hope.

Nick and the caravan leaving the small town and headed to the Big City. A little more than halfway they pass a sign that reads 'Next Gas 5 Miles' as it passes what seems to be a broken down 38 Ford off the side of the narrowest path of the road just past the old single lane bridge, they all pass safely. A view from a higher location, would show Tony's car well ahead of Nicks car, maybe 2 miles ahead

Still Traveling

Jesse – (Sitting in the back seat of Tony's car) Marianna?

Marianna – Yea...

Jesse – Are you excited as I am?

Marianna – Probably more, I never been to anything like this in english.

Jesse – Yea me neither.

Marianna – In spanish yea, but in english no way.

Tony – What about you're rukita? Is she gonna be there or is she gonna be square? Ahh ha

Jesse – Yea she's coming in back of us, somewhere (as he turns back but doesn't see nothing but dust)

Marianna – She could have rode with us Jesse.

Jesse – Yea but I didn't want her old man to find out about that, and I don't think neither did she, it could be hazardous to my health (they all laugh)

Laura's car – as Moose drives, Laura sits tight next to Moose, with Julie and Cindy in the back seat

Cindy – So he say's to me, Why don't you just stay home I can be there by 9, and I said, uh uhh hey dadio I'll be at the Rock & Roll show...

Julie – So is he from town?

Cindy – Nah, he's from North Town, he graduated last year.

Moose – North Town? What's his name?

Cindy – Eddie, Eddie Hernandez... you know him?

Moose – Yea I know who he is, he's half Mexican.

Cindy – Yea I know, he's hot like a chili jalapeno pepper (all girls laugh)

Julie – ooooooh Cindy, likes em hot!

Laura – (looks at Moose) Yea well I like em big (Moose swerves a bit and they all laugh)

Tommy's car

Tommy – Wow looks like Moose is drunk (as Tommy looks in review mirror and Maryann turns to see)

Maryann – Why? What do you mean?

Tommy – He's swerving ready to crash.

Maryann – It's probably Laura grabbing him I bet ya.

Tommy – Grabbing him? With others in the car? No way!

Maryann – O.K. maybe it's him grabbing her.

Tommy – Now that makes more sense (they laugh)

Nick's car

Stew – I thought as a lawyer you represent anyone with issues with the law?

Josephine – Well it's like a doctor, you're a doctor for a certain health issues, right?, either, bones, eyes, ears and nose, or blood or nerves and muscles or even allergies.

Jimmy – So the law is the same? How so?

Josephine – Well there's civil, criminal, business lawyers to oversee contract negotiations and settlements or divorce which are called familiy law attorney's...

Nick – O.K. boys enough law talk, change the subject man.

Josephine – Nick, there young boy's trying to learn something...

Nick – No they're trying to plan for the future, on how they can use you to save their hides.

Stew – O.K. music! What is your type of music Josephine?

Josephine – Oh yes, I love Rock & Roll...I was raised listening to Frank Sinatra, Perry Como, Dean Martin which I love it really... but when I started high school everybody was listening to rock & roll and my parents did not approve at all!

Jimmy – So what did you do?

Josephine – I eventually convinced my father that it's what the teenagers are into ... and he understood.

Nick – Yea well that's even starting to change.

Stew – Change? In what way?

Nick – Ah man it aint even close to where it use to be anymore.

Jimmy – Like the surf groups and all?

Nick – Man all that garbage, surfing and all this bubble gum crap.

Josephine – Nick, first of all it's isn't not ain't, and you don't know if Stew & Red like that type of music, (she turns to them) Thats just his opinion, you don't have to listen to him.

Nick – Yea but mark my words it's only gonna get worse, watch and see, or listen rather.

Jimmy – I hear that there is some bands coming from Europe with long hair and everything!

Nick – Long hair? guys with long hair? that'll never work, they'll get booed write out of America... I'm telling you, long hair? No way!

Stew – What kind of music can long hair Europeans possibly make – blahhhh blah blah, cheez

Josephine – I think they'll be interesting, that's what I think, you have to give them a chance.

Nick – It's givem.

Josephine – What?

Nick – You said give them, the proper way is givem and gonna and wanna and Ima, that's the proper lingo dear (they all laugh as Josephine whacks Nicks arm)

(Quietly Stew tells Jimmy)

Stew – Is this just great or what?

Jimmy – (smiles and gives Stew another thumbs up)

Nick leads the caravan of cars into the Big City. They travel into the city 3 blocks and circle the block and park 1 block past the JC auditorium on the side of the street facing home. As they all park and get out of their cars, fear seems to be the farthest thing from their minds. Although Nick keeps looking around expecting the unexpected

Josephine – Come on baby relax (as she grabs him by the arm)

Nick – I am relaxed.

Tommy – Here we are man, ready to rock & roll?

Nick – Yea, hey everybody's hip to our plan right Tommy?

Tommy – Oh sure Nick, we told them, this is the way it's gonna be or we ain't going, right Moose?

Moose – That's right, I told them if they get out of line, they have to deal with me before they deal with you.

Nick – Boy, I bet that really made em shake in their boots, huh? (Moose looks at Tommy as if to say say, chee wiz Nick)

As Nick and Josephine walk to the corner everyone follows close behind, Nick spots Tony's car parked two cars from the corner with no one in it

Nick – There's one of the Muchacho's, Senor Antonio (Nick turns towards everyone) Hey listen up! I know Tommy and Moose already told you guys, but I'm gonna say it again just so you know you heard from me. We all stick together, inside, outside or even trips to the bathroom or the refreshment stands, got it?

When we leave, we all leave together, no one cuts out alone unless you have an emergency or something, got it? Let's do this.

Stew – Hey don't worry Nick I'll keep my eyes on them for ya.

Nick – Right, you'll be to busy keeping your eyes on Julie's…

Josephine – Nick! (yanks his arm)

Nick – What? I was gonna say, ahh ah blouse, I was gonna say blouse, cheez louise.

Scene from inside the auditorium where Tony and Marianna and Jesse all sit as Nick and the group walk in

Jesse – Hey Nick! (Jesse waves them in to a section of tables in the corner, on the side of the stage) Over here!

(As the group led by Nick head to the corner, Katie breaks away to run to Jesse, they talk and greet one another with a hug. Tony greets everybody)

Tony – Orale, Nick, how goes it homeboy, everything alright?

Nick – Yea evrerything is peachie keen as they say, where's ah, Juan and company?

Tony – Ahh they'll be here ese, you know the Mexican old ladies always running behind schedule.

Marianna – Heeeyyy!

Tony – Is this the twinkle toes vato? (as Tony points over to Stew and Stew walks up to Tony with Julie at his side)

Stew – Hey Tony, this is Julie, Julie this Tony and?

Tony – Marianna, Hello Miss Julie (they all exchange greetings)

Marianna – So I hear you can dance?

Stew – A little, I hear you can cut it as well?

Marianna – Aaaa, I like, love to dance, I don't how good I am.

Stew – Like me, I love it too, but it's got to be a boogie woogie type song, you know? something that really swings.

Tony – Hey if you promise to keep your hands off of her, I might let you dance with her.

Josephine – Oh my goodness, Promise him, this I got to see (Josephine says with overwhelming joy)

Julie – Oh he'll promise alright, or else (she makes a fist at him, (they all laugh)

Cindy – Wow! Look at that stage, it's like wild man, wild!

Laura – Yea, wouldn't you like to go up there singing and driving the audience crazy?

Cindy – Not the whole audience, just the boys!

Laura – Oooohh !

Moose – You girls are way too much...

An office within the auditorium location down a hallway from the bathrooms and a nurse's station. In the back ground the MC gets the show started. The school superintendent and a couple of school security aids talk with Capt. Billings

Security #3 – (Walks in during an ongoing conversation) Excuse me sir... They're here.

Super – O.k. thanks.

Capt. Billings – Where about are they?

Security #3 – They are all together sir, sitting up front a long side the northwest wall, sir.

Superintendent Billings – Did you notice about how many there are?

Security 3 – I didn't count but if I were to guess I would have to say about 25 or so sir.

Security #2 – Did you want an exact number, cause I…

Capt. Billings – No need, that's o.k. Ahh, let's make sure they don't spread out… Well never mind, just make sure you keep the peace while on the premises, huh?

Superintendent – Captain?

Capt. Billings – Yea?

Superintendent – What about the immigrant kids, did you find out if they were coming?

Capt. Billings – From what I've been able to find out, they didn't come, If I'm not mistaking I (turns and looks at security #1)

Security #1 – Yea from what I observed, there are only 3 of them here, a couple and a third wheel guy.

Superintendent – Do we know who it is?

Security 2 – It's that one guy who played wide receiver for South County but quit by his senior year.

Security #3 – Tony Mendez sir and his girlfriend or wife and the third wheel is Jesse Ramirez.

Superintendent – The running back kid?

Security – That's him.

Superintendent – We're going to try and recruit that kid, he'll be our version of Speedy Gonzalez. (smiles)

Capt. Billings – (looks concerned) Well wherever little brother is, big brother can't be too far behind.

Security #1 – If that's true, we'll find them I have 30 security guy's in the parking lot and on the streets, they'll tell me if they spot them, sir.

Capt. Billings – O.K. gentlemen, let's talk about this tomorrow morning on how we had a successful evening last night, (nods head) Fred.

Super – You got it Frank.

Security #1 – (looks at other 2 security guys) Lets go to workguys.

Back to the auditorium where there is dancing going on. Fast dancing changes to slow dancing and back to fast dancing, as time moves on. Outside in the parking lot of the auditorium, through the shadow, the feet of someone walking in the parking lot, approaches a car with a slim jim tool, opens a car door and plants a couple of objects under the driver's seat. The feet moves quietly to the front end of another car as a security guard approaches. After the coast is clear the same person plants something again in another car. Shadow image looks to be Alberto.

Meanwhile back in the show, the MC introduces The Killer Jerry Lee – Jerry Lee takes the stage and greets the crowd, sits and starts to play 'All Night Long'. After the his first song, the audience is still in amazement as Jerry Lee says:

Jerry Lee – You know, as I travel all over this great big 'ol country and all over the world, people wanna make me feel sad, How so Jerry Lee? you may ask, and I'll tell you, I play dancin music, understand? I play music that makes your feet wanna move to groove, it makes you wanna swing and shake that thing baby... understand, If you know what I'm talking about let me hear you say Rock & Roll Jerry Lee!... (everyone shouts it) O.K., I think we're on the same page now... I want all the dancin couples up front here in front of the stage, come on now! You know who you are. All the dancin couples up here and ready to show Jerry Lee you appreciate his music, come on! are you ready? come on let's do this... Is everybody ready? O.K. here we go, all the pretty girls and all the pretty boy's, I want to tell you that you Shake my nerves and you rattle my brain (Breaks into Great Balls of Fire)

About 10 couples hit the dance floor

Josephine – O.K. guy's here's your chance, come on! Get out there! Tony, Julie tell them!

Julie – Come on Stewie show em how it's done!

Tony – Go, baby make me proud mama!

Stew and Marianna take to the floor with smiles of confidence on their faces, as their piers shout words of encouragement

Stew – O.K. here we go, you lead.

Marianna – Me?

Stew – Yea, do what you do, anyway you want, I'll keep up don't worry.

Marianna – O.K. then!

As Jerry Lee plays 'Great Balls of Fire' the 10 couples dance with a few stopping after 1 ½ minutes due to the caliber of dancers. As Great Balls Of Fire ends, Jerry Lee moves right into 'Whole Lotta Shakin Going On' and 3 more couple fade out, with 1 minute to go in the song 1 couple remains with Stew & Marianna. Nick talks to a stage hand and hands him a note. Stew & Marianna give way to the remaining couple to show what they have left. After 15 seconds, Stew & Marianna take over and blow their competition away, with Stew dropping 3 splits in a row and Marianna really shaking it up. The song comes to an end, with the crowd going nuts with excitement for the final couple Stew and Marianna.

Julie – Oh my gosh Stew! (she hugs him as they come off the dance floor together)

Stew – I've been waiting for that moment ever since the day I learned to walk!

Tony – That's my baby! (Hugs and spins her around with pride)

Marianna – Man o man, that loco can dance!

Josephine – Are you kidding me, Oooohh! And they're from South County! Yea! Ooooohh !

Nick – O.K. get a hold of yourself girl.

Josephine – Didn't you think that was dynamite?

Nick – Yea I did (laughs and holds her)

Moose – Wow!

Laura – Chee wizz, do you think we can do that big guy?

Moose – Sure, as long as we're asleep when we do, cause the only way that's gonna happen is in our dreams! (Moose, Laura,

Jimmy and Cindy, Tommy and Maryann all laugh)

Jerry Lee – Now that's what I'm looking for right there, let's give it up for that couple once again (Jerry Lee stands and applauds them) that's what Jerry Lee's music is all about baby... wooh hooh!

Jerry Lee – O.K. I gotta a request here from a guy, who wants to let his girl know that he thinks you are the best thing that ever happen to him... are you listening? and her name is Josephine, and turn around honey Nick wants to ask you something (Breaks into Hello Josephine)

Josephine – (Josephine turns around to Nick) Niiick!

Nick – (On 1 knee with an engagement ring) Josephine Coletti, will you marry me?

Josephine – (With tears of joy streaming from her eyes) Yes, of course I'll marry you baby! (they kiss and hug, then slips the ring on her finger as their group applauds them and swarms them with hugs and congratulations)

Stew – (Turns to Jimmy) I feel like this is my last night of life!

Jimmy – Why do you say that?

Stew – Man this is like the greatest night of my life, I feel like the Duke of Earl man, first Julie, then we ride with Nick & Josephine, Then I get to rip it up on the dance floor, then we get to see the greatest proposal in the history of life itself! Man what a night!

What a night, dadio!

Jimmy – Yea it's something we never expected that's for sure!

Cindy – (Asks Jimmy) Hey hip cat, wanna dance? (pulls him to the dance floor)

Jimmy – Looks like I got no choice!

Julie – You're gonna have to start teaching me how to dance like that so we can go to more dances and Rock & Roll shows.

Stew – I never thought you'd ask!

Julie - I'm asking, I'm asking (laughs and hugs Stew and he shakes his head in disbelief for he truly believes this is the greatest night of his life)

Julie – (Leans to talk to Josephine and Stew nonchalantly leaves to the bathroom) Can I see your ring? Oh my stars, it's gorgeous!

Josephine – My father is going to have a heart attack and my mother is going to have a cow! (they both laugh)

Moose – Tell me Nick, how long have you had this planned man?

Nick – I didn't plan big man, It was just a spontaneous thing.

Moose – Well it sure worked out for you man, what a night huh?

Nick – Yea I'll tell you man...

Moose – So next question...

Nick – Oh no, let's not jump the gun so fast, or should I say jump the broom, cool it with the questions Moose man.

Moose – Hey we have to know man, dont'ya know your bachelor party is going to take some planning, Jeepers dude.

Nick – It's going to be at least a year or 2, so I can save some bread and get the businesses rolling to my satisfaction.

Tommy – Hey, is what my dad said true Nick?

Nick – It all depends Tommy Boy, what did he say?

Tommy – That you're buying old man Celetti's station and property?

Nick – Yea, looks that way guy's.

Moose – (Pauses and thinks a second or two) That's why you said back at the station that maybe you would sell it to me one day...

Nick – Ughhhhhh, (laughs) Why else would I say that genius?

Tommy – (Both Tommy and Moose hug Nick and congratulate him) All right Nicky my man...

Moose – Cool McCool, hey maybe now I can get my old part time job back?

Nick – Yea come down and fill out a job application and we'll see (they all laugh)

Moose – (Quietly asks Tommy) Hey Tommy,

Tommy – Yeah

Moose – You got an extra ah, ah you know man an extra rain coat for my friend?

Tommy – Oh feeling lucky are ya?

Moose – Well I don't know about lucky, but I do know I'm feelling...

Tommy – Spare me big boy, yea lets see if we make are way to the men's room and I'll cover you.

Moose – Ah, I just need the coat man, I can cover myself (they both laugh)

Tommy – Yeah I hope you can, it be too early in life to have a little Moose running around (laugh)

Moose – Nooooo! Not yet at least (smiling and making a scared face)

Paul and Andrew approach

Paul – Hey have you guy's seen Stew?

Tommy – He was just here... is he out on the dance floor?

Julie – No, I don't think so.

Jimmy – I'll go check the floor

Nick – Paul, you and Andrew go check outside, maybe he went out for some fresh air, Tommy, Moose check the John!

Cindy – I notice he wasn't here when we got back from the floor, but I thought you guys knew...

Jimmy – No he's not out there!

Nick – Great! (sarcastically)

Josephine – Oh baby I'm sure he's o.k.

Nick – Hey where's Tony and Jesse?

Jimmy – There out on the dance floor, I just saw them.

Julie – I don't see him towards the refreshment stand either.

Maryann – I need to go to the bathroom...

Laura – Come on, I'll go with you, Jimmy can you come with us?

Jimmy – Sure, I'll run for help in case you girls run into trouble...

Maryann – Oh that's great Jimmy (Jimmy snickers)

They run into Tommy and Moose on the way to the bathroom

Jimmy – Any sign of him? is he in there?

Tommy – No! we didn't see him...

Moose – Man if he's playing a joke, the joke is going to be on him when I get a hold of him.

Laura comes running back to Nick, Tommy and Moose

Laura – I just saw a lady heading to an office, might be an infirmary past the bathrooms... she had some ice and towels and she was running, and 2 guys came running out of the boys bathroom after you guys came out and ran towards the back with her!

Nick – Paul, Andrew stay here with the girls!

Paul – You got it!

Nick – Let's go!

Nick, Tommy and Moose head pass the bathrooms and around the corner they notice some adults perhaps some security standing guard and a gentleman approaches them

Security IV – I'm sorry no one allowed in this area (stands to block them from proceeding)

Moose – That's nice! (Moose shoves him unto the floor as though he was a child)

Nick, Tommy and Moose open the door and find the superintendent and some security along with 2 ladies who are playing nurses to Stew, as he lays on the infirmary bed banged up pretty bad holding his ribs and has 2 black eyes and a large fat lip and a towel saturated with blood.

Superintendent – Hey what's the meaning of this?

Nick – To retrieve our friend (Nick decks the Superintendent) and expose your play Jack!

Tommy lay's out another security, while Moose head butts one and stopping another with a straight right hand

Moose – (Looks at the nurses) You want's some?

Nurses – No please! (they run off)

Tommy – Then get out!

Nick – Come on kid, you o.k.?

Stew – Oh Nick, I think I have some broken ribs, I'm not sure...

Nick – Alright Stewart, we're gonna get you out of here kid... come guy's grab underneath his arms be careful he's hurt man, we're walking out, I'll go in front, we drop anyone who isn't with us... got it?

Moose – You got Nick!

Tommy – Let's do it!

Jimmy and Cindy come running their way

Cindy – Oh Lord is he o.k.?

Nick – You 2 go back and gather everyone up and meet us out front, now! I mean now! (as they go running back) No one stays behind!

Tommy – You o.k. Stewie boy?

Stew – I'll be alright eventually man, I got a lot going for myself now, don't I? I mean with Julie and all...

Moose – You sure do man, hang in there little buddy, we'll be out of here soon...

Stew – Hey what about my pretty little angel eyes?

Moose – It's o.k. little buddy, I'm right here (Moose smiles at him)

Nick – It's good to keep a sense of humor even in tough times.

Nick, Tommy, Moose and while carrying Stew walk outside to wait for the others

While they wait outside they all check in with Stew

Nick – O.K. listen up! Everybody to your cars, nobody splits, we stay in order just the way we came, we'll stop at the corner, Tommy when we get there, you get off make sure everyone is in line ready to roll... got it?

Tommy – No problem Nick, Everybody to your car lets go, start em up fast, let's go!

Josephine – (AS they walk in front of Moose and Tommy carrying Stew) What about Tony and Marianna and Jesse?

Nick – Looks like they already cleared (Nick looks at where Tony's car was parked and its gone)

They all get to their cars and start them up and Nick pulls out to the corner and stops and waits for Tommy to get out of his car and checks to make sure every last one of them are in line and ready to head back home

Tommy – O.K. Nick, we're all set man everybody's accounted for and in line.

Nick – O.K. Tommy get to your car and let's get the hell out of here.

Tommy goes to his car and gets in, and Nick leads the caravan back home on it's a 20 mile journey

Nick – How's he doing back there?

Josephine – Are you o.k. Stew, considering?

Julie – (Who is attending to him) Doing o.k. sweetie?

Stew – Ahh yea, it hurts when I breath, but I'll be o.k.

Jimmy – Hey you don't worry about talking Stew, just hold on Nick's going to get you to County General, you'll be o.k. (as a tear drops from Jimmy's eye)

Stew – Man things were going so good...

Nick – Hey don't waste your breath partner, hold on to all those thoughts at least for another 20 minutes buddy.

Stew – Is my face pretty banged up (as he looks up at Julie)

Julie – Shhhh, don't worry about that, they couldn't ruin this gorgeous face (Nick looks in the rear view mirror with a half smile)

Josephine – That's right Stew, those punks couldn't dance like you so they tried to re-arrange your cute little face and they couldn't even do that... right Jimmy?

Jimmy – (Looking very distraught with tears in his eyes) I mean, I know I probably would have gotten my butt kicked too, but at least he probably wouldn't have gotten beat up this bad.

Josephine – Oh it's not your fault, Don't blame yourself Jimmy.

Stew – You're lucky you didn't go with me, otherwise we'd both be on our way to the hospital.

Nick – Man Stewie! Why did you...

Josephine – Nicky! baby not now, come on things are bad enough right now.

Stew – I'm sorry Nick, I'm sorry for ruining everybody's evening (as he struggles to talk)

Julie – O.K. Stewie shhhh, hold your words... we'll be there before you know it.

Stew – All those guys laughed at me, (struggling to talk) even that Capt. Cop Billings guy when they took me back there.

Julie – Shhhh, relax Stewie, don't talk (As Nick looks into the rear view mirror again, this time with anger in his eyes)

Tommy's car

Maryann – Man I don't believe this (with tears in her eyes)

Tommy – Hey sweetheart it could have been worse...

Maryann – Man, when is this stupid rivalry going to end Tommy?

Tommy – As soon as the goonballs grow up... probably never!

Laura's car

Moose – Ughhh! (Moose slams his hands on the steering wheel) Those dirty sons of...

Laura – Hey come on big guy, don't let it get to you!

Cindy – Yea, calm down, there's nothing that can be done now about them or about Stew, just relax I'm sure Nicks gotta a plan.

Moose – Yea well if he don't, I'll come up with one, I'll just go over to their school and beat the crap out of the first guy I see... I mean look what they did to that poor kid, he can't even defend himself, why didn't they jump me?, Oh my dam stinking socks, why didn't they jump me?, I would of... (slams id hand again and looks straight with tears in his eyes)

Paul's car

Andrew – Poor Stewie man, poor guy, I don't believe this even happen to him, after he lit the crowd up for Jerry Lee, man did you see him on that floor with Tony's girl, man they were great!

Paul – Man, I feel bad... for the bad time I gave him last night at the party, teasing him and all, him and Jimmy...

Connie – That's why you should never do or say bad things to or about anyone cause of stuff like this, you never know.

Andrew – Yea he was pretty upset with you last night... you know?

Paul – Yea, I know, I'll make it up to him.

Andrew – How? How you gonna make it up to him Paul?

Paul – If I know Moose and Nick, they'll be going for some payback, and I'll be with them... You can count on that!

The caravan traveling in the dark... The next few minutes go buy

Josephine – Is he doing o.k. how's his breathing?

Julie – It's a lot softer now, more calm (as Stew's head rests on Julie's lap)

Josephine – Ah that's good, that's a good sign.

As they approach the single car lane that is about a quarter of a mile long they near the bridge and Nick notice's the old 38 Ford blocking the bridge and begins to slow up, quickly looks in his rearview mirror when out of nowhere an older 2 ton truck plows into Nicks driver side door at a high speed, pushing Nick's car into the large ditch and unto it's side. With blood curdling screams from Josephine and Julie, Nick yells 'Hold on!

Simultaneously from the left and right side other older pickup trucks and large trucks plow and hit some of the cars and bang them up with injuries to the passenger's. 5 out of 7 cars are smashed up. The 2 remaining cars backed up fast and headed back towards the big city passing a few more trucks that tried to run them off the road

Nick, yelling for Josephine as she seems to be hurt and unconscious, Nick calls out for Jimmy and Stew and Julie

Jimmy – What just happened? Stew!

Julie – (Half unconscious herself) Stewie! Oh my god, Stewie! (start's to cry)

Jimmy – Stewart, come on man... is he breathing?

Julie – I don't know... I can't tell... please God!

Nick – (Nick listens for Josephine's breathing) I'm gonna get you home baby, don't worry, Jimmy come on! (Nick climbs out the driver's side window as the car sits on its side with the passenger door on the ground. Jimmy follows Nick)

Jimmy – What'll we do Nick (As 2 guys get out of the truck and attack Nick and Jimmy with 3 ft. 2x4's)

Nick – Get behind me Jimmy, stay close (Nick meets one of the guys straight on with a tackle and jumps to his feet and punches guy #2) Grab the board Jimmy protect yourself... hit em!, hit em hard on the head! (Nick is intense and angry)

Jimmy – (cracks one over the head and knocking him out cold) Yea... take that you jackass!

Nick – (Takes the other 2x4 and clobbers the other guy) Come Jimmy! (Runs toward Moose who is fighting 4 guys) You son of a... (and clobbers another guy)

And all out fist fight occurs with the big city guys out numbering the small town boys 2 to 1. Big Moose fights off his opponents and Nick and Jimmy clobber others but are getting whacked right back as well. Paul and Andrew fight to protect their girlfriends.

Paul well in control, while Andrew struggles a bit. Their enemies begin to retreat as a gunshot blast fills the air as everyone freezes and Paul goes down. Moose runs down the slowest of the opponents and begins to punch him relentlessly in the face 5,6,7,8,9,10 times and Nick tackles Moose to push him off. Jimmy lay's on the ground with blood on his face but seems to be o.k.

The big city guys go running to their cars in the dark celebrating their victory. Moose has blood on the back of his head and shirt.

As Moose and Nick attend to Paul, while Andrew cries emotionally "Don't die" "Please Don't Die Paul, I love you" Paul lies lifeless.

Connie screams in shock of what just took place with her boyfriend and her sisters kathy and Katie cry as they hold her."Stay with him Jimmy!" says Nick to Jimmy. Nick and Moose run over to Tommy's car

Nick – Tommy!, Tommy boy! Maryann! (No sound as they are both underneath the flipped over convertible.

Moose – Come on Nick, let's try to push it over!

Nick – No Moose! we don't know how they lay under there man, one slight move could . . . Oh my God... Go check Laura and Cindy... Tommy! Tommy boy! (Nick lie's on the ground trying to see through the dark) talk to me... somebody!

Jimmy – (Back at Nicks car) Julie can you hear me?

Julie – (Crying) Yea I can hear you Jimmy...

Jimmy – What's going on in there?

Julie – I think Stewart and Josephine are dead Jimmy, I think they died I don't know (continues to break down)

Nick – (Gets back to the car) Come Jimmy boy, let's try to push it back on its wheels (They push and push and Moose arrives to help)

Moose – Laura and Cindy are o.k. they are just stunned and groggy man (with a couple of big pushes, the car ends right back on its wheels) Her car starts Nick!

Nick – Good, (Nick climbs through the window) Josephine, Josephine baby are you o.k.? please baby...

Josephine – (moans and groaning with pain) What happen?

Nick – We got ambushed baby, but it's gonna be o.k. I promise

As Julie holds Stewarts lifeless body in the back seat, she sobs quietly

Julie – He's gone! This sweet, funny and gentle boy is gone! I should have known this was too good to be true...

Jimmy – No! (Walks off crying in disbelief)

Nick – Damn! (puts his head down and starts to cry for Stew and the situation they are in)

Josephine – Come (She grabs and hold Nick with her left arm. Seems like her right arm is broken)

Josephine – Julie honey are you hurt? Julie (Quietly) Just my heart.

Nick kisses Josephine on her forehead, and sits down and tries to start the car, but it won't start – Just then a barrage of guns sound off in the distant night about 30 to 40 rounds, Nick urgently says

Nick – Moose!

Moose – Yea!

Nick – Go check those others, the other cars see if there are anymore casualties, see if any of those cars start!

Moose – O.k. (Runs off)

Nick – Jimmy boy, I need you to hold it together guy, got it, I need you man!

Jimmy – What do you want me to do Nick (as he wipes away his tears)

Nick – You come with me Jimmy boy (they run up the ravine to push the 38 Ford out of the way, they successfully move it enough for a car to pass)

Person in Car – What happen here?

Nick – We got ambushed heading back home... from a bunch of guys from...

Person – Oh my Lord, anyone hurt?

Nick – We got a few dead bodies Mister... can you get to town and call for some help please?

Person – Sure thing son (roars towards the big city)

Moose – They got one car that starts, no one seriously hurt although lots of blood Nick.

Nick – Jimmy can you drive?

Jimmy – I will!

Nick – Go help Andrew get Paul in the car and drive their car to the hospital, but follow us, got it?

Jimmy – Gotcha Nick (runs to help Andrew with Paul)

Nick – Moose get those other guys to pile in the one running car, take someone if you have too in Laura's car

Moose – O.K.

Nick –(Runs to one of the old pickup trucks and starts it up and drives it close to the edge where his car sits in the ravine) Come on Julie honey, come out of there so I can put Stewie in the back of the truck, come on baby… you're gonna be o.k. we're gonna make it despite all of this.

Josephine – O.K. baby, I'm coming, come Julie, come on (they head to the truck up the ravine, While Nick puts Stew over his shoulder and carries him up to the bed of the truck and lays him down)

Nick – (Runs one last time to Tommy's car and calls out) Tommy! Tommy boy! Maryann can you hear me? (waits, drops his head, no answer and runs to the truck)

Moose and the other 2 cars are filled with the remaining South County students as the wait for Nick to lead once again. They head to County General Hospital rapidly

As they approach the city limits coming off the county road they notice several police cars and a couple of ambulances heading towards the ambush area

Nick and the others pull into the emergency area of the hospital parking lot with Moose driving Laura's car with Laura and Cindy and Jimmy driving Paul's car with Andrew in the back seat holding his brother and Connie in the passenger seat and one of the other cars carrying Connie's sisters Kathy and Katie.

Nick quickly gets out of the car and run's into the E.R. entrance to get help . . . Out comes a group of nurses, doctors and assistance's with gurney's and wheelchairs

2 nurse's on the phone making calls to parents. Nick sits with Julie as everyone else is being treated. Other patients and family sit waiting their turn. 2 ambulance's arrive rushing Tommy in who is clinging to life, and another gurney with the covered up body of Maryann

Nick stands up and approaches the 2 arriving body's and notices Tommy being treated, then notices another covered up, knowing in his heart it was Maryann. Nick bows his head and cries as Julie hugs to comfort Nick as they both cry.

Julie – (As they sit back down) This seems like a nightmare.

Nick – I've had nightmares most of my life Julie, believe me this is worse than any nightmare I ever had.

Tommy's parents rush into the E.R. and go straight to the front desk

Tammy McCall - (Nervously) We're here for Tommy McCall (Nurse checks her chart)

Nurse – Tommy has been rushed into surgery Mrs. McCall I presume?, please have a seat and we will be with you as soon as we hear something… please.

They approach some seats when they notice Nick and Julie

Bill McCall – (Walks up to Nick and Julie) Nick? Nick what happen son? (as Nicks bloody forehead and dirt ridden clothes tells of a horrific event)

Nick – (Sits there with his head down and tears flow down his cheeks) This towns worse nightmare Mr. McCall, that's what happen man! (as Mrs. McCall joins her husband)

Like a stampede of wild horses, in rushed Josephine's parents and the parents of Maryann, Moose's mother and the parents of Connie, Kathy and Katie

Gina Coletti – Where's my baby girl? (She says with a desperate and panic voice) Where is she? (In a hysteric)

Joe Coletti – Gina! Calm down now (hugs her)

Nurse #2 – You're here for?

Joe Coletti – Josephine Coletti mam.

Gina Coletti – There he is, there's that no good monster (as she breaks for Nick)

Joe Coletti – Gina! Gina! You're going to need to calm down right now Gina (refrain's her from attacking Nick)

Nick stands up to confront Gina Coletti and Julie and the McCalls stand in shock

Nick – That's o.k. Mr. Coletti let her go.

Gina Coletti – I knew you were nothing but bad news from the day I met your drunken parents, and I was right!

Joe Coletti - Gina that's enough!

Todd McCall – Joe! Do something Joe!

Tammy McCall – Oh my word Gina, how can you say such a horrible thing?

Julie – You witch! (runs outside)

Security – Mam, you're going to have to hold it down or I'm going to escort you out of here, understand me?...

Gina Coletti – I hate you Nick! (screams at Nick as Nick heads outside to check on Julie)

The head nurse in the back ground informs Maryann's parents of her passing

Mrs. Swenson – No! No! (she faints into her husband's arms)

Mr. Swenson – Honey please! (as he too begins to become weak with shock) Don't do this, I need you too.

The McCalls run over to help them cope Moose's mother is talking to a doctor's assistant

Doctors asst. – So his injuries are serious, but not life threatening mam, he'll be o.k. we're still checking him out.

Mrs. Flannigan – Oh thank you so much doctor (she walks over to have a seat)

Stew's parents enter into the E.R. room looking around for Stew, they walk up to some people and ask if they had seen him, then they approach a nurse

Mr. Combs (Bob) – Hi, is our son here?, we heard he was brought here, do you know if he's hurt' or?...

Nurse – Ah, what's your son's name? (as she looks at her chart)

Mrs. Combs (Susan) – Stewart, they call him Stew, do you know if he's o.k.? (In a calmly manner)

Nurse – (Finds his name and next to his name on her chart it reads, deceased. The nurse looks stunned for a quick second and excuses herself) Let me go check, real quick, I'll be right back.

Nurse heads to the back section and sits down and begins to cry, another nurse and doctor come to her aide

Doctor – What's wrong Chris, are you o.k.?

Nurse 4 – Chrissy, what's wrong honey?

Chrissy – I can't tell them…

Nurse 4 – Tell who honey? Can't tell who?

Chrissy – The folks of that young boy they brought in, that Stewart boy, his parents are asking for him and they seem as though they feel he's o.k. and I can't tell them…he died!

Doctor – That's alright Chris, I'll tell them, what's there last name? (looks at the chart) Combs (walks out to tell Stews parents)

Doctor – (Calls out) Combs, Mr. & Mrs. Combs?

Bob – Yes right here doctor! (they approach the doctor)

Doctor – Folks, I have some bad news.. your son Stewart was in a terrible accident and he didn't . . .make it, I'm so sorry.

Susan – (Grab's the doctor and says) No! please don't tell me please (breaks down crying)

Bob – Are you sure doctor, are you positively sure?

Doctor – Yes Mr. Combs I'm afraid so, there was nothing we could do for him, he had died prior to their arrival with him, I'm so sorry. (walks away)

Bill McCall – (Walks over to Andrew who sits all alone in a corner of the waiting room) Andrew, Andrew? What ah…

Andrew – They killed him Mr. McCall, they shot and killed Paul (somberly)

Bill McCall – Oh my Lord Andrew, I'm so sorry… where are your folks?

Andrew – They are out of town, they're not due back until tomorrow I think or the next day (cries)

Bill McCall – (Embraces Andrew) O.K. son let it out, It's going to be alright (Bill McCall cries)

Time elapses 2 hours pass – still in the E.R. room

A surgeon and a nurse from the operating room come out to the waiting area

Nurse – Mr. and Mrs. McCall?

The McCall's – Yes! (They approach quickly) Is Tommy o.k.?

Surgeon – He's out of surgery for now, he's is not out of danger by all means, he has major injuries both to his head and back and neck. We drained blood and fluids from his brain and we're doing all we can do to reduce the swelling of his nerves in his neck, all we can do is watch and hope he can make some improvements on his own, only time will tell, Now if you'll excuse me, I have to assist back in the O.R. (He turns and leaves)

Nurse – We're keeping a close eye on him, he's surrounded by nurses, we're doing all we can for now, he's a strong young boy (She turns and leaves as well)

A woman doctor – (Comes to the waiting room area and calls out) Nick?

Nick rushes towards the doctor and Mrs. Coletti who is asleep wakes up when she see's Nick approaching the doctor

Gina Coletti - Hey, don't you dare try to act like you care... you barbarian!

The woman doctor – Who is this lady?

Nick – This is Josephine's mother and father Mr. and Mrs. Coletti

Joe Coletti – Gina, can't you maintain yourself for one minute? Please! I'm sorry Doctor ...

Woman doctor – For the sake of your daughter Mrs. Coletti now is not the time to unleash your feeling or opinions, we have a lot of issues with several other people and their families, so don't be so damn selfish and be more considerate, please.

Nick – How is she doc?

Woman doctor – She is doing well, resting, we've run several test and examinations on her, and we put a cast on her broken right arm, luckily it was a clean break, we placed it back and put a short cast on it. Now she did suffer a pretty serious concussion, but x-rays show no bleeding of the brain, and outside of some bumps and bruises, she is going to recover quite well... and Nick she is in recovery and she's asking for you, but don't stay to long o.k.?

Nick – Thank you so much (he hugs the doctor) Mr. and Mrs. Coletti, please you guys go ahead and go first, I'll wait (Mrs. Coletti starts to cry more)

Joe Coletti – Nick (puts his arm around Nick) Why don't you come with us (Gina walks ahead, Nick and Joe walk behind)

As they walk to visit with Josephine, sheriff detectives and police arrive at the hospital to investigate and interview all who were involved and to discover the losses by the group from South County, as Mr. and Mrs. Combs complete release papers for the mortuary, a detective approaches them

Detective Mitchell – Hi folks, my name name is Det. Mitchell with the Midland County Sheriff's Dept. I understand your son Stewart was a possible victim at the crime scene on Country highway...

Bob Combs – look, I know you have a job to do, but we haven't slept all night and my wife is not feeling up to this, I hope you can understand...

Det. Mitchell – I do understand, and my condolences to your family for your loss, ah, would it be possible to stop by later at your residence to chat a bit?, I promise it won't take long...

Bob Combs – Yea that be fine ah, our address is... (fades out to the McCall's and the Swenson's

Det. Carson – Hi folks, I'm Det. Carson with the Midland County Sheriff's dept. I understand you lost a daughter this, last night correct? And your son is in critical condition I believe, right?

I have a few questions if you don't mind, I know it might not seem appropriate but we need to start this investigation to see of any of this chaos and madness can be brought into perspective, so...

Todd Sewnson – First of all, we lost a daughter, the Combs lost a son as well as the Styles, but you say into perspective?, chaos? and madness?, I have a question for you, Why are you here and not over at Midland asking questions there?

Det. Carson – I would be Mr. Swenson, but as for now there is no one to interview or question over there... as of yet.

Mrs. Swenson (Philys) – What do you mean, they are the murderers that did this, they took some of our children's lives!

Det. Carson – It seems that way, but we have no way of proving that yet Mr. Swenson because...

Bill McCall – You need to start your investigation over there

Detective, not here!

Det. Carson – Well you have more living witnesses here then they do...so...

Tammy Swenson – What do you mean by that?

Det. Carson – Yea, it seems like there were about a dozen of kids from Midland involved, but 8 or 9 are dead and 3 suffered serious gun shot wounds and are clinging to life right now.

Bill McCall – Oh my dear God! What?

Det. Carson – Yea, so you see we need to find a starting post to find out what's going on and who did what to who and so on...

Julie's mom is entering the E.R. room as Bob and Susan Combs are walking out, Julie sits in the corner with Andrew

Susan Combs stops Terry Bennett at the door front

Susan – Terry?

Terry – Oh, Susan (surprised)

Susan – Is your daughter here Terry?

Terry – I hope she is, they called me to come pick her up.

Susan – Because she was with our son tonight…

Terry – Ohh, I didn't know that… what happened?

Bob – Our son Stewart was killed tonight…

Terry – What, oh my God, Susan, Bob I'm so sorry, oh my goodness I am so so sorry, but where's my daughter?

Susan – I don't who she is… is she in here?

Terry – There she is… Julie!

Julie – Oh mom, I'm so sorry mom, I'm sorry for not telling you about the rock and roll show, I didn't tell you because…

Terry – Oh honey, it's o.k. it's o.k. honey… (pause's) this is Stewarts mom and dad, she was a friend of mine from high school.

Julie hugs Susan and Bob and weeps uncontrollably

Josephine's room, as Gina and Joe sit on each side and Nick stands at the foot of the bed. Josephine here's the soft subtle voice of her father

Joe – Hey sweetheart… are you awake?

Josephine – (Waking up slowly) Mmmm, papa? (struggle's to open her eyes)

Gina – We're here baby, mama and papa are here sweetie, you're o.k. baby...

Joe – Josephine? Nick is here too... Come Nick.

Josephine – (Opens her eyes, squinting) Nick, baby are you o.k.? (begins to cry)

Gina – Maybe you should wait outside... (stares directly into Nicks eyes)

Joe – Nonsense!

Nick – Hey baby I'm o.k. how are you? I'm o.k. Josephine...

Gina – Can't you see how she's doing?

Detectives Carson and Mitchell stand at the door of Josephine's room listening

Josephine – You know what mama (says in a crying voice) if it wasn't for Nick we'd all be dead, you know that... you know that now, Nick saved everybody out there that is still alive, and we have him to thank mother...

Nick – (Nick hugs Josephine) Shhhh calm down baby, don't get yourself worked up please, relax baby...

Joe – Nick, thank you (shakes his hand them suddenly hugs him and cries) thank you Nick, I can't thank you enough son...

Gina – (crying, with her head down) I'm sorry, I'm so sorry Nick, she's our little girl, she's all we got (embraces Nick)

Nick – It's o.k. Mrs. Coletti, Josephine is going to be o.k. that's what counts, I'm sorry too for whatever I have said or might have done to you to make you feel this way.

Det. Carson – Nick, can we talk to you out here for a minute?

Nick – Sure (Walks out the door) How can I help you?

Det. Mitchell – Nick, I'm Detective Mitchell and this is Detective Carson... Can you tell us what in the world happen out there Nick?

Nick – A bunch of us went to the Rock & Roll show right? at the college, we went with a plan to stick together no matter what, and ah, Stewart disobeyed the order and wondered off to the bathroom alone and lo and behold no witnesses, but got his face smashed in and his ribs kicked in and couldn't walk when we took him out of the nurses quarter with a bloody face and could barely breath (Nick say's with a cracking voice)

Det. Carson – No one seen him getting beat up?

Nick – He went to the bathroom from what he told us, and he said he got jumped by 2 guys, he's not a fighter man, he's not a threat to anyone, and a couple of our people seen 2 guys run out of the bathroom in the other direction towards where we found them hiding Stewie.

Det. Mitchell – O.K. you need to tone it down Nick, where trying to get a grip on what and who was behind all these murders.

Nick – Who's behind them? Why don't you ask the head that college and the Capt. Of that worthless police dept. why don't you ask them?

Det. Carson – Why them Nick?

Nick – Cause Stewie said when they took him from the bathroom to the nurses quarter, that Capt. Billings guy was standing and laughing at him, in the hallway, why would they take him to the nurses quarter when they knew he was from South County... Why? Knowing that he had friends with him yet they didn't even come looking for us... why?

Both Detectives look at each other

Det. Mitchell – Did anyone else hear Stewart say that he saw Capt. Billings in the hallway?

Nick - Yea, Josephine here and Julie and Jimmy, they were all in the car when Stew told us man, he was set up, this whole mess was set up man, they planned this out from the get go!

Det. Carson - Easy Nick, I'm going to ask you son to hold it together o.k.? can you do that for us, and for everyone else?

Nick – (Rubs his hair back and grabs his neck) I don't... the more thought of what happen and what could have happen, is driving me crazy man... Look at Stewie man, he's gone, Maryann, gone,

Paul... Tommy boy hanging on, I mean (breaks down as Det. Carson the elder of the 2 detectives holds Nick as he cries)

Det. Mitchell - Hey Nick, Did you see who shot the boys from the city?

Nick – (Pulls away from Det. Carson wipes his eyes) What do mean who shot the boys from the city? What do you mean?

Det. Carson - Yea Nick someone shot the boys that attacked you guys, as they drove back to Midland...

Det. Mitchell – They were ambushed and over 70 rounds killed 7 out of 10 and the other 3 are in pretty bad shape, it looks pretty bad.

Nick – (Sits down and hold his head and remembers to himself when he, Moose and Jimmy heard a series of gun shots fired off in the distance)

Det. Carson – You didn't know about the shootings Nick?

Nick – No, no I, I ah (pauses as he thinks)

Det. Mitchell – Did you see anything Nick or anyone that had guns? You look like you remembered something, what is it, what were you going to say?

Nick – No, I just can't believe all of this happened, it seems like, I died and was placed in another planet that's all (gets up and walks back towards Josephine's room) You guys need to go talk to those punks from the Big City, before I do.

The E.R. waiting room – Jimmy sits half asleep with Andrew who is asleep in a corner as Moose comes out from the E.R. area

Moose – Hey Red bird (Quietly)

Jimmy – (Wakes up) Aye Moose, you o.k.?

Moose – Ah, some stitches and x-rays and crap like that...

Jimmy – Let me see (Inspects the back of Moose's head) Oooo!

Moose – How's Andrew hanging?

Jimmy – A nurse gave him a sedative to relax him, but I think Mr. and Mrs. McCall are going to take him home until his parents get back tomorrow

Moose – Ah that's good, poor Paul man, and Andrew and the parents man, they are going to be floored by all this crap.

Just then 2 Police from the Big City approach Moose

Police 1 – Are you Clendon Flannigan?

Moose – Yea, why?

Police 2 – Can you stand up please?

Moose – Sure (Stands up) What's going on?

Police 1 – Can you turn around and place your hands behind your back?

Moose – Yea I could but you're gonna...

Police 2 – Just do it (grabs Moose and Moose pushes him away and a ruckus breaks out, Moose throws the other police man to the floor and Jimmy stands side by side asking what's going on? Soon Bill McCall, Joe Coletti, Nick and 3 male assistance and 2 nurses run to the fiasco going on)

Police 1 – (Places his hands on his gun and orders) Get on your knees and place your hands on your head!

Police 2 – Do it now!

Sheriff Coleman and an assistant and Det. Mitchell and Carson arrive at the scene

Moose – Screw you!

Sheriff Coleman – What on earth is happening here?

Police – We're here to apprehend the suspect for a murder!

Jimmy – We kept asking them what's going on and they just tried bullying Moose without answering his question…

Moose – I don't trust these dirt bag no good for nothing crooks!

Sheriff – You mind explaining to him and now to us what the charge is and what evidence you have against him?

Police 1 – We were ordered by Capt. Billings to come down here and arrest Clendon Moose Flannigan for the murder of a one Daniel Mills last night sheriff.

Sheriff Coleman – And you have evidence of Moose here is the one that committed this murder?

Police 2 – According to Capt. Billings, yes.

Sheriff – Well fellas, inlight of what's taken place in the last 8 hours I'm going to overrule the arresting of Mr. Flannigan here, and I will take it up with Capt. Billing myself, so you guys are excused from my jurisdiction (The 2 officers turn and walk away)

Det. Mitchell – Son, what murder are they talking about?

Moose – I don't know, how about Maryann, huh? Maybe Stewie huh or Paul, huh who else maybe Tommy? You tell me...

Det. Carson O.k. son settle down... did you do any shooting?

Sheriff Coleman – O.K. Moose its o.k. (looks at his wounds) You alright Moose?

Moose – Yea with these (shows both of his fists) I'll be alright when I go back and smash them punks up, then ask me that question again!

Det. Carson - Take it easy son...

Nick – Moose, somebody blasted those guys full of holes man, after they left us.

Moose – No, really? (Look of concern)

Nick – Yeah like 7 out of 10 man were killed and the other 3 are like Tommy boy, hanging on for dear life.

Jimmy – Ahh man those were...

Nick – Yeah those were the same guys (as he raises his voice to over ride Jimmys voice) that ambushed us your right!

Moose – (Looks at Jimmy and shakes his head no)

Jimmy – (Sits down) Wowie I can't believe this man...

Det. Carson – Well believe it son, it's for real and we have to solve who did what, to whom and why.

Sheriff Coleman – I can give all those answers in a paper bag in a short while detectives, but I'm going to need your help.

Det. Carson – Sure, you got it John.

Det. Mitchell – Hey we're here for you Sheriff...

Sheriff Coleman - O.k. come with me, we'll see you guys in a bit.

Moose's mother arrives back in the E.R. and see's Moose and runs to him

Mrs. Flannigan – Oh... Moose are you hurt?

Moose – No mama I'm o.k. it's just a scratch, no worries mama.

Mrs. Flannigan – (Hugs him and cries) Oh what would I ever do without you Moose, your sisters and I would be devastated.

Nick – We'll talk in a bit (looks at Moose and Nick and Jimmy and Joe walk away)

Jimmy – I'm sorry Nick, Mr. Coletti, with all that's going on and spinning in my head, I haven't even asked how's Josephine?

Nick – (Puts his arm around Jimmy) Oh, she's gonna be fine Jimmy boy, She's gonna be fine, a few broken parts and bumps and bruises but she's o.k. man.

Joe Coletti – She's good and so is Nick here (he puts his arm around Jimmy too)

Jimmy – Boy not only is she smart and pretty, but she's tough as well.

Joe Coletti – Yea well I think Nick wouldn't have it any other way.

Police try to keep reporters out of the E.R. for the sake of the parents and the injured on behalf of the doctors and nurses request at the front entrance

As police walk in and out of the E.R. area Susan Combs sits with Julie and her mother Terry as Bob Combs went for coffee

Julie – So then it finally happens the opportunity for Stew to dance and team up with Tony's girl Marianna... and so they went out to the dance floor and I mean they took on about 10 other couples (laughs along with Susan and Terry) and by the time you knew it, It was down to them and another couple and Stewie stopped and told the other couple to dance... and then him and Marianna broke into their final moves and they saved their best for last (laughs and cries) and Stewie ended it by doing 3 jumps and splits while Marianna spun around and they stopped as if they had planned it all out, it was fantastic and the crowd went crazy and even Jerry Lee stood and applauded them (they all cried with smiles)

Susan – (Wipes her tears) I always knew Stewart was gifted, but he seemed to have a little self-esteem issue, that no one liked him and yet everybody has nothing but good things to say about him.

Terry – I'm so sorry Susan (they hug) for everything, really I am.

Susan – Thank you Terry, thank you so much.

Julie – Mrs. Combs

Susan – Just call me Susan, please.

Julie – I thought I had hit the jackpot with Stewie, I really did, I mean as far as being with him and all.

Susan – Ah thank you sweetie, and I'm sure, if I know Stewie he was more than likely head over heels for you too.

Jimmy – Hi Mrs. Combs (As Jimmy greets Susan she stands and they hug and cry) What am I going to do now Mrs. Combs? I don't know...

Susan – Now, Now come now honey, it's going to be fine, I have to be strong for Stew and so do you, we all do and look, he's not the only one, there are a few others that also suffered loses here, I know it all seems like a bad dream and we'll all grieve together, but he left us a lot to be happy about, don't you think?

Jimmy – Boy Mrs. Combs, I wish it would have been me, Stewie was a good kid you know.

The Rev. Williams arrives as Bob arrives with the coffee coming out of a hallway

Bob Combs – Hello Reverend, would you like a coffee?

The Rev. Good morning Bob, no that's fine, but thank you Bob.

Bob – I was wondering if anyone had called you.

Rev. – Well as a matter of fact I received a few calls, so I couldn't sleep after that bad news so I thought I'd make my way over here to see how I could be of any help, and Bob I am so sorry to hear about Stewart, I am so so sorry...

Bob – Thank you Reverend, It's kind of hard to believe at this point and I would imagine it's going to take some time to set in, but I'm sure it will, but we're not the only ones that lost someone either, so...

Rev. – Well your being very strong Bob and that is very important especially for Susan at this point... Hello Susan, I am so sorry for your loss (As he hugs Susan)

Susan – Oh thank you Reverend, thank you so much, ... Reverend I don't know if you remember Terry?

Rev. – Sure I remember (embraces her) How are you dear? Welcome back...

In front of Josephine's room

Joe – Nick I think you should go home and get some rest, Josephine has been given another sedative to help her sleep so...

Nick – Ah I appreciate the thought Mr. Coletti but I would just go... I wouldn't be at rest, I need to be here at least for a while longer, my blood is just...

Joe – Son, I know this is a total disaster with some exceptions, but you need to rest... get some rest and clean up, did you have the doctors take a look at you?

Nick – They tried Mr. Col...

Joe – Please Nick call me Joe.

Nick – Eventually I will, you know but I'm going to have some trouble dealing with this situation here, you know cause...

Joe – Nick, there is no reason to put yourself through all this agony Nick, I know you feel responsible for what happen but it was out of your control and to put yourself through the pain and blaming yourself is not a good thing, it wasn't your fault as to all this tragedy, son...

Nick – Look, I know I'm not at fault, but to see Josephine, I mean she could have gotten...

Joe – That's what I'm saying son, that's exactly what I'm saying here, your saying she could have but she didn't.

Nick – Yeah but look at Stewie man, Maryann and Paul, Tommy hanging on by a thread (starts to cry as Joe embraces him to comfort him and Gina comes out of Josephine's room and witnesses Joe's affection for Nick and develops tears in hers eyes)

Gina – Nick, come home with us... so I can fix you something to eat and you can get cleaned up and rest up a bit and we can come back later, Josephine will be asleep for a while, please... come on...

Nick – (Hugs Gina) Thank you Mrs. Coletti, but I'm going to hang out here in case she wakes up I don't want to not be here for her, so you guys go and get some rest, I'll be here, I'm good, honest I am...

Joe – Are you sure Nick?

Nick – Yea I'm good and if something comes up I'll call you guys, go ahead.

Gina hugs Nick and cries and apologizes for everything and Joe hugs and thanks Nick and Nick sheds some quiet tears with a smile – The Rev. Williams finishes up a circle of prayers with some of the families – Everyone embraces one another

As the morning sun begins to rise, detectives, police and reporters still linger around the hospital

Sheriff's office

Sheriff John Coleman – And this dates back 21 years ago.

Det. Carson – Wow, yea I remember when it happen, I heard it when I was over in Bakersfield.

Det. Mitchell – Unbelievable I tell you, but do you think this all culminates from that time?

Det. Carson – I think so just based off of all the talk I've heard over the years.

Sheriff Coleman – The truth is fellas, I believe it only exists because of 2 people, because they won't let it go, and they have been keeping this beast caged up and feeding it, and I believe this is going to prove my theory is correct (Sheriff Coleman pulls out a pack of pictures he had Max Tolbert of

Maxwell's Pharmacy get out of bed at 4 a.m. to give him some finished film he developed for Sheriff Coleman late Saturday night)

Det. Carson – Hmm, that's Capt. Billings brother Fred (as he combs through the photos and hands them to Det. Mitchell) This is dated when? Yesterday?...

Det. Mitchell – This is where?

Sheriff Coleman – In back of the police station in Midland.

Det. Mitchell – And this was yesterday huh?

Sheriff Coleman – Yesterday afternoon gentlemen.

Det. Carson – And these trucks in the back ground... look like the ones that were used in the ambush (puts the pictures down and looks at Sheriff Coleman with a shocked look on his face) Is there motive?

Sheriff Coleman – Uh huh... keep looking.

Det. Carson – (looks through 3 more pictures and comes across a photo that has Fred Billings the superintendent of the college showing the truck to 4 of the boys that were involved in the ambush and were shot in the second ambush going home to Midland) Oh my Goodness John, how in the world did you come across these?

Det. Mitchell - Amazing, simply amazing Sheriff!

Sheriff Coleman – Well you credit that to experience and good detective work ... or simply luck and at this point I'd have to say luck

Det. Carson – Intuition I think.

Sheriff Coleman – Well this whole rock and roll show has bugged me from the very beginning of the talk of this show coming to the city right ... So I was concerned and I began to ask around of the boys from South County were planning on going, but I also know Billings and his brother, you see it was their little brother Phillip that was killed by Steve Bennett while his good friend Dominic Pagani stood by and watched... So I would say revenge is there motive.

Det. Mitchell – Ohhh, hmmm

Det. Carson – So over the years...

Sheriff Coleman – Over the years these brothers along with others have kept this fire burning and refused to let it die.

Det. Mitchell – Revenge...

Sheriff – Revenge has always been the motive, except for the fact that they had to grow up and get jobs, get married and have kids, but they never forgot, never forgave and always thought payback, and here it is!

Det. Mitchell – So how did you get the pictures?

Sheriff Coleman – After my shift yesterday morning, I had breakfast at Tina's and I seen some of the dads there and I chatted with them a bit and I guess you can say I left there with a little bit of curiosity on my mind, so I jumped into my car, I always have my camera and I decided to go check out the scene at the college and I happen to drive by the police station and I seen Billings out back talking to some of his officers and I noticed Fred there in the back row looking over the trucks with some students I guess and Frank only 20 feet away, so it wasn't like he was unaware of his brother and young men 20 feet away, and those are the same trucks used in the ambush, so I had a couple of my detectives fingerprint the steering wheels of those trucks and I had Max print the date and time of the pictures I took.

Det. Carson – So my next question to you John, How do you want to handle this?

Sheriff Coleman – I think we need to find a witness like from there side of the road to talk to us and collaborate the fact that they were put up to this by the Billings and with what evidence we have, I believe we can solve this case and hopefully put a stop to the 21 year old grudge war.

Det. Mitchell – Let's hope... Let's hope it's the end and not the beginning of the second half.

Det. Carson – And the ten victims from Midland?

Sheriff Coleman – Not at the risk of sounding inconsiderate but, I think if we solve part 1, we'll solve part 2.

All 3 stay looking at each other

Back at the hospital, Nick sits outside and talks to Juan

Juan – I'm sorry to hear about this whole mess man, I can't believe Maryann and Stewie and Paul ese... I liked Paul man he was o.k. with me you know, he respected everybody aye...Damn!

Nick – It's hard to believe, I'm just waiting to wake up from this bad dream (hangs his head)

Juan – I woke up early this morning cause I thought I was dreaming too ese...

Nick – What do you mean?

Juan – Yea, the cops aye, came pounding at my door wanting to search my car and my room and from what I heard Sergio and Tony's pad and Arturo's pad...

Nick – Nothing?

Juan – Nothing ese, I guess we disappointed them, but my little bro. came home and told me that some plato came down at the concert so Tony got Marianna out of there early.

Nick – Yea, well I'm not going to ask why you weren't there but... maybe it's better that you weren't.

Juan – (smiles and looks off into the distance) Who says we weren't there carnal?

Nick – (Stares at Juan as Juan still looking away, Nick shakes his head) You mean...

Juan – Did you see Tony and my carnal?
Nick – Yea they were there.

Juan – And at the first sign of trouble, where were they?

Nick – they were gone ... whooo! Dissapeared like magic...

Juan – They had your back holmes, they were looking out for you and all your troops ese...

Nick – Where were you Juan?

Juan – Lets just say, paying you back brother like I said I would (Juan and Nick stay starring at each other)

Midland City Hospital parking lot

Det. Mitchell – Sheriff... (As Sheriff Coleman is walking to the entrance of the hospital) Sheriff!

Sheriff Coleman – Hey...

Det. Mitchell – I just spoke to an investigating officer and he tells me that they discovered some pretty incriminating evidence sheriff...

Sheriff Coleman – Really, like?

Det. Mitchell – Like guns and marijuana in the cars of several of the boys…

Sheriff Coleman – Who's cars?

Det. Mitchell – The cars are all from the boys that were shot from the Midland.

Sheriff Coleman – The city boys?

Det. Mitchell – Yep!

Sheriff – Was there a search on the South County boys?

Det. Mitchell – Oh yea, clean, every one of them, they even had search warrants for the Mexican boy's cars, and they too were all clean.

Sheriff Coleman – Good, where's Carson?

Det. Mitchell – He's getting copies here in town of the preliminary reports, so they don't end up getting changed before you know who finds out.

Sheriff Coleman – Good, hey listen, are you busy right now?

Det. Mitchell – What do you need?

Sheriff Coleman – I need for you to interview, or at least find out which one of these city boys will talk, you know.

Det. Mitchell – Gotcha, you got it...

Sheriff Coleman – I'm going to head back to South County, I'll catch you later.

South County Hospital, Sal and Sofia Celetti and Ron Tomkins Sr. and Junior sit with Nick

Sal – I'm so sorry Nicky for all this you had to endure...

Ron Tomkins – You'd think those big city people would have had too much on their agenda's to carry this grudge this far and this long (rubs his head in disbelief)

Nick – Yea it seems everyone from here knows that.

Sofia – It's like your Raymond Ron, he was set up by those monsters.

Sal – Sofia, there was never no...

Ron – She's right Sal, he was set up, that girl had him go over there to meet her and then she lured him to the location where he was beat up according to an eye witness.

Sal – Then why didn't you file charges Ron?

Junior – Cause Mr. Celetti, they changed the reports to cover it up.

Sal – Who?

Ron – The cops Sal, the police from the city changed or had the reports changed to make it look like it was a fight instigated by Ray, that was the farthest thing from the truth...

Junior – Yea, and then what happen to him was his own fault according to those slime balls then all of a sudden, no witness anymore...

Sal – So they're all in on it, all of them, from the people to police, to the D.A and even the judges, all of them!

Sofia – But how long is this going to continue?

Ron – That's why for this last year Sergio, poor boy, thinks it was his fault as to Raymond dying (as he stares out a hospital window) when Raymond got to that party he asked Sergio to give him a ride home, but Sergio had been drinking and was afraid to get caught again, and told Ray just to drive slow, Serge didn't know Raymond was hurting from his head, he thought Ray had just been drinking, so when Ray left he passed out behind the wheel and hit, the (starts crying)...

Junior – (Hugs his dad) Dad come on now, don't get yourself all worked up again, its o.k.

Nick – Well Mr. Tomkins I know Sergio has had a lot of trouble dealing with that but he's...

Ron – I know Nick, I don't blame Sergio for nothing, as a matter of fact I've been so heart felt for him because of his feelings, I love that boy, I love all them boys, and all of you guys because you guys are all friends, and that means a lot to me.

Sofia – You too are special to everybody in this town Ron, because you always are the first to extend your hand to help others... Marge would be so proud of you.

Sal – That's right Ronny.

Nick – You're a good man Mr. Tomkins.

Junior – I love you dad...

Ron – I love you too son (as they embrace)

Sal – Son, You better get home and clean up and get some rest, don't let Josephine see you all torn up with blood on you son, it'll only bring back bad flashes, you know.

Sofia – Let us give you a ride home Nicky...

Nick – Yea I guess you're right Mr. C, you're always right...

Sofia – Well it's like he says, He's not always right, (they both say it together) but he's never wrong (as they begin to walk away)

Sal – You guys coming Ron?

Ron – In a bit, I'm going to check on the McCalls and others I'll see you guys later...

Sal – O.k. then (Sal walks with his arm around Nick as Sofia walks holding Nicks hand)

Parking lot of the Midland police department

Officer Hamilton – You wanted to me sir?

Capt. Billings – Yes I did, I understand you're the one who's done the initial preliminary reports?

Off. Hamilton – Yes sir...

Capt. Billings – I want them on my desk a.s.a.p.

Off. Hamilton – They should be there soon sir, I've turned them in for processing and copies will be on your desk a.s.a.p.

Capt. Billings – You turned them in so soon?

Off. Hamilton – Just the pre...

Capt. Billings – I know what the preliminary is Hamilton, I wanted to view it before it was submitted...

Off. Hamilton – Sorry sir, it's just other agencies wanted a scope of what was discovered by us so they can compare notes.

Capt. Billings – O.K. O.K. is there anything I should know?

Off. Hamilton – Well sir we confiscated some guns and marijuana from Dan's car and a gun and marijuana in James, Brian and Zachary's car sir...

Capt. Billings – Guns? Where they or had they been fired?

Off. Hamilton – Looks that way sir...

Capt. Billings – Is that in the reports?

Off. Hamilton – Yes sir it is.

Capt. Billings – (Gets into his car, rolls down his window) What other agencies Hamilton?

Off. Hamilton – South County Sheriffs, State Department or FBI and our department as well as our sheriff detectives sir.

Capt. Billings drives away with a worried look on his face

Moose's house, as Laura's mother and father (Chris and Larry Snyder) visit with Moose and his mother (Margaret Flannigan and his 2 younger sisters Marlene and Lana)

Margaret – More coffee Larry?

Larry – Oh thank you

Margaret – Like I was saying when I got the phone call at 3:30 this morning, I couldn't comprehend anything, I thought Moose had already come home so I was completely thrown

Chris – I know, I could imagine Margaret, I mean how much can one person understand at 3 in the morning and then a call from the hospital that your child is there, I mean come on can you be more considerate?

Larry – The way they said it you know 'Your daughter is here at South County Hospital emergency being checked out, there was a horrible accident please come down as soon as possible, please thank you' What are you supposed to do, or think, my God...

Margaret – That's what I'm saying, you freeze, your brain, the train of the thought, you can't think or act...

Chris – I guess we're the fortunate ones however...

Margaret – In my call they told me my son had been injured in the accident and was receiving emergency medical treatment, for me to rush because the doctor needed to make some decisions, I couldn't even (starts to cry and Moose hugs her as Moose's younger sisters look on with tears and Laura gets up and hugs Margaret as well and then comforts the girls)

Moose – They couldn't hurt me mama, not this time.

Margaret – Then they tell me you're under investigation for killing someone?

Laura – Mrs. Flannigan the detectives and Sheriff Coleman all said it was all done in self-defense, he was being attacked by 4 guys hitting him with 2x4's, what was he supposed to do sit there and wait for the cops and get beat?

Chris – Police Laura, not cops

Larry – Those miserable creeps are cops… keystone cops!

Moose – We were set up, we were set up good and Nick thinks those punks are too stupid to think up a plan like this, he feels someone else is behind it.

Larry – You know I went to City college and I played football, as a matter of fact, I played with Fred you know Capt. Frank Billings brother and it was their little brother Phil that was killed by Mike Bennett in what we thought was a straight up fair and square fight, he just happen to fall and hit his head on a bumper of a car then the cement… (pauses) those guys, those brothers never forgot, I know because me and couple of other guys from South County were given a rough time but we were some of the best players so we were favored by the coaching staff…

Margaret – That is a terrible thing to do if indeed it was revenge after 20 years or so…

Laura – I'm happy in so many ways that you're o.k. (hugs Moose and Moose hugs her back) but I'm sad for all the others… our friends and their families, it won't be the same without them.

Moose – I know, I'm glad too that you didn't get hurt, especially on our first official date, but my buddy Tommy and his girlfriend Maryann are gone, my buddy Stew, he was like the brat little brother I never had (stays hugging Laura in the middle of the living room while everyone looks on, as Moose sheds more tears)

Nicks house, Sheriff Coleman knocks and knocks on Nicks door

Nick – (Nick awakens from his sleep as he is all cleaned up) O.K. I'm coming (opens the door) Uhh, it's you…

Sheriff Coleman – Sorry Nick for waking you up…

Nick – It's O.k. I was just hoping that when I woke up it was gonna have all been a bad dream, you know?

Sheriff Coleman – I understand Nick, but I need to get you're take on the incident, you know step by step on every event of the evening, can you do that?

Nick – Sure, I can do that… you're going to make me live it all over again and again and again, aren't you?

Sheriff Coleman – Sorry Nick… First of all, just off the record, who do you think did this, I mean master minded this whole ambush?

Nick – I don't know who master minded this whole thing, but I do know it wasn't those young punk guys from the city, (pauses) In my opinion it was somebody who still wants revenge from 20 years ago…

Sheriff Coleman – What about the city boys that did the attacking and then were shot on their way back to Midland, do have an opinion on that?

Nick – Maybe the same person who tried doing us in, did them in to cover their tracks, I don't know…leave no eye witness thing, you know.

Sheriff Coleman – Like I said Nick this is all off the record, do you know where Juan and the muchachos were last night?

Nick – (Looks confidant) Well, they weren't there except for Tony, Marianna and Jesse, you know Juan's little brother?

Sheriff – (Looks in thought) Yeah… Tony said soon as they heard Stewart had been jumped they left because to him that was a bad sign to the small towner's and especially to them, he wanted to get his wife out of there, well he said his old lady, old? She's only 17 (chuckles)

Nick – Yeah that's right… especially to them, and Tony wasn't about to let anything happen to his wife and to Juan's little brother you know…

Sheriff Coleman – O.K. on the record, you said Stew told you and who else about seeing Capt. Billings laughing at him in the hallway…

Nick – Me, Moose, Tommy… then he told Josephine, Julie and Red, you know Jimmy and me again…

Sheriff Coleman – O.k. (as he writes down the information) I'm going to have to get statements from them as well…

Nick – You think that big city copper had something to do with it?

Sheriff Coleman – Do you know the story of the event that took place?

Nick – Way back when? Uhh bits and pieces you know over the years... and who knows what the real truth or what's been fabricated, you know like when you hear stories of how much a bank robber steals from a bank, you know he really stole 100 dollars, then a week later it was 1000 dollars, then a month later it was 10,000 and after a few years it was 10,000,000.00 you know how it goes,... who knows?

Sheriff Coleman – Mmmm. You're right Nick, who knows ... O.k. let's see...

Tina's diners where Det. Carson and Mitchell are having coffee

Det. Mitchell – How's those reports look?

Det. Carson – Not good...

Det. Mitchell – Hmm, not good for who?, the city boy's or the small towner's?

Det. Carson – Not good for the Billings brothers, adding you're interview with the Bradley's, it doesn't look good for the Billings brothers at all...

Det. Mitchell – Those pictures that Coleman took of the police station Saturday afternoon catching them all on film was amazing huh?

Det. Carson – It's called intuition Mike, a sheriff like John has been around for long long time… just goes to show you when you think about something or something crosses your mind, don't ignore it, either you're conscious or your intuition is telling you to investigate it, see it through…

Det. Mitchell – That comes with experience I guess huh?

Det. Carson – No… (sips his coffee) passion Mike, it's called passion, leaving no stone unturned, you got a gut feeling, which comes from loving your job and what it stands for, go with it.

Fred Billings driveway as Capt. Billings and his brother talk

Capt. Billings – Well what do we do know?

Fred – What do you mean Frank?

Frank – I don't know if you've heard Fred, but it's chaos out there in regards to your little plan…

Fred – Oh now it's my little plan, excuse me?

Frank – You know, in all honesty, I too wanted to get back at those ignorant inbreads that took our little brothers life, but sometimes like mother said, it isn't worth the time or the efforts one takes towards revenge, because you'll be the only one that will end up suffering in the end... remember that?

Fred – Well you know what? Who better to lie than the law themselves... just do what you do best Frank, Lie and deny any involvement, that's all, plain and simple brother.

Frank – Preliminary reports have already been turned in, there's 5 different agencies corroborating in this investigation and now guns and marijuana have been found in some of our boys cars Fred and they were shot down by someone and no one knows who Fred after the ambush they were ambushed...

Fred – Well it sure in hell wasn't me and it wasn't you, was it?

Frank – No, what are you talking about?

Fred – There it is, that's all we need to say, is no, we don't know anything, there is no evidence that traces back to us and now no witnesses, so why are you worried?

Frank – Coleman, that's why.

County General Hospital in Josephine's room with Reverend Williams and Nick walks in

Reverend – And so often times situations arise in our lives, and we don't know why or the reason for that matter, but be assured that God knows, and often he wants to see in which direction are you going to go in, in the midst of the storm, are you going to draw towards him or away from him (as the Reverend sits next to Josephine's bed holding her hand Nick walks in) Oh hello there Nicholas...

Nick – Hello Reverend...

Reverend – (Stands to shake and hug Nick) How are you doing son?

Nick – Better now Reverend, thank you.

Josephine – Hello sweetie, I've been worried about you...

Nick – I'm o.k. I think.

Josephine – Reverend came in and I awoke to him saying a beautiful prayer for me and all of us really, it was so comforting.

Nick – Thank you Reverend, sometimes the prayers come a little to late it seems though huh?

Reverend – Well Nick, sometimes yes and sometimes just in time, I do have to run now I have more stops to make, however son, I would like for you to stop by my house at you're convenience, just to talk… o.k. you have to talk Nick to come to an understanding and to give you some perspective, otherwise it will drive you crazy, o.k. son?, you take care of yourself (turns and kisses Josephine on the forehead) you get well and rest up you here?

Josephine – O.k. I will Reverend, thank you…

Nick – Goodbye Rev. I'll stop by in a day or 2…

Reverend – You do that, bye bye, God bless you both!

Nick – Hello baby – (Nick leans in to hug and kiss Josephine and Josephine hugs him tight with her left arm and they both cry in each other's arms – 30 seconds)

Josephine – Thank you baby...

Nick – For?

Josephine – For saving the rest of us, you were like a mad crazed man, but you kept it together, and you got Jimmy to become something that he isn't or wasn't, you were all of our hero baby...

Nick – Well Moose too and Jimmy...

Josephine – Yea but if it wasn't for you Moose or Jimmy didn't stand a chance Nicky, you were the glue, you saved us baby, I'm so thankful for you...

Nick – O.k. I'll be your hero... as long you'll still be my wife?

Josephine – Oh yes baby, of course, I asked the nurse where my rings are and she put them in a bag here in my drawer...

Nick – I'll get it (opens the drawer to take out the ring and place it back on her hand) do you want the other 2 rings?

Josephine – Not now, this is the only one I want to see on my hand, it is so, beautiful.

Nick – I know your mom and dad didn't see it because the nurses in the E.R. had taken it off you along with the other 2, did you tell your mom?

Josephine – No I was waiting for you so we can tell them together.

Nick – Yea, I told Sal and Sofia and he told me I should go to your house and ask for your hand in marriage, he said that's the proper way of doing it.

Josephine – Yes it is, but the way you did it was you, I mean you got Jerry Lee to dedicate my song to me and it was you baby, I loved it, it was like I was dreaming.

Nick – I love you (kisses her hand) then the nightmare happen.

Tina's house with Tina and her husband Doug sits in Connie's room along with her sisters Kathy and Katie, all trying to comfort Connie

Tina – (Has her arm around Connie trying to comfort her) It's something no young person should have to go through...

Kathy – He was so young with his whole life ahead of him.

Connie – He was so brave out there, when that whole thing happen he jumped right out and protected us with no questions (continues to sob)

Doug – Maybe to brave honey, for his own good…

Katie – Why did this all happen daddy, what's it all about?

Doug – Some useless feud sweetheart, that happen a long time ago and through the years seems like some people just carried this grudge and refused to forgive and forget, I mean…

Katie – I think the new girl's father died in that fight years ago, that's what I heard…

Kathy – Oh yea that girl… Julie

Tina – Yea, how did you guys here about that?

Connie – She just started school this past week, I guess her and her mom use to live here or something, anyway that was all the talk at school this past week, and she was with Stewie at the dance and they were getting along like they had known each other all their lives and this goes and happens…

Tina – You know their mothers were like best friends back in high school and when Terry's boyfriend died in that fight he didn't know Terry who is this Julie girl's mother, was pregnant with Julie's older sister who is off in college back east somewhere...

Kathy – Oh o.k. a lot of people thought it was Julie's father that died...

Doug – No it was Joann I believe, right honey?

Tina – Yes I believe so, she should be about 20 or so now...

Doug – Then Julie's dad and her mom Terry were divorced last year and Terry and Julie moved back here to South County.

Tina – See dad was friends with Joann's father and Nicks father back in that time and dad knows Julie's father because he works for the high school in North Town so they see each other at conferences and meetings.

Connie – Poor Andrew has to bare all this on his own until his folks get back.

Kathy – They are always going on vacations those 2, while Paul and Andrew practically raise themselves this past year...

Doug – They don't vacation honey, they have a new business that they run and it requires for them to be on the road quite a bit trying to get clients, but I'm sure this will at least put a stop to Deborah going on less trips.

Connie – I'm going to call the McCall's to see how Tommy and Andrew are doing.

Katie – Andrew's at the McCall's?

Tina – I'll call honey, I had plans on stopping by, but I'll call and check in with them, I want to take them some food.

Sheriff John Coleman's office with 2 FBI agents, and Both Det. Carson and Mitchell along with 3 Sheriff deputy's

FBI agent 1 – (Looks at pictures and interviewed testimony from young patient/participant) This is solid evidence, testimony, the trucks that were used, finger prints, the Billings brothers at the police yard with some of the ambushers and then they were killed themselves, and that portion of this case still remains a mystery.

Sheriff Coleman – I think we need to get the Billings brothers before they find out we got some evidence on them so they don't fly the coop or others end up dead from them trying to cover their tracks.

Det. Carson – I think your right John, I think we need to get some warrants and get these jokers off the streets…

FBI agent 2 – As long as they're in custody we can then work on them to see if they indeed shot and killed the very same kids they used for the ambush… we need answers to this theory.

FBI agent 1 – That's the way it looks so far but who knows…

Det. Mitchell – I wouldn't bet against it, that's for sure…

Sheriff Coleman – Me neither, but we'll see.

FBI agent 1 – Get me a copy of this entire investigation and after they're arrested and you guys interrogate them we're going to also interrogate them as well, so let the fun begin gentleman, go get them!

Juan's house, as they all sit around the drive way

Juan – Damn, a hell of a night that's for sure…

Tony – It was all going so smooth too, huh?

Jesse – Man I can't believe this whole mess happen to our friends ese...

Sergio – That goes to show you homie, whenever there is unrest between 2 villages anything can happen even if it takes 20 years aye...

Juan – Orale la verda...

Tony – It also goes to show you, when things are done right, whether there right or wrong, if you back some ones play you back it with intentions to help them no matter what it takes.

Juan – What's done is done, never to be mentioned again, it's forgotten, we move on, I'm square with Nick, and old man Tomkins owes us one (Look of confidence) (others say) La verda, Orale, That's it.

The loading docks at Tomkins Farms, Alberto taking a sack from the front seat of Ron Tomkins Jr. truck to his trunk and place's the sack into the little brown suitcase and closes the trunk door as a diesel truck loaded and heading out of town pulls up next to Alberto's car. Alberto places the suitcase on the passenger side

of the diesel truck floor board and closes the door and pats the door twice and the diesel truck leaves out of town. The door of the diesel truck says, Tomkins Farms – Mr. Tomkins is at the intersection in his pick-up truck watching one of his Diesel Truck leave town

Josephine's room at the hospital

Josephine – So you think I might be able to go home by tomorrow then?

Nurse – I think so, the doctor will examine you in the morning and if all looks o.k. to him, I think he might let you go...

Josephine – I hope so (as Joe and Gina enter her room to visit) cause I could do this at home (giggles)

Nurse – That's true, but the head injuries have to be monitored for a couple of days, Oh hello, I'm Helen Josephine's nurse for the evening

Gina – Hello, there not releasing her are they?

Nurse – No she was asking...

Gina – Oh no sweetheart you need to rest and make sure...

Josephine – Mother, mama I know that...

Nurse – O.k. I'll be right out here if you need me.

Josephine – Didn't I tell you?

Nurse – (Smiles) I'll be right out here if you need me.

Joe – Where's Nick?

Josephine – He went to check on Tommy's condition...

Gina – What did you mean when you said to the nurse, didn't I tell you? What did you say to her?

Josephine – Nothing mama, I just told her you guys watch out for me like a mother grizzly watches her cub...that's all.

Gina – I bet you did (Josephine and Joe laugh) look what I brought you, your favorite fresh bake corn bread and some butter, and before you go on, I brought enough for Nick too...

Josephine – Oh mama you are so sweet, (pauses) when you want to be of course, I love you!

Joe – There he is, all cleaned up, are you rested up?

Nick – Hi, well I tried sleeping when Coleman came knocking and woke me up...

Joe – Yea those guys are really trying to put this case together, there all around town, they been in and out of here all day.

Gina – Here Nicky have some warm corn bread with butter...

Nick – Oh Mrs. Colletti that's smells great!

Josephine – Nick, how's Tommy boy doing?

Nick – (Takes a bite of corn bread) He's stable, ah man this is the greatest, ummm, the doctor said the first 24 hours are the most critical, if he makes it through the day he's got a good chance for the bleeding to stop and you know little by little (puts his head down) he'll make it Tommy boy's tough...

Joe – You know Tommy's a fighter Nick, you know that...

Gina – Yea but what will be his reaction when he finds out Maryann has passed?

Josephine – Oh that's right... well like the Reverend said we can't stop praying... praying builds our faith in God...

Nick – That means we have to start praying, and praying hard... for Tommy and everyone else...

Joe – That's right.

Moose's house, getting ready to leave with Laura, Julie and Jimmy back to the hospital, as Moose approaches Laura's car, Det. Carson and Mitchell pull up

Laura – oh o, it's the cops (as she looks through her rear view mirror and gets off the car)

Jimmy – Oh man you think they're there going to arrest Moose? (Jimmy gets off and Julie jumps off)

Det. Mitchell – Clendon?

Moose – That's me...

Det. Carson – Well we seen you at the hospital but we hadn't introduced ourselves to you, I'm Det. Carson and this here is Det. Mitchell (they all shake hands)

Moose - This here is Jimmy Spiderman Tolan, Laura my girlfriend, and this here is Julie, she was out for the first time with Stew last night, what a way to break up huh?

Det. Carson - We're sorry for your loss all of you, really we are, but now that I got you all here we just want to get a quick statement from all of you just to lock up the first portion of this event and to be able to arrest some suspects.

Jimmy – We heard the so called suspects were shot and killed, you found out who it was that did that to them?

Det. Mitchell – No not that portion Jimmy, but we're pretty sure we know who put them up to the ambush, and maybe we'll find out through that who did the shooting too.

Moose – I was hoping you wouldn't find out until after I found them first…

Det. Carson – I know how you must feel Clendon…

Moose – Call me Moose please...

Det. Carson – Moose, but those exact feelings is what kept this fueled in the first place, you got to let it go son because people have and people will continue to die if you don't.

Det. Mitchell – That's the truth... 2 wrongs don't make a right, a made up mind and a smart decision makes it right.

Julie – Come on Moose, we're all hurt, I'm hurt and I barley new him one day, I can imagine you guys who knew him practically all your lives.

Jimmy – I'm not one to tell especially you Moose what to do, but I don't want to lose you either o.k.?

Laura – Yea you big lunk, me neither...

Det. Carson – You see, listen to your friends...

Moose – Yea, I guess your all right (with tears in his eyes)

Det. Carson – O.k just a few questions I won't keep you.

Det. Mitchell - Real quick, where you guys off too?

Moose – The hospital, to go see who's left and to check up on our friends.

Det Carson – O.k. when you guys first left from South County at? (fades out)

Sal's house, on the phone

Sal – Yea it was a shocker to everyone... Yea we lost 3... Well just call Alan for me and tell him to hold off for tomorrow, I'll call you in the afternoon and we'll see how Nick is doing, and we'll get it done when he's ready... Yea ... O.k. Molly thank you huh, and I'll call you tomorrow, o.k.? ... O.k. (hangs up)

Sofia – She was shocked?

Sal – (Rubs his mouth) Oh yes, she was...

Sophia – Yea, she's probably wondering why she came back here instead of taking the job with that big company in San Diego...

Sal – Well I think it was to pick up where her daddy left off as far as building his book keeping business and adding on all the stuff she learned in college... that's what I think, I could be wrong.

Sofia – Molly is a real go getter just like her daddy was...

Sal – Oh yea... that she is.

Back at the hospital

Joe – And her mother didn't want to have nothing to do with me and would try talking Gina into breaking it off with me.

Josephine – Oh mother, you never shared that with me...

Gina – That's because...

Nick – (Laughs) Oh no! I don't think I want to hear this (covers his ears)

Joe – That's because Gina knew what she had in me and her mother didn't, God rest her soul,... I realized it early on in your relationship, but I figured I'm not going to remind Gina, maybe it will come to her, when she reminisces about her past...

Gina – And it took this near tragedy to realize that we could have lost you and your right, it was this precious jewel that saved more lives than there were lost, and I thank you and I ask for your forgiveness again! Mi dispiace (I;m sorry) (They stand and embrace)

Nick – I already forgave you Mrs. Colletti and I never held anything against you anyway, cause I knew my reputation was kind of shaky and I didn't blame you for wanting to protect your daughter.

Josephine – (Cries) This is what I have been waiting for, for so long...

Joe – Me too sweetie... me too.

Nick – And now that I have you both here, I can't wait any longer (reaches into his pocket and pulls something out) Mr. and Mrs.

Colletti, (they stay looking at Nick and Josephine as Nick takes a knee next to Josephine's bedside) May I have your daughters hand in marriage? (Nick holds her hand ready to place the ring back on her finger)

Joe – On behalf of my wife Gina, Nicolas Pagani we would be honored to have you as our son in law! (Gina cries and hugs Nick and Josephine (Nick place the ring back on her, and kisses her)

Nick – Thank you Mr. and Mrs. Colletti... thank you so much!

Joe – Welcome to our family Son, we are honored (they hug)

Detectives and police arrest Fred Billings at his house with search warrants, confiscating items that may be used as evidence against him as well as his office at the college

Detectives also arrest Capt. Billings at a restaurant while having dinner with his wife and another couple

Back at the hospital as the celebration goes on in Josephine's room, Moose, Laura, Julie, Jimmy and Molly all arrive to visit Josephine and join in the celebration (Hugs and tears fill the room)

Nick – Listen everybody, thank you for all being here for this memorable moment, thank you for your well wishes and all your love it means the world to us, you made this real special by showing up here, you know despite all the friends and lives that were devastated by this tragedy, I just want to thank you all and especially Mr. & Mrs. I mean Joe and Gina my in laws to be, and to Moose and Jimmy for your bravery and trying to help save our friends, I will always be ever so thankful to you guys man and to you 2 girls who stuck it out with us and help keep things under control, Thank you, I love you guys (they embrace and share sentiments)

Tommy's Room

As one nurse changes his I.V. bag and the other changes his bedding out

Nurse 1 – Can you Imagine how Northland or Memorial hospital which ever got all those others that were shot, I can't imagine the chaos...

Nurse – Oh I know, I mean we had 3 that were killed (Tommy's eyes open, his head is bandaged up except for his eyes and nose) and those from the city had 7 or 8 I heard...

Nurse 1 – Yea, what a shame for all the families...

Nurse 2 - And this poor boy here when he wakes up...

Nurse 1 – If he wakes up...

Nurse 2 – Oh poor thing, fighting for his life and his family on pins and needles...

Nurse 1 – Terrible, simply terrible, then to find out that his girlfriend was one of the ones that didn't make it (as both nurses leave the room)

Nurse 2 – Oh I know, how sad is that, my goodness!

Tommy's eyes... Begin to tear up as if he heard what the nurses said... His eyes streaming with tears... his heart machine showing aheart beat...15 seconds pass and Tommy flat lines – A code blue is on, as doctors and nurses rush to Tommy's bedside, after a few minutes The McCall's show up only to find Tommy's room filled with exhausted doctors as a nurse escorts the McCall's away from the room and sits them down in the hallway – A doctor comes out from the room and explains to the Mc-Call's that they did all they could do, but they lost him – The McCall's are stricken with grief as they hold each other along with Tommy's young brother and sister

A nurse enters Josephine's doorway and calls Joe out and gives him the sad news about Tommy

Joe – (Looks devastated as everyone notices)

Gina – What is it Joe?

Joe – The nurse just informed me that Tommy just passed away.

Josephine – Oh no, a nurse told me earlier that he was strong and that the doctors said he had a good chance because he was a fighter (begins to cry as Nick comforts her)

Moose – (Cries with Laura comforting him) Tommy boy! (Moose cries)

As everyone shattered by the news continues to cry

Joe – Gina, let's take a walk and see if we find the McCall's...

Gina – O.K. (as she cries they leave the room)

Jimmy – (Hugs Moose) Hey Moose I'm so sorry...

Moose – It's o.k. Red bird, if he was going to stay messed up, it's probably better that he went home man, you know?

Laura – He probably knew that Maryann had gone before him and she came and got him, that's what I feel...

Nick – I like that Laura, that's a good thought to hold to.

Josephine – That's a beautiful thought Laura, you just made all of us feel so much better about Tommy leaving us.

Julie – Death is such a tragic event when it happens like this, but it seems to bond every ones heart together, bringing every one closer...

Jimmy – Your right Julie and I hope we can all stay friends so that we don't feel that emptiness that just occurred in our lives...

Nick – Hey you got that right Red, I never want to lose any of you guys as a friend, got that, none of you!

Josephine – I want you all to know that when Nick and I are married we want you guys there, when we have our own house you guys are welcomed anytime no matter what, you hear me? and I truly mean that.

Jimmy – Thank you Josephine (Everyone begins to embrace and agree on their friendship)

The town begins to hear of Tommy's passing, the town folks begin to show up at the hospital to help comfort the McCalls, led by the Reverend, the Swenson's, (name of few more)

Los Muchachos and most of their parents show up at the hospital to pay their respects and Juan his girlfriend Gloria, Tony and Marianna Arturo and his girl and Sergio and his wife show up at Josephine's room to check in on Josephine and Nick

Sheriff Coleman's office where he meets with FBI agents, and County Detectives as they arrange interrogations with the Billings brothers

FBI agent 1 – We will conduct the interrogation tonight separately with both brothers, now it's going to go all night I guarantee you that, and we will strictly stay on collecting evidence through testimony until we get a confession, excluding any and all coercion, we don't need to give these educated fools any open doors to take advantage of.

Det Carson – That's fine agent, will we have access to your interrogation as far as preparing for the second part of the investigation… right?

FBI agent 2 – Well let's just say, we will let you know if we should need to use you guys to draw out any more information...

FBI agent 1 – The way we will work it, as soon as we get a confession on the first half of the event we will begin to seek out information on who killed the boys from the city, if we get it from them, then we'll have enough to convict them for life, if we can't get it, then we'll sit down with you guys and develop a plan for you guys to become their friend and we'll draw it out from them from that angle.

Sheriff Coleman – I'm sure there will be more arrests to follow so I would like everyone to be available as we make those arrests.

Det. Mitchell – Agent what about this charge on Moose that Capt. Billings made...

FBI agent 2 – As Sheriff Coleman and I discussed already, the testimony is that no charges will be made against the Flannigan boy, it was clearly self defense... and that's that!

FBI agent 1 – O.K. let's get this started (both agents go to separate rooms where Frank and Fred Billings are being held)

Det. Mitchell – What others do you think will be arrested John?

Sheriff Coleman – I think most of the security team he had at the college for the show and quite possibly some of his officers... Well I'm going to put some coffee on...

Det. Carson – We'd better get a team together ourselves, I have a feeling it's going to be another long night.

Sheriff Coleman – I'll be here all night gentleman, I'll contact you through radio or phone as soon as the names start dropping on my desk...

Det. Carson – You got it John (both detectives depart)

Scene FBI agents interrogating the brothers in separate rooms as this dreadful day comes to an end -

Early Monday morning 6 a.m. at Sal Celetti's house – Sal pours himself a cup of coffee on the stove and hears a knock, and walks to the front door

Sal – Nick... What are doing at it so soon? It's only 6.

Nick – Sorry Mr. C ... I knew you'd be up...

Sal – No need to apologize son, come on in, come get some coffee (Sal grabs a cup and pours it for Nick) What brings you by son?

Nick – Oh I was just thinking if we could wait on signing those papers for a couple of days at least til Josephine comes home.

Sal – Oh sure, I already put that off Nicky, I called Molly and she was going to call Allen and get that pushed back, no worries son.

Nick – O.k. I'm going to go open up...

Sal – Nonsense, you take a couple of days off and get yourself some rest, you too have been pretty banged up you know...

Nick – No... I can't rest that seems impossible, I'll go nuts at home Sal, I'm better off at the station, I have some cars that need to go out this week and I have a big truck engine coming to over haul from Santiago Trucking and so...

Sal – Well if you feel your better off down there but you take it easy on yourself, you here?

Nick – I know Sal, thank you and Mrs. C so much for being there for me I appreciate it...

Sal – Hey, that's what family is for you know... Hey and listen I hear Gina Colletti's cold heart melted down, huh Nicky boy?

Nick – Yea, man that was shocker I'll tell you...

Sal – You know, between that miracle and the fact that these detectives and John Coleman, I think they're going to finally put the fire out between South County and Midland, at least it looks that way.

Nick – Let's hope Mr. C, I sure hope so.

Sal – You and Josephine set a date yet?

Nick – Ah we talked about it but nothing set in stone you know... there's still a lot of planning she says...

Sal – Well you plan it out good son, and take your time and let all this grief pass... you got yourself a good one there, she's a lot her daddy... your lucky...

Nick – Oh yea for sure... It's probably going to be next summer after this her 3rd year of law school...

Sofia – (Walks in the kitchen) Oh good morning Nicky! (hugs him)

Nick – Oh good morning to you Mrs. C

Sofia – Would you like some breakfast?

Nick – No Mrs. C, I'm not hungry right now...

Sal – Nicky's going to go open up...

Sofia – I'll tell you what, I'm going to make you some breakfast and I will send it with Sal, enough for you and Jorge, how about that?

Nick – Yea, that's sounds good, thank you (kisses Sofia on the cheek) well thanks for the coffee, I'll see you down there.

Sal – O.k. son I'll be there in about an hour...

Nick – O.k. (leaves for the station)

Sal – Well he looks sharp, I was a little worried about him...

Sofia – Ah he's better off keeping busy, remember his daddy?

Sal – Yep... I sure do...

Sofia – His daddy was a quiet loner and the only friend he turned to was the bottle and it ended up ruining him...

Sal – I know, I won't let that happen to Nicky... you can bet on that!

Sofia – Now about this so called retirement home you want to build for me...

Sal – Yea what about it?

Sofia – When do they start construction on it?

Sal – Next week, why?

Sofia – And how long is it going to take for them to finish it?

Sal – 6 to 8 months depending on the rain, why?

Sofia – Just in time for Nicky's and Josephine's wedding perhaps?

Sal – Could be...

Sofia – Well...

Sal – Well what?, you having second thoughts?

Sofia – Oh no, go ahead and build it, but I don't really want to leave our little house here Sal...

Sal – Yea ... I know what you mean...

Sofia – How about, we give the new house to Nick and Josephine for a wedding gift!

Sal – (Gets a big smile on his face) Hey you know that sounds great!

Sofia – But lets don't tell them until the wedding day

Sal – Good idea, that's a great idea! I didn't want to leave here either, but I thought you did...

Sofia – You had this house built for us 30 years ago, I don't want to leave it (they hug in agreement)

Sal – Hey... do you think Gina's going to get offended if we out gift them?

Sofia – You know what... I hope she does, cause I am dying to put that woman in her place (throw's a punch into her hand)

Sal – I'd better warn Joe (Sal laughs)

Sofia – You'd better... I'm warning you to warn him (Sal still laughing)

At the mortuary where Ron Tomkins visit the owner of themortuary

Ron – (Talks to the receptionist) Good morning...

Receptionist – Oh good morning to you sir, how can I help you?

Ron – Ah... is Russell here?

Receptionist – Yes Russell Grant, just one minute sir, and whom may I say is asking for him?

Ron – Ron, Ron Tompkins.

Receptionist – (Goes into an office with Mr. Grant sitting at his desk signing papers) Mr. Grant there is a Ron Tompkins asking for you...

Russell Grant – Oh sure Martha send him in, send him right in...

Martha – Mr. Tompkins right this way (shows him in)

Russell – Hey Ron, how are you?

Ron – Hey Russell, Is it any good when one visits a mortuary?

Russell – Oh I know, it's just a routine question unless you were just stopping by to say hello, but I truly know what you mean…

Martha – Mr. Grant can I bring you some more coffee and coffee for your guest?

Russell – Yes Martha, yes indeed, Martha is new here only a few weeks, Martha Pena this is my good friend Ron Tompkins, Ron this is my new receptionist and right arm Martha Pena…

Ron – Thank you… It's a pleasure meeting you

Martha – It's a pleasure for me as well Mr. Tompkins

Ron – Thank you…

Martha - I'll be right back with your coffee (smiles and goes for the coffee)

Russell – Ah, Ron does this visit have anything to do with the McCall's boy and the Swenson's girl?

Ron – Well unfortunately it does Russ as well as the Combs boy and Paul's Styles boy too, Paul Jr.

Russell – Oh?... I wasn't aware of those 2 others, I thought the other deaths were from the Midland area?

Ron – Well they too had 7 or 8 and we had 4, thank God no more than that...so far.

Russell – Oh my goodness, I am so not happy about getting business this way, you know that Ron, I mean when a person has lived their life and is ready for the eternal rest that's natural you know, but when in this case when one goes way before their time, well it's not... well you know Ron you went through it...

Ron – Yea I know, I ah... unfortunately been through it quite a bit already...

Russell – I'm so sorry, you know, but what do all of these tragedies have to do with you Ron?

Ron – (Martha comes in with the coffee) Well your ... thank you dear...

Russ – Thank you Martha...

Martha – You are welcome enjoy.

Ron – You're probably going to start hearing today or tomorrow from all these families, and I want you to give them your cost of the funerals and services and what not, and then tell them when they ask for the price that it is paid for...

Russ – Oh, and it is paid for by?...

Ron – Me, but you don't need to tell them that if you don't have to, unless they absolutely want to know, then tell them it was me.

Russ – My goodness Ron that is awfully thoughtful and considerate of you... but may I ask why are you paying for all 4 funerals?

Ron – (Sips his coffee) Oh good coffee... It's just something that I want to do Russ, you know Paul and Deborah just starting their business, the Combs are young and barely first time home buyers and you know the McCall's boy and the Swenson girl were boyfriend and girlfriend so I want to lighten the burden of pain for all of them that's all...

Russell – In all my years Ron I must say this is a first...

Ron – Yea it's a first for a lot of things Russ, I just hope it's a last also.

Officers and detectives arresting security guards at the college and a couple of staff members and 3 police

officers at the City police station 10 in all

Sal's Gas and Garage – Jorge pumping gas and Nick working on an engine on an engine stand in the garage

Nick – (Phone rings) Sal's... Yea this is Nick ... No I don't think I can this week and I think next week also is going to be tight... o.k. thank you anyway (Hangs up as Jorge walks in)

Jorge – Hey Nick this old man's car is giving him problems and it's having problems starting can you look at it real quick?

Nick – Yea lets go see (Nick walks out with Jorge to check the car) Hey how's it going? Can you try to start it, (Nick pops the hood and the old man starts the car while Nick is in the front of the car and the man tries to run Nick over and Nick jumps out of the way and falls to the side as the man drives straight ahead and stops to get out and close the hood)

Old man – You! it was you that killed my grandson... you'll pay for this you hoodlum!

Nick – (As Jorge comes to Nicks aid) Go call the sheriff Jorge and give him a description of the car, hurry he's probably going back to the city heading south! (Jorge runs to make the call)

Old man – I promise you, you're gonna pay (gets in the car and peels out)

Nick – You're the one that's gonna pay you old fool! (Nick stays on the ground holding his knee)

Jorge – (Jorge comes back) Are you o.k. Nick?

Nick – Every time I think I am, something else happens to tell me that I'm not (Jorge helps Nick up)

Jorge – Nothing broken amigo?

Nick – No, at least I don't think so

Jorge – Lets go sit down… that old fart he play on trick on me amigo (Walks Nick inside) After this weekend, this is the last thing you need my friend, que hombre!

Nick – Thanks Jorge … don't worry who knew that old fart was going to do that, huh? I was wanting to talk to you sometime today, so I guess this is a good time…

Jorge – Si como no amigo…

Nick – I ah, I'm buying the gas & garage station off of Sal… Jorge

Jorge – Oh yea! That's good, no?

Nick – Yea, that's good si, muy bueno, si?

Jorge – Oh I'm happy for you Amigo!

Nick – Good, thank you Jorge, I want to give you a raise, you know more money?

Jorge – Oh o.k. mas denero si si o.k. good…

Nick – Yea mas denero, more money, but more responsibility too o.k.?

Jorge – Yes amigo, whatever you want or need Jorge is here for you…

Nick – Good I know Jorge, we're gonna make a good team you and I and we're going to hire a couple of more people and you're gonna be a boss man too o.k.?

Jorge – Ohh o.k. o.k.

Nick – O.k. we'll sit down later this week and start on a new plan to grow this business…

Jorge – O.k. amigo, I go to work now (as a car and truck pull in for gas)

Nick – Go get em amigo.

Sal Celetti drives in to the station and parks on the side his usual parking space and Nick comes out to greet him

Sal – Hey Nicky, pretty soon this will be your spot huh?

Nick – Yes sir...

Sal – You know Nicky, I didn't know how I was going to handle all this retirement stuff, but in light of all this tragedy this past weekend, I'm looking forward to spending the rest of my life with the Mrs. You know that?

Nick – I don't blame you Sal, I thought for a few minutes there on Saturday night that I had lost Josephine, cause she was unconscious, and ah, my life was for a quick minute was at a standstill, I was trying to think, you know what was going on, what had just happen and what was going to happen and what should I do... I couldn't grasp it all in my head...

Sal – When time stood still...

Nick – Yea, it was like the whole world had frozen up

Sal – In every one's life, that moment will occur at one time or another son, for us the

Mrs. And I it was when we found Madelyn cold in her crib, she was only 5 day's old, our only baby, our only child...

Nick – And you were about my age?

Sal – 21... yea 21 years old...

Nick – You and Mrs. C were the only ones that have ever given me a chance Sal, you guys at that time and now are everything to me, I mean that (They embrace as Jorge looks on)

Sal – You are the son that God has blessed us with Nicky, we love you and we are expecting for you and Josephine to have some little babinos running around and calling us grandpa and gramma you know, Sofia and I have been talking about how nice that would be (wipes tears from his eyes)

Nick – Oh you know that's gonna happen for sure (Jorge walks up to them)

Jorge – Hello patron

Sal – Hello Jorgie, this is your new patron here...

Jorge – Yea he told me, I will miss you and Sofia much senor...

Sal – Oh speaking of that, she send you guys some breakfast (goes to retrieve it from his truck)

Jorge – That's one reason why I will miss you guys so much, especially for her food...

Sal – Well ever since your Mrs. taught her how to make tortillas she cooks them all the time now, here you guys go... go eat... Papa's, scramble huevos and some bacon and tortillas Jorgie just the way you like them...

Jorge – Ah thanks you to much patron, come on amigo, how you say, lets grubb, andale... I have some salsa in the refrigerator

Nick – Lets eat hombre...

Sal – I'm going to go talk to Allen and Molly, do you think Thursday son would be a good day?

Nick – That should be, Josephine should be out tomorrow or Wednesday, so yea that sounds good...

Jorge – As long as no more locos try to run him over...

Sal – Like last Saturday?

Jorge - No like a little a while ago, just before you come...

Sal – What? What's he saying?

Nick – Some old guy from the city came in and I was checking his starter, cause Jorge told me to come check it after putting gas, which he never paid for, I popped his hood and told him to try to start it and he started it and shoved it in drive and almost ran me down...

Sal – Who was this old fart?

Jorge - We don know, but he yell some crasy things, that Nick kill his grandson or sometine like that, hombre loco...

Sal – Did any one...

Nick – Jorge here ran and called the sheriffs station...

Sal – Well I'm headed that way now, I'll stop to see if they caught him, you guys gave them a description of his car?

Jorge – Oh yes, yes yes!

Nick – It's o.k. they'll get him I'm sure...

Sal – Yea well you guys make sure you keep an eye out on all out of town cars you here me?... this might just be the beginning of a damn feud starting up all over again,,, dang it man! (Sal heads out)

Jorge – Oh he not's to happy... Its good yes?

Nick – Very good (as they eat their breakfast)

Reverend Williams brings Andrew home and stays with him to await the arrival of his parents who have been out of town on a business trip

Andrew – Come in, I haven't been home, the last time I was here, Paul and I left for the show together.

Rev. Williams – Hmm, it's going to be hard at first Andrew, the grieving period, it will take some time to adjust not having Paul around, but eventually you'll receive closure and you'll adjust...

Andrew – It's going to be hard (starts to cry)

Rev. – Yes at first it will be son...

Andrew – You know my mom and dad have been working really hard trying to get this business off the ground and they've been fighting a lot over money and stuff...

Rev. – Your parents have been faithful members of the community and have helped a lot of folks here in this town and many times God will send people to bless you in times like this and many times he does little miracles in our lives just to show us that he cares in times like this for us, for his word tells us that he will never leave us or let us down, so... (a knock at the door, it's Kathy, Connie and Katie)

Connie – Andrew (hugs him) Hello Reverend...

Rev. Williams – Hello girls...

Kathy – (Hugs Andrew they cry) Your parents aren't here yet?

Andrew – No, not yet, I called the Reverend to come bring me home so he can tell my parents when they get home.

Connie – Why do you suppose tragedies like these happen Reverend? What significance does it have if any?

Rev. Williams - Often times Connie, the purpose reveals itself immediatley and yet many times it comes with a waiting period or perhaps a slow revelation, but the significance will always be a divine message, reason and even example not only in the spiritual being but often in the physical as well...

Katie – So you're saying, that something good will come out of something so bad?

Rev. – If God sees fit for it to be a lesson to others or if he sees fit to bless one or many for whatever his purpose is, we don't know, but if we are patient and we draw to him rather than run away from him, we will see that he is in control and he will bring understanding to us in time... Remember he too knows what it feels like to lose a son... it's been said that He will close the eyes of one, to open the eyes of many (all have a look of being in deep thought)

Sheriff's station as Sal enters the office

Deputy Sheriff Burt – Good morning Mr. Celetti

Sal – Good morning Burt, can you tell me if they caught that man that tried running down Nick at the station?

Deputy Burt – They did, he's in custody, as a matter of fact Mike just left to get a statement from Nick and Jorge and to see if Nick wants to press charges against him...

Sal – Press charges? What do you think?

Deputy Burt – Well it don't matter what I think Sal, it depends on what Nick thinks, it's not our call...

Sal – Who is this old fool?

Deputy Burt – I can't tell you who it is, but he is from Del Rey and he's the grandfather of the kid that they say Moose punched his lights out, for good Saturday night...

Sal – Well they said this might be the guy who shot and killed Paul, I don't know...

Deputy Burt – Nobody knows Sal it was dark plus there was no gun found on the kid, however he had hit Moose a few times with a 2x4 and Moose turned around and caught him before he could run away...

Sal – I'm not saying he deserved it no, but I am saying when you make wrong choices the consequences could cost you dearly...

Deputy Burt – Yea that's true, it's like playing with fire, eventually you're going to get burned...

Sal – Something needs to be done about this nonsense between these 2 communities, there has been far too many deaths already and if anything isn't done it's going to continue to grow and go on and more people will die.

Deputy Burt – We're discussing that now Sal with Sheriff Coleman, but perhaps some of you citizens can come to a council meeting bring it up and demand something be done, I don't know the answer, but you're right it needs to stop.

Sal – It's gonna come to a point where our wives or kids, grand kids can't go to the city for anything without looking over their shoulder or worrying about being attacked or ambushed on the way back home, it's ridiculous!

Deputy Burt – Your right Sal, you ain't going to get no argument from me.

Sal's Gas & Garage

Deputy Sheriff Mike Santucci – So you're just going to let him get away with it? I don't understand...

Nick – Like I said, I don't understand why you don't understand Mike, there are a lot of emotions flying high all over right now man, and this grandfather is proof of that man his grandson is dead and he feels someone is to blame... when he comes to his senses he will realize what he did was wrong, I don't blame him man he's old and all emotional, let's just let it alone and not keep making this fire bigger...

Deputy Mike – Pressing charges and finding them guilty is a law abiding process so they're punished for their crime, let's hope we don't turn this stir crazy man free and then he accomplishes his goal Nicky...

Nick – Let him sit it out for a day or so, let his family come get him and when they see no one is pressing charges maybe they'll see someone is trying to put an end to this useless waste of time and lives, huh...

Deputy Mike – O.k. Nick I'm with you man, you know that, by the way how's Josephine doing?

Nick – She's doing good, hopefully coming home tomorrow or at least by Wednesday...

Deputy Mike – Glad to hear it, and Nicky I know you been through quite a bit this past weekend but I'm really glad nothing happen to you man, we go back a long way and you and Johnny were my little brothers and all I have left is you (puts his arm around Nick) so you take care and be careful... huh?

Nick – (Nick hugs him back) I know Mikey, you and your family are like my family and guess what?

Deputy Mike – What?

Nick – I need you to be my best man...

Deputy Mike – What? Your kidding right? Mr. I aint never getting married (embraces Nick) of course I will wild cat you know that!

Nick – Thank you man thank you and ah just hold that note between us because I'm pretty sure Josephine is going to ask Kristine to be her maid of honor so it'll all work out perfectly.

Deputy Mike – Oh yea no problem, so you got a time frame in mind?

Nick – Well probably next June, July perhaps...

Deputy Mike – Oh oh oh oh, just hope Kristine isn't gonna be baking bread in the oven at that time...

Nick – Hey that's up to the baker man (they both laugh)

Deputy Mike – O.k. man back to official business now, I'm going back to report to Coleman hopefully he'll understand why you're doing this Nicky, I'll catch you later gator...

Nick – Yea o.k. Earl

Jorge – Earl?

Nick – Yea that's Earl amigo, when we were punks together me, him and his brother Johnny we use to refer to him as the Duke of Earl, cause he was so cool with his greasy duck tail hair, leather jacket, cigarette in his ear and all the girls he could of handle man he was the coolest dadio in town and his brother Johnny was too...

Jorge – Y el senor Johnny?

Nick – Johnny? – Johnny died in a car wreck racing some punk from Northland in 57, I was supposed to be in the car with him Jorge...

Jorge – Ah but God he had another plan for you amigo...

Nick – Yea amigo I guess he did, even my mama told me that cause I couldn't stop from crying for Johnny, I couldn't even go to his funeral, I was so broken by him dying.

Jorge - I sorry for you amigo...

Nick – No don't be sorry for me Jorge, I'm good because of people like you (hugs Jorge with a smile)

Reverend Williams embracing Mrs. Styles and Andrew embracing his Father Paul Sr. as the girls cry in the living room

Paul Sr. – We had such a very successful business trip, I figured we'd come home and share the news with the boys and maybe our lives would turn back to some what a normal life again without all the stress (sobs with a broken heart)

Reverend Williams – In time Paul, In time all the reasoning will come together for you, I know it's hard and it's a hard thing to understand right now, so grieve, but grieve with Gods peace...

Mrs. Styles – Thank you Reverend for looking out for Andrew...

Rev. Williams – Well, the McCall's took Andrew home from the hospital with them, to clean him up and eat and stuff, so you'll need to express your appreciation when you see them, as the girls said they lost Tommy as well last night and the Swenson's lost Maryann and the Combs lost Stew on Saturday night along with Paul Jr.

Deborah – This is not right… it's just not right (breaks down again)

Paul Sr. – I know Deb… I know.

Rev. Williams – (Glances out the window) Looks like more company…

Connie – Oh yea mom and dad were coming over to bring some food for you guys because they knew you'd be tired from your trip…

The Reverend greets Doug and Tina Collins at the front door as they bring some trays of food

Rev. Williams – Hello my lady, Doug welcome… come on in they just arrived about ten minutes ago…

Tina – Hello Reverend, Connie, Kathy can you take these… thank you… oh Deborah I am so sorry (Tina and Deborah embrace and share a good cry, Doug and Paul Sr. embrace as Paul breaks down in Doug's arms)

Doug – I'm so sorry Paul (tears flowing)

Paul Sr. - Thank you Doug, thank you for everything...

Doug – Your welcome my friend.

Another knock on the door, Connie opens the door to find the McCalls and the Combs and the Swensons, all with more food and deserts, coming to discuss funeral arrangements – They all greet one another and share hugs and tears as they're welcomed in Ron Tomkins office as Sheriff Coleman visits

Sheriff Coleman – (Walks up to Ron's door to his office) Knock knock...

Ron – Hey Sheriff come on in...

Sheriff Coleman – Ron... busy?

Ron – Always busy John, have a seat

Sheriff Coleman – Thank you... I didn't mean to intrude...

Ron – Not at all... how can I help you?

Sheriff Coleman – Well, I just wanted to know if it is a possibility Ron, If I... If I can bring by a list of the boys that were shot Saturday night , the city boy's you know...

Ron – O.k.

Sheriff Coleman – For you to take a look at the list to tell me if you recognize any of the names on the list Ron of the boys who might have jumped Raymond a couple years back in Midland...

Ron – It's been a few years John, but I'll look at it, bring it in... or I can swing by your office, let me know. Is there an particular reason why John?

Sheriff Coleman – Well there's always a reason why, but I ah, just need to know for the sake of the investigation... just making sure that no stone goes without being turned overas they say...

Ron – Yea I understand Sheriff, I understand... but do me a favor as well John...

Sheriff Coleman – Sure thing...

Ron – Don't let any of these young detectives participate in the investigation and start to presume, and speculate and manufacture a wild story cause the're looking to buck for a promotion based on a theory John, because that's what happens with inexperience.

Sheriff Coleman – I know what you're saying Ron, that won't happen here... I think I'm the only one asking right now, just so I can close that door in my conscious...

Ron – Well John, you can always close that same door the way Billings closed the door on me and my family, to protect their tight community...

Sheriff Coleman – I need facts and evidence Ron, I don't arrest anyone without evidence and I don't make any assumptions without facts (stands up to leave) and I sure as hell never send an innocent person to prison... I'll call you Ron.

As Sheriff Coleman makes his way to his car Juan and Tony notice him leaving Ron Tomkins's office

Tony – Check it out ese, Coleman was in the old mans office aye...

Juan – Ah don't worry carnal, ese viejo didn't get rich by being dumb ese, he got rich because he's smart and he cares for people, plus his plan was full proof, que no?

Tony – Full like in filled up or fool like in... hey fool!

Juan – Ahh ha ha fool proof, another words you can investigate fool but you'll never find what you're looking for...

Tony – Orale, ain't that the truth, that vato knows his stuff holmes (they shake hands)

Moose knocks on Laura's front door

Laura – Hey big guy what's up? (she hugs him)

Moose – Hey... I couldn't sleep that good you know...

Laura – Yea I know what you mean, come on in, I was...

Moose – No it's o.k., can I talk to you out here for a minute?

Laura – Sure, just let me go shut off the stove (she runs to the kitchen and comes right back) o.k. what's up sweetie?

Moose – I have something really bothering me in the midst of all this chaos and all this sadness...

Laura – What is it?

Moose – I know you've liked me for a long time and all this time, you know... the rumor was that I was in love with Cindy and just waiting for the right time to make my move and stuff right?... but

Laura – But?

Moose – Well the truth is... is that even after this past weekend and all the tragedy and all, I was so amazed by you, your personality and everything really, Laura... I ah, I don't

Laura – You don't want to be boyfriend and girlfriend, is that what you're trying to say? (a sad look on her face)

Moose – No! not at all, that's not what I'm saying, I'm saying... I guess what it was I was giving it so much thought and I thought maybe Laura and I were just holding on to each other through this tragic event and now when the dust settles maybe everything will go back to normal and just being friends, and I ah

Laura – Moose, I have liked you since the 4th grade and I fell in love with you or at least my interpretation of love in the 7th grade and I have turned down other guys asking me out just so I could be available in case opportunity presented itself and it finally did, but I'm not going to let my world stop just because you don't want to be boyfriend and girlfriend with me...

Moose – No Laura, that's just it, I want to be with you... I guess it would be another heart break for me if all of this was just a friendship thing cause I really do love you, I do (with tears in his eyes)

Laura – (Kisses Moose) I've always loved you forever, it seems...

Moose – (Kissing) O.k. then it's official, you're my girl and I'm your guy?

Laura – You betcha! (still hugging and kissing) finally!!

Nick walking to Josephine's room with a bouquet of flowers and chocolates and sees a nurse walking Josephine in the hallway

Nick – Hey! You're not planning on escaping from me are you?

Josephine – Oh hey baby... just getting some exercise... apparently it's mandatory...

Nurse – Hello Mr. Pagani...she's doing quite well I must say...

Nick – Yea? Well enough to go home?

Josephine – Hopefully tomorrow morning baby, they are going to do some concussion tests on me this afternoon, if all goes well I can go home in the morning.

Nick – That's good… I brought you some flowers because you're so pretty and some chocolates cause you so sweet!

Josephine – Oh you're so sweet… I love them and I love you (hug and a kiss)

Nick – I was gonna bring me some corn…

Josephine – Some corn?

Nick – Yea corn…

Josephine – Why corn?

Nick – Just in case you thought I was corny…

Josephine – Well then you should of brought goofy instead (hugging and laughing – Nick helps Josephine back into bed)

Nick – Yea you're right, I am goofy I guess, goofy for you…

Josephine – That's a part of you that I'm the only one who knows that, you know that… nobody knows you like this but me, and that is so special to me, Nicholas Vital Pagani

Nick – Well Josephine Carolyn Coletti… there's some stuff that only I know about you too that no one knows either so…

Josephine – Huuh! You better not ever…

Nick – Well you never know Josephine… I mean if you don't do what I say you're in big trouble…

Josephine – That's black mail… oh my goodness you'd resort to breaking the law (hits him with her pillow)

Nick – Hey you're messing up the doo! (they laugh together)

Josephine – Can I tell you something?

Nick – Sure baby anything…

Josephine - I was really worried sick these last 2 days here…

Nick – Why is that?

Josephine – Because I knew this was a lot of pressure and stress even for Nick Pagani, Mr. fix it, Mr. Tuff as nails, you know, and I was just hoping to God that you wouldn't go home and pull out that old bottle of whiskey that your father left behind, that you have been keeping it hidden to remind yourself of who he was and how he died and I was so scared Nick, I prayed like I never had prayed before baby...

Nick – I can see why people turn to the bottle, they feel the deeper you go into it, the deeper and further their problems go, but when you sober up one realizes that they were just hiding from you but they're still there, so they try it again, and again and again, because they realize if they are not going to go away, let's keep them hidden for as long as we can and the next thing you know... your liver, blood, memory take a train out of town, and bam! You're done.

Josephine – Wow baby... this whole time I always worried about that, about you and here you had it figured out this whole time, I am impressed... I really am...

Nick – You know what?

Josephine – What?

Nick – You're my escape

Josephine – Oh?

Nick – You helped me get through that night, you helped me make it through the day yesterday and you got me up and going this morning and I got so much to be thankful for, having you in my life Josephine (they hug)

Jimmy sits alone at the booth him and Stew use to in at The Malt Shop

Linda (waitress) – Hi Jimmy… Mr. Robertson said this is on the house… It's a cherry coke Stewie's favorite…

Jimmy – (Starts to cry) Thank you Linda (puts his head down) (Since you been gone by the Dreamers is playing on the juke box)

Julie – (Julie walks in) I thought I'd find you here…

Jimmy – Hi Julie… I'm sorry, I just can't seem to hold it together.

Julie – Hey I understand… you're too young for all this guy, we're too young and no one expects us to know how to hold it together… so what do we do? We come down to our favorite watering hole and drink til we can't see straight… Thank you (reads her name badge as Linda brings Julie a coke) Linda…

Jimmy – Amazing… you're just like him, quick witted, never short with words and a sense of humor at the peak of his character.

Julie – I've often been asked since I was a little girl it seems… Why are you always laughing?, why are you so happy?, why do you make light of everything? All of my life I've answered so many of those questions… huuu man.

Jimmy – So what's your answer?

Julie – I'd rather laugh then cry…I'd rather be happy then sad… I'd rather avoid misery then to live in it…

Jimmy – Wow Julie… I would have never known you have sadness in your life…your smile and charm paint over it very well, but may I ask what brought on this sadness so young?

Julie – Well as a kid my mom and dad were always fighting, you know arguing…

Jimmy – Fighting over what?

Julie – Over stupid things like money, cause my dad was always getting let go or fired and seemed like he was home more than working… arguing over my sisters father, for some reason his name was always coming up, his name was Steve Bennett he died in that clash with the city boys 21 years ago, and my dads name is Lyle Bennett, he was first cousins to Steve my sisters father and my mom was really in love with him and I guess she was just looking for security when my dad came into the picture.

Jimmy – Did your parent's divorce?

Julie – No they were never married… but sometimes my dad would leave, then come back and fill my mom with promises and sometimes my mom would kick my dad out, even call the cops to do it if she had too…then again he would eventually come back and here we go again… a miserable merry-go-round.

Jimmy – Man Julie, I'm so sorry to hear that…

Julie – But… through all that and then moving a hundred times going to different schools and never really having any friends, I thought this was it, I'm older and I know what's going on, I come here and right off the top I meet cool friends and then Stewie and pow! Just like that a week later it all changes for the worse (Julie tears up)

Jimmy – What's the answer Julie?

Julie – I don't know... I have no clue...

Jimmy – Do you believe Stew can see us now?

Julie – I don't know that either (starts to cry)

Jimmy – I believe he can... and I believe he wants to get a message to us...

Julie – And what would that be?

Jimmy – I don't know yet... but I believe he will get it to us pretty soon... I just feel that in my heart.

Julie – You know if anyone else other than you and Nick, I'd say you're crazy... but I think you are a pretty a smart cat and I believe you...

Jimmy – Me and Nick huh? Why me and Nick?

Julie – Nick because he's Mr. Cool and you because you're Mr. Brains and together with Ally Oop you guys cleaned house the other night.

Jimmy – Oh wow Julie don't ever let Moose know you called him Ally Oop!

Julie – Why not?

Jimmy – Because then he would know either me or Stewie told you that, because it was Stew that gave him that name years ago... but Moose never liked it and he would beat us up even if he thought we called him that name so don't, please don't...

Julie – O.k. I won't... now I have something on you... I'll make you do all my homework or otherwise I'll tell Moose you told me (begins to laugh)

Jimmy – Oh no! I've created a monster... I'll do your homework it's better than getting beat up by Moose.

Julie – I only got to sit one time here with Stew... and to think I'll never see him here again just breaks my heart...

Jimmy – Can you imagine... I've sat here over a hundred times with him, I don't know if I could come back here anymore without getting depressed...

Julie – (Julie grabs Jimmy's hand) We can Jimmy together you and I... for Stewie?

Jimmy – I guess (Julie looks and smiles and gives Jimmy a thumbs up – they both giggle) so what's your sisters name?

Julie – Joann… she's supposed to be coming from back east any day now…

Jimmy – Do you guys get a long?

Julie – Ahh… sometimes, we use to fight a lot when we were kids and stuff… I have'nt seen her in a few years… but her and my mom hooo… world war 3.

Jimmy – Wow! So she's like Nick and Josephines age then right?

Julie – Well she's about 20.

Jimmy – Does she look like you or you like her actually…

Julie – Oh her and I look nothing alike… she's a looker, gorgeous!

Jimmy – So are you Julie, don't kid yourself silly…

Julie – Ahh thank you, you're so sweet.

The Sheriff's station, the family of the old man that tried running Nick down is trying to get him released

Daughter Jennifer Mills of the old man and her son Donny Mills

Daughter (Jennifer)– (At the front desk) We received a call that my father had been arrested...

Deputy Gene – O.k. that would be Nathan Forrest ?

Jennifer – Yes...

Grandson (Donny) – Why was he arrested?

Deputy Gene – Attempted murder...

Donny – What?

Jennifer – Oh my God... what do you mean attempted murder?

Deputy Gene – Mam... he is being held right now for trying to intentionally run down a worker at a gas station here in town, now...

Donny – Was it the guy who killed my brother? because...

Deputy Gene – Now stop! There is no proof that anyone killed anyone here, how can you guys know that, if you weren't there, we don't even know and we've been investigating the case since this has all happened so...

Deputy Mike – What's going on here?

Deputy Gene – This is the daughter of the man who tried running Nick down and this is the grandson...

Jennifer – Are they sure it was intentional because...

Deputy Mike – Look... we have 48 hours to hold him until we find out the entire details of the case... we're still investigating it.

Donny – O.k. these guy's from South Town killed my brother and my grandfather is old and very distraught over this whole situation... he's just in shock that's all, he didn't know what he was doing man...

Deputy Mike – O.k. take it easy now... you can't go around saying this guy or that guy killed my brother... look a lot of people lost their lives this past weekend and everybody has been effected by this whole mess, understand?... now look, the guy that your grandfather tried to run down does not want to file attempted murder charges on him because he understands the old man's reasoning... he's supposed to come down and either file lessor charges or a release form to drop the whole thing...

Jennifer – So what do we do in the mean time? Can we go talk to this guy?

Deputy Mike - No mam you can't... you'll just have to wait it out, but he should be here shortly... now you can wait here or outside in the grass area, there are some tables out there or go have some lunch or coffee at the diner, it's up to you...

Donny – Well if we go to the diner, we might miss him, so let's just wait here mom...

Daughter – O.k. (Mother and son walk outside)

Deputy Gene – What a mess huh?

Deputy Mike – Yea... a lot of lives ruined... and they'll never be the same again.

The Mortuary, where all 4 families are arrive to make funeral arrange-ments

Martha – (Confronts all four families in the waiting lobby) Mr. Grant will be with you folks in about 5 minutes and he will be meeting with you in our conference room... if you would follow me please

They all follow Martha to the conference room

Martha – Make yourself comfortable, there is some fresh coffee and water as well, he'll be with you in a minute or so and once again, I'm am so deeply sorry for your loss...

(They all thank Martha for her hospitality)

Nick getting ready to leave from his visit with Josephine

Nick – O.k. baby I'm going to get going... gotta get back to work and I have to stop by and see Mikey to sign some papers...

Josephine – At the sheriff's office?

Nick – Yea...

Josephine – Ahh... well I guess some type of witness statement for the investigation report or something?

Nick – Or something like that, I'll see when I get there...

Josephine – O.k. sweetie... I'll see you later?

Nick – Oh yea...I'll be back after closing, love you...

Josephine – Love you too... Hey baby (as Nick heading out the door)

Nick – Yea...

Josephine – Are you eating?

Nick – Yea…why?

Josephine – Cause I know you, that's why…

Nick – I'll tell you what… I'll bring some burgers and fries and a shake from Howie's and we'll have dinner together, how bout that?

Josephine – (With a big smile) It's a date Mister! You'll have to sneak it in now…

Nick – I know… bye (whispers) (Josephine smiles)

At the mortuary with owner Russell Grant meeting with the 4 families in the conference room

Russell – Individually or as a group or combination of any of you the price is paid and covered for all of you…

Bill McCall – By whom?

Todd Swenson – Well it doesn't matter by whom, I mean it's paid for, it's paid for right? Either way?

Todd – Yea I know but I do know we both have life insurance policies… but I don't know if either the Combs or.. do you guys Paul have a policy on Paul Jr.

A knock on the door from Martha

Martha – Mr. Grant

Russell – Yes Martha what is it?

Martha – There's a Molly Anderson here that has some information for the Styles…

Russell – Oh yes, yes show her in…

Martha – Come on in Miss Anderson…

Molly – Call me Molly and thank you so much…

Russell – Hello Molly…

Molly – Hello Mr. Grant how are you sir? (a quick hug)

Russell – Fine, fine have a seat…

Molly – Hello folks I'm Molly Anderson, I would imagine you're all aware I've taken over my father Jim's business here in town, since his passing… I am so so sorry for all of you for your tremendous loss and I do have copies of the McCall's life insurance policy as well as Mr. Swenson family policy and Paul, I don't know if you know this, but when you left your job 3 months ago your boss covered you with a 1 year health and life insurance policy and Paul Jr. is covered (hands Paul Sr. and Deborah a policy for the amount of $10,000.00 – They begin to cry)

Paul Sr. – Oh my Lord... and we don't have to use it because the funeral cost is paid for?

Russell – That's exactly right Mr. Styles, but the money is yours.

Deborah – The Reverend said...

Paul Sr. – I know... I know (they cried)

Russell – O.k. so I guess the question is, how do you folks want to do these funerals? together, individually or combinations?

Sheriff's office as Nick arrives

Nick – Hey Mel... Mikey around?

Deputy Mel – Yes sir, here he comes now.

Deputy Mike – Hey there's my man...

Nick – What's happening Duke?

Deputy Mike – Oh you know dadio, just another day at the zoo man… so ah, did you think on it anymore? you know Sheriff Coldman ain't to happy about you dropping or should I say not filing charges on this old character man…

Nick – Yea well we got to get the ball rolling somehow mending these broken fences so…

Deputy Mike – Well just to let you know there's the daughter of this old man here and her son, the brother of this Daniel Mills guy… and here they come now… step in here Nicky (opens the door to let Nick into a room) hold on mam…

Jennifer Mills – Is that him?

Deputy Mike – (Closes the door to where Nick is) Hold on, hold on… we are still talking to him in regards to whether he will be filing charges for attempted murder or a possible lessor charge or dropping it all together, so just hang on…

Donny Mills – Can we just have a word with him… I mean it would mean so much to us to just have a chance to…

Deputy Mike – He just got here so, I'm going to go get Sheriff Coleman... Oh here he comes now, and we'll see if we can get this whole thing straightened out... Sheriff!

Sheriff Coleman – Yes Mike...

Deputy Mike – Sheriff this is Jennifer Mills the daughter of Nathan Forrest the man that tried running down Nick and this is her son Donny... folks this is Luet. Commander Sheriff John Coleman

Sheriff Coleman – Folks... how can I help you?

Jennifer – Sheriff we just want to talk to the gentleman that was involved in this situation sheriff that's all...

Sheriff Coleman – Now look mam... These charges can be very serious, your father could have killed this gentleman or injured him severely, now it's against my better judgment to allow someone to break the law and get away with it... so my advice to Nick would be to press charges to the fullest extent of the law... but unfortunately it's not my call, but Nicks... I'll need a few minutes with Nick then I'll come out and talk to you 2 (leaves to go talk to Nick in an interrogation room where Nick is waiting)

Jennifer Mills – Oh Lord...

Donny – This would crush the remaining family we have.

Sheriff Coleman – Hey Nick...

Nick – Hey Sheriff...

Sheriff Coleman – That mother or daughter of the old man that tried running you down and her son are out there sweating it out... and like I told them I don't advice letting someone off the hook for a crime especially one as serious as attempted murder Nick... now I know it's not my call, but I hope you have thought this decision out thoroughly...

Nick – I have sheriff... I think it's the right call. Now if you would like to charge him for a lessor violation that's fine, one that won't let him do know jail time you know? but again one that he'll regret making a dumb choice based on letting his emotions get the best of him...

Sheriff Coleman – O.k. Nick... I'll let you talk with them with me and Mike here in the room... but I will charge him with excessive speeding and evading a police officer, resisting arrest and minor asault, which would call for a 2 year probation and a 1 year suspension of his license... how's that?

Nick – Knock yourself out sheriff

Sheriff Coleman – Well if I did that Nick, I'd have to arrest myself for aggravated assault... I guess I'm going to have to get use to this lingo sooner or later (opens the door and calls Mike) Deputy Mike can you bring The Mills in please and step in here yourself?

Deputy Mike – Sure thing... come on in folks right this way.

Sheriff Coleman – Folks, this is Nick Pagani the victim of this here near fatal crime... Nick this here is Mr. Forrest's daughter Jennifer and her son, Mr. Forrest's other grandson Donny...

Jennifer – Mr. Pagani I would like to apologize on behalf...

Nick – Hold on here... (Nick looks carefully at Donny as Donny sit's next to his mom) Hold on just a damn minute... you, you're one of the guys who had jumped Juan Ramirez last month at the hardware store in Midland... remember me?

Donny – I don't know what you're talking about...

Nick – Yea of course not because now you're gonna try to run like you did when I popped you in the face... I'm sure you remember that...

Sheriff Coleman – Hold on Nick... is that true son?

Donny – I, I ah

Sheriff Coleman – You know Capt. Billings called me to inform me of that altercation and he said it did indeed happen... now are you one of the boys that jumped Juan, yes or no?

Nick – Go ahead tell him...

Sheriff Coleman – Hold on Nick... well were you?

Jennifer – Donny...

Donny – (With a scared look on his face) Can I tell you why it happened sheriff? Nick...

Sheriff Coleman – Please do... but tell me first were you one of the boys?

Donny – Yes I was... we were across the street at the coffee hut and Capt. Billings and his brother Fred were there having coffee, when the Captain called us over...

Sheriff Coleman – Now who's us?

Donny – Me and Jason Knight and my brother Dan

Sheriff Coleman – O.k.

Donny – Well he Capt. Billings told us that there was a beaner from South County across the street in Millers Hardware store and that we should go over to the side parking lot where he parked and wait for him to come out and give him a hard time... and that if he acted up, to give him a big city send off, and then him and his brother laughed... Jason asked him, what do we get from this besides the pleasure of beating a Mexican and Fred said to us... points with us, which add up to favors owed back to you... understand? He said...

Jennifer – Oh Donny, I am so disappointed in you...

Sheriff Coleman – And where is Jason Knight?

Donny – He's dead sir… along with Dan and 6 others… so far

Sheriff Coleman – You know Nick was not going to file charges against your father mam… Nick

Jennifer – (begins to cry) I am so so sorry for all of this, I truly am…

Nick – Just for you lying I have in mind to change my decision to press charges, to teach you a lesson… but I feel sorry for your father, your grandfather and your whole family, and all the families and towns people that were effected, by this stupid rivalry or grudge or whatever you want to call it… the old man was just emotional… and I'm not going to press charges on him, if you testify against the Billings if need be, right sheriff?

Sheriff Coleman – We will be charging him however with a few other charges, but no jail time… just probation and a suspension of his driver's license… he'll need to appear in court next week here in town… Mike you want to book him and turn him over to his family?

Jennifer – Thank you Nick, thank you so much, you're so kind (hugs Nick with his permission) may I?

Nick – Sure...you're welcome mam... I'm sorry for your loss...

Donny – Thank you (shakes Nicks hand)

Nick – I know it don't bring your brother back, but I too am sorry for this whole mess, we lost 4 close friends too...

Donny – I'm sorry too (hugs Nick)

Two FBI agents walk in

FBI agent 1 - Donald Nathan Mills?

Donny – Yea...

FBI agent 2 – You are under arrest my friend, for the murders of Tommy McCall, Maryann Swenson, Stewart Combs and Paul Styles Jr. you have a right to remain silent anything you say can be held against you in a court of law (as they cuff and walk away with Donny)

Jennifer – Oh Donny, oh my God... sheriff! (as she cries in the sheriffs arms)

Nick – (Nick says to deputy Mel) So much for kindness huh? (Nick walks away)

Reverend Williams South County Community Church

Moose – (Walking into the church with Laura, Jimmy, Julie and Cindy) Hey do you guys know if Nick and Andrew were invited?

Jimmy – I would think Andrew would be here...

Laura – I'm sure he is (Moose holds the door open so all could enter)

Rev. Williams – Ah here they are now... hello youngens

(All respond to the Reverend with hello's)

Rev. Williams – O.k. it seems all 4 families have agreed to a joint funeral this coming Friday, being all 4 were friends in our close knit community and all have agreed that the 4 of them Maryann, Tommy, Paul Jr. and Stewart would have preferred it like this in the event they would have had a say so. With that being said we will commence a standard funeral service here at 10 a.m. after the opening portion of the service, the families would like to open the floor for family or friends to come to the podium and say a few words on behalf of our friends that have gone before us.
Andrew...

Andrew – Hello guys, thanks for coming... all our families would like whoever would like to come forward on Friday and say some good things about each person that we will be celebrating their lives... but we want to be somewhat organized and not make it too long and drawn out... so what we have decided is that everyone agreed to have Connie lead this portion of the service and if whoever wants to say something, or perhaps write or read a poem or even sing a song, please get in touch with Connie no later than? (looks at Connie)

Connie – No later than 12 noon on Thursday, so we can have the programs for the service printed up by Thursday evening ready for Friday morning...

Andrew – O.k. also depending on the response of the rest of the community and our fellow high school students there is a good chance we will be having this service at the high school gymnasium as well as the celebration banquet/reception at the high school cafeteria... we should know more about that by tomorrow... Mr. McCall...

Bill McCall – Hi guys, thanks for being here... this is such a hard thing to do... but I thank God we have all of you to help get us through this entire ordeal, so again thank you... In leu of flowers if you or your families are planning on buying flowers, we would appreciate if you would just make a cash contribution to the funeral fund, we would greatly appreciate that very much.

Rev. Williams – The announcement will be in this Wednesday's paper for the funeral service and it looks like it will be moved to the high school because they will be cancelling school for Friday, so if the high school classmates attend, well this church obviously would not be able to hold that amount of people, so the school would be much more appropriate... O.k. anyone else have anything to share? (pauses) O.k. God bless you all and thank you for coming.

(As the meeting disperses everyone begins to converse)

Moose – Hey Connie (Moose hugs Connie as well as Laura, Julie and Jimmy) Are you o.k.?

Connie – Yea I think... still in shock, you know...

Moose – Yea... it's hard to believe, even til now I just ah...

Connie – I think it would be less dramatic if I had not seen him get shot... I mean my last vision of him alive was getting shot in the back and going down (Laura hugs Connie)

Laura – It's o.k. baby, everything will turn out good eventually… all your memories, all the silly things you guys did and things he said, you'll see…

Connie – (Still hugging Laura) Thank you guys…

Jimmy – For what it's worth Connie, we're here for you… always.

Moose – That's right…always.

Connie – Thank you so much…

Moose – Did you happen to talk to Nick?

Kathy – I tried calling him twice at the station and twice at the hospital, but everywhere I called I just missed him or he hadn't got there yet so…

Moose – O.k. I'll stop and see him and see if he's gonna want to say something… I'll talk to him and I'll have him call you.

Sal's Gas & Garage

Nick – (walks in and finds Jorge cleaning up) O.k. amigo let's get her closed up… it's quitting time…

Jorge – Oh o.k. o.k. orale amigo how's Josephine?

Nick – Oh she's doing great… she'll be coming home manana…

Jorge – Oh Thanks God… I am happy for her and my new boss…

Nick – Thank you amigo… muchos gracias. Hey listen Starting tomorrow my friend $2.10 cents an hour and on December 15th of every year a Christman bonus as well as annual raises… how's that sound?

Jorge – Si? That's o.k. fine to me amigo that's (thinks for about 10 seconds and says) hijole amigo thas about $140.00 a month and about $1700 a year more… are you sure?

Nick – Dang Jorge, you should be working at the bank not at a gas station, that's some fast adding, man… yea I'm sure, but remember, you are going to be having more responsibility too o.k.?

Jorge – Oh yes, yes amigo… you tell me, I do it…o.k.?

Nick – You got it Jorge… go home to mama and tell her the good news… I'll finishes locking up… go ahead.

(Moose pulls in and up to the office area)

Jorge – O.k. amigo hasta manana... Hello Mr. Moose (pats Moose on the arm as he gets off Laura's car) Aye que grande ese muchacho, se come puros frijoles y tortillas... hijole mano...

Moose – Hey Jorge ... man I wish I knew what he was saying...

Nick – Yea well some things are better left unheard... what's up Moose man?

Moose – Ah just coming from the church, with all 4 families and stuff, you know making the arrangements and all...

Nick – Oh... o.k. so when is it?

Moose – Friday... probably at the high school gym...

Nick – Oh (Nick tries to occupy himself searching for keys and papers)

Moose – Did you hear me?

Nick – Yea, yea I heard...

Moose So uh... Kathy tried a few times reaching you here and the hospital but you either had just left or hadn't got there so...

Nick – So what did she want?

Moose – To let you know about the meeting with families this afternoon at the church with Reverend Williams...

Nick – Oh... well I got a business to run here and a fiancée that's in the hospital... in case no one knew...

Moose - Everybody knows Nick... How's she doing?... we were just gonna stop by and see her...

Nick – Well she's doing good... and you don't need to stop bye and see her on my behalf...

Moose – On your behalf?... no we planned it since this morning Laura and I... if you get a chance give Connie a call if you want to say something at the funeral (turns to leave as he sees Nick a little agitated)

Nick – Well like I said... I have a business to run...

Moose (turns back around and faces Nick) You mean... are you saying you're not going to the funeral?

Nick – That's right... that's what I'm saying, that's exactly what I'm saying...

Moose – For Tommy boy and...

Nick – I know who it's for! (Nick says with an angry voice) What do you think I'm stupid that you have to remind me?

Moose (Moose stays shocked) Excuse me Nick... all this time I thought we were friends, sorry to bother you (turns and walks away)

Nick – Friends! Friends! (angry tone) You think I want to go and see 4 dead people in their coffins, huh? Friends don't let friends die Moose... you call me a friend?

Moose – (With a loud response... as Mr. Celetti pulls in) You're like our big brother Nick... more than a friend, unless we were the only ones that seen it that way from our side... and nobody is holding you responsible for what happen to them or us, so get off your pity potty...

Nick – My pity huh... I'll show you my pity potty (as Nick starts at Moose and Sal cuts him off)

Sal – Nicky! Fermati! (stop it)

Moose – Come on... you wanna to hit me... go ahead... if it will make you feel better... do it!

Laura – Moose stop… get in the car!…get in the car!

Sal – Step back now Nick!… what the heck is going on here? (as Nick walks back into the office)

Laura – One minute their talking and the next yelling and then you seen what I seen…

Sal – Moose? What uh…

Moose – Lets go (Moose gets in the car)

Sal – Hey I'm talking to you son… what's going on here?

Moose – We ah just stopped by to (Moose tears up)

Laura – We just came from the church with a meeting with all the families for the funeral service on Friday… we stopped to tell Nick about the arrangements and that he should call Connie who is in charge of the Eulogy and the program coordinator for all those who would like to say something…

Sal – Yea yea…

Laura – So Moose told Nick and he got upset and said he wasn't going Mr. Celetti cause he has a business to run and they got in an argument...

Sal – Oh man... well I'll...

Moose – He's still blaming himself for all this mess Mr. C...

Sal – I'll talk to him Moose... you guys go ahead, I'll talk to him, I know he's really bothered, I just hope he don't go overboard with this whole thing... o.k. we'll see you guys later...

Laura - Bye Mr. Celetti

Moose – Take care Mr. C.

(Sal approaches Nick who sits with his head down at the desk)

Sal – You know that would have been one hell of a fight... between 2 pretty good friends...

(Nick remains silent)

Sal – You remind me so much of your father Nicky...

Nick – Oh come on Mr. C, don't go there with this...

Sal – To late Nicholas, we're already here, and there's not a damn thing you can do about it son... what took place on Saturday night has come and gone and there's four less people in our town and we can grieve, cry, we can hurt together or alone... but it still doesn't change anything...nothing! It's not going to bring them back... it's not going to make the pain easier or make it go away, facts are facts and the truth is the truth and we as a people have to deal with it whether we like it or not... everybody in their own way have to deal with it... It's no different then a fight, a battle something you know about... If a guy walked in here right now and attacked you, you gonna just lay down and let him whip you? No, not Nick Pagani, you are gonna rise to the challenge and fight that guy with everything you got... I know you Nick... If 2 guys came in or 3 guys came in you are going to take em all on with everything you have... I've seen you so I know what I'm talking about... and they couldn't beat you Nicholas... because you have it in you, you're a fighter son... it's the way you are, cause you were made like that by the man upstairs... why?

Only he knows, but know you have 4 guys called death... and you have to rise Nick...

you have to rise son and take them out before they take you and everything you love...

Nick – (Nick stairs with a blank look on his face) You know, sometimes I can see why my dad drank and my mom for that matter... even if it was a temporary fix... I keep the last bottle of his in the cabinet to remind myself of the pain and the promise I made to my mom and my brother Mark... but so many times I wanted to lose myself in it, even for a little while but then I thought, it would be a lousy excuse.

Sal – My father told me when I was young and always looking for excuses to get out of trouble... he said, Excuses don't make men, truth makes men, failures and determined attitudes make men, real men... That wife to be of yours came to me a few months ago and asked me if I ever seen you hung over or smelling of heavy booze in the morning...

Nick – Why did she do that?

Sal – Because she loves you Nick and cares for you... that's why and so do all these kids coming up... they look to you like a roll model... don't disappoint them Nick or yourself or Josephine...fight son, with everything you got (hugs Nick) your papa and mama loved you so much, just like me and Sophia too... we love you son (tears up)

Nick – I love you too... all of you.

Laura visits Josephine as Joe and Gina get ready to leave

Josephine – Hey Laura, how are you? (Joe and Gina greet her as well)

Laura – Hello (hugs everyone) I was good til about 15 minutes ago

Joe – Well we'll be here bright and early sweetie... see you then.

Gina – bye bye baby... bye Laura... tell mama and daddy hello for us...

Laura – O.k. Mrs. Coletti, I will... bye.

Josephine – What's going on?

Laura – Well Moose and I were on our way here after the meeting at the church with Rev. Williams and the 4 families for the funerals... so Moose volunteers to stop and deliver a message to Nick regarding if he wants to say something at the funeral, to contact Connie so he can be put on the program, right?... that's all... and kaboom!

Bid old argument breaks out between Nick and Moose and my God, I thought they were gonna take to blows, but thank God Mr. Celetti pulled up and prevented them from fighting... man I tell you that was scary...

Josephine – Oh my God... what the heck happen?

Laura – I jumped out of the car because I was shocked, I couldn't believe it... I mean they almost fought Josephine...

Josephine – What was the argument about?

Laura – I tried asking Moose on our way here but he gave me the silent treatment... but what I picked up, it looks like Nick isn't or doesn't want to go to the funeral... that's what I got out of it, so...

Josephine – What? His own friends and he... oh oh oh oh oh...

Laura – What is it?

Josephine – You know... where's Moose by the way?

Laura – Oh he dropped me off and said he would pick me up in a half hour...

Josephine – You know what... Nick didn't attend his best friend Johhny Santucci's funeral and he didn't even attend his father's funeral... so I'm thinking...

Laura – Why?... does he have a fear of funerals or something?

Josephine – No... I don't think it's that, it's more of that he doesn't want to see his loved ones dead... you know what I mean?

Laura – Ohh... I see, yea that might be it because when they were yelling at each other, that's what Nick said... something like why? So I can see them dead in their coffins or something like that...

Josephine – Oh Lord... that's got to be it...

Laura – Josephine, I'm not here throwing Nick under the bus or anything... I hope you or him don't think I'm ratting him out...

Josephine – No honey... not at all, I won't say anything don't worry... I'm glad you told me so I can try to soften Nick up... I know he's hurt and feeling guilty and just way to emotional you know?

Laura – Well thank you for understanding... I too would like to try and help them iron things out, but as long as Moose doesn't let me in... what can I do?

Josephine – I know... where is Nick now?

Laura – Oh Mr. Celletti stood with him there at the station, he said he was going to talk to him, so...

Josephine – Oh that's good... Mr. C will straighten him out, I hope...

Laura – O.k. well I'm sure Nick will be headed this way, so I'm gonna cut out and you are going home tomorrow right?

Josephine – Yes! First thing in the morning they said... Nick was supposed to bring me Howie's, I hope he doesn't forget, I can't stand this hospital food anymore...

Laura – Oh I know, I got my tonsils out a couple of years ago and this girl I shared a room with, we were eating trying to swallow our food and she said, that they brought whatever food they didn't eat or finish at the old folks home over here for us... and that was it for me, I mean barf, barf city girl... oh I was done...

Josephine – Thanks for sharing...

Laura – I'll tell you what, I'll be home in about an hour and if Nick doesn't come, call me and I'll bring you Howie's... o.k.?

Josephine – Oh that's so sweet... if I don't call you that means Nick came and brought me Howie'e... or I ate this food again and now I'm in a coma...

Laura – Oh no! (laughs) bye... call me! (they hug and Laura walks out)

Josephine – I will... bye!

(Moose sits in the parking lot waiting for Laura, listening to 'Crying In The Chapel' by the Orioles – as Moose listens to the song, tears begin to run down his face as he reminisces of hime Tommy boy as kids playing all the way to high school and some of Stew as well, with feelings of emotional loss and now thinking his friendship with Nick is damaged, remembers him and Nick fighting off 4 guys at the gas station... a bit confused)

Laura – (Laura gets into the car) Hey baby, you o.k.?

Moose – (Sniffles and laughs) Yea I'm o.k. although I lost some things, I gained something precious... you...

Laura – (Hugs Moose) So did I… you… we'll get through this baby, I promise…

Moose – (Moose weeps with a painful smile on his face) I know we will.

The Celetti's show up to Josephine's hospital room with Howie's, a cheese burger, fries and a chocolate shake as Josephine is reading one of her law books

Sofia – Bella ragazza (beautiful girl)

Sal – Mio prezioso (my precious)

Josephine – Oh you scared me…

Sal- Perdonami… (forgive me)

Josephine – It's o.k., I guess I was just startled… you brought Howie's!

Sal – Yes… Nick sends this… he said he would be a little late and he didn't want you to starve…

Josephine – Yea well, he was supposed to come eat with me, so I could make sure he's eating…

Sofia – He was going to go talk to someone and then go shower up he will be here soon enough… promette (he promises)

Sal – So you are headed home tomorrow?

Josephine – Yes… first thing in the morning… thank God…

Sofia – And the doctor examined you and all?

Josephine – Oh yea… they did a complete concussion test and other eye tests… so it all came out good they said…

Sal – Ah questo e buono (that's good)

Josephine – (dives into her food) Oh my goodness…mmm!

Sofia – Buono? (good?)

Josephine – Ohh! Mucho bueno

Sal – That's Spanish…

Josephine – Spanish, Italian or even Japanese… it's delicious!

(Sal and Sofia laugh)

Sofia – Japanese! (laughs more)

Josephine – Mr. Celetti... I don't want Nick to know, but what started that lotta (conflict) between Nick and Moose?

Sal – Ahh, you heard already?

Josephine – Yes I did... but I don't want Nick to know that I know... I want him to tell me himself...

Sofia – Sangue Italiano bambina (Italian blood little girl)

Sal – No no... you know Nick Josephine... he has a lot to be thankful for ah, from where he came... you know... he'll tell you that himself... but anything that takes him back to those depression years... those years that he was hurt and felt that God couldn't be real, because he would not let bad things like this happen... that's what Nick is battling right now...

Sofia – Another words he's allergic to bad things that happen, negative things... things that cause him pain in his heart...

Josephine – So Moose didn't say anything bad to Nick to hurt him?, cause Moose doesn't know this side of Nick...

Sal – No Moose was just dropping by to give Nicky the news about the funeral, and Nick snapped... Moose probably still don't know why he snapped...

Josephine – Poor Moose, he's got to be hurt himself...

Sal – Oh yea... he's gotta be, these boys from here look up to Nick, you know?

Josephine – I know... but what do we do?

Sofia – Sal had a good talk to Nick and scolded him too...

Sal – He has to face these adversities, bad news, situations that are negative... he has too... I told him, like when he use to fight... he needs to meet the challenge and defeat it... that's all!

Josephine – And what did he say?

Sal – He's stood quiet... starring off into the distant, like always.

Sofia – Your mama and papa came?

Josephine – Oh yea, they were here earlier and they left as Laura got here, but no Moose, just Laura...

Sal – Yea Moose... he's hurt.

Nick arrives at Rev. Williams house which is next to the church – Nick rings the door bell

Rev. Williams – Nick... I was hoping you'd stop by, come on in Nicky have a seat... good to see you again...

Nick – Hi Reverend... thank you... yea I ask myself if this tragedy didn't happen, I know for a fact I wouldn't be here right now... you know...

Rev. Williams – Yea well that's probably true... but unfortunately it did happen and even tough guys got to talk... you need to express your feelings, it's a matter of importance to the soul Nick, rather than releasing it in negative ways...

Nick – I'd prefer not too... but everyone seems to think I need too, I'd rather just not bother anyone with my feelings and keep it to myself, you know?

Rev. Williams – I do know... and I do know because I have dealt with it for many years Nick even before you were born, that it's not a healthy way of doing things, I mean bottling things up...

Nick – I guess I'm just private that way, that's all...

Rev. Williams – Nick... When you were a child, did you ever take a bottle of pop and shake it up... then suddenly open it or remove your finger from the opening?

Nick – Sure, what kid didn't?

Rev. Williams – And what happen Nick when you let go?

Nick – It blew up... exploded...

Rev. Williams – Why do you think it does that?

Nick – Well... I guess all that different stuff they put in it, when it gets shaken up it erupts...

Rev. Williams – That's right ... and what about a pot on the stove when it has liquid in it and it reaches temperatures beyond its boiling point, what happens?

Nick – Boils over?

Rev. Williams – And one last analogy...you're into cars, what happens when you don't put water in the radiator or oil in the motor or even gas in the tank, what happens Nick?

Nick – It breaks down or stops running right...

Rev. Williams – It breaks down... and even when it comes to the maintenance of it, perhaps flushing the water out of the radiator, or changing the oil, rotating the tires, putting new brakes and even washing the car... in many ways it's needs are similar to us as humans... some things need to be taken out and some things need to be added in and some things need to get changed, cleaned and even rotated and shifted and a necessary change to keep things running right... do you understand?

Nick – So you're saying that I should remove the old unnecessary things and replace them with good things necessary to keep me running right?

Rev. Williams – That's correct Nick...

Nick – In you're opinion, what are some of the old things I should take out?

Rev. Williams – Only Nick and God know that son... my opinion doesn't matter... be true to yourself and that way you can be true to everyone in your life...

Nick – How do I be true to myself Reverend?

Rev. Williams – You know when someone brings you their car or truck because it's got some issues and it's not running right?

Nick – Yea...

Rev. Williams – Well Nick, it's the same way... you look, listen and locate the problem, then you share with the customer as to what's wrong and what it's going to take to correct it, right?

Nick – Yea... true...

Rev. Williams – O.k. do you ever lie to them?

Nick – No never!

Rev. Williams – Why not?

Nick – Because... that would... only hurt them and could be a dangerous situation to them down the road...

Rev. Williams – And could that danger kill them or gravely injure them?

Nick – Sure!

Rev. Williams – So being truthful to them could only help them then, right?

Nick – Yea, right...

Rev. Williams – And the bible tells us that the truth will set us free... and, we are to walk in truth throughout our lives so we could be better off dealing with ourselves as well as others.

Nick – Wow... I guess this God guy has it pretty much in check, if we just pay closer attention to him huh?

Rev. Williams – Yea pretty much... we have a tendency of taking matters into our own hands and messing them up and then blaming him or someone else for the problem...

Nick – (stays thinking) hmm...

Rev. Williams – What are you thinking Nick?

Nick – I need to overhaul my life Rev. from the ground up...

Rev. Williams – That's the first step to correcting anything is the admission of the problem... Can I pray with you son?

Nick – Sure (Nick stands as the Reverend places his hand on Nicks shoulder)

Re. Williams – Dear Lord we come to you this evening, honoring you and giving you thanks for this encounter.... We ask Father to fill Nick with your wisdom and...

The Styles residence

Paul Sr. – (Paul Sr. and Deborah sit at the kitchen table drinking coffee) On Thursday before we left, Paul said to me, 'I'm going to do something dad, I don't know what, but I am going to make a contribution to this business' amazing... 2 days later he leaves us and 2 days after that he makes a $10,000 contribution from a policy he didn't existed and neither did I...

Deborah – Yea, way more than what was needed for the house and yet plenty to purchase inventory for us to make a bigger percentage on all these first orders... unbelievable...

Paul Sr. – That's our son for you...

Deborah – So do you think we can buy Andrew a car?

Paul Sr. – Looks that way, we're going to have to and you too, because I'll be on the road and you'll be here ordering and shipping and he needs to get to school and practice so... yea...

Deborah – Maybe you can talk to Nick, he has connections right?

Paul Sr. - Yea that's right… I'll stop by tomorrow and talk to him to see if he can start looking for a couple of good quality used cars so we can get 2…

Deborah – Good… Paul…

Paul Sr. – Yea…

Deborah – Are we going to be o.k.?

Paul Sr. – Of course we are, why you ask that? (hugs her)

Deborah – It's just that, in a blink of an eye our lives have changed forever…

Paul Sr. – Yea… but we still have another son, we still have a business to grow and we still have each other (they remain holding each other)

Nick pulls up to Moose's house at dawn

Margaret – Honey… (as she looks out the window) looks like someone just pulled up in front of the house…

Moose – Hmm... looks like (as Moose heads outside)

Margaret – Do you know who it is dear?

Moose – Yea it's Nick mama...

Margaret – Oh... well invite him in... I'll serve you guys some ice- t...

Moose – Hold on mama don't go serving nothing... just hold on...

(Nick gets out of his truck and leans on his fender facing away from Moose's house)

Moose – You lost... or just coming to yell at me some more?

Nick – Huh (chuckles) look man... I was wrong man for my actions back at the garage... and ah, I just ah, wanted to come by and apologize to my friend Moose, that's all (stares up into the sky)

Moose – (Pauses) Ah don't worry about it Nick...

Nick – I didn't say I was worried about it Moose man... I said... I'm sorry big guy (turns to shake his hand) I had no business talking to you the way I did...

Moose – (Moose shakes Nicks hand) Can I ask you a question Nick?

Nick – (Chuckles again) How did I know you would eventually ask me that?... yea sure go ahead...

Moose – Is there something bothering you about this whole mess... I mean more than what we all know?

Nick – Ah it's complicated Moose... I mean I don't know if you would understand it even if I told you... cause most of it I just found out myself you know... it's ah to deep but really to petty, it's just something I know now I need to get over it or through it and move on... bottom line...

Moose – Try me... if I'm your friend ... try telling me and maybe, just maybe we can both find some kind of closure or solution ... maybe... who knows, stranger things have happen...

Nick – I'll tell you what... you come back and work for me part time to get yourself some spending cash for your new chick-a-dee and we can talk little by little and get everything back to normal... what do you say?

Moose – Really?

Nick – Yea – Yea really… I'll work around your football practice and you can do some hours during the week and you can work weekends, I'm gonna open on Sundays to cause there's a lot of new people in town so there's more gas to be sold man…

Moose – Oh man Nick that be cool man… I could use some spare change and I only got a couple of more weeks of football and I don't know how it's gonna be without Tommy boy… man…

Nick – Hey it'll work itself out… believe me…

Moose – You got it big boss man (hugs Nick) thanks man I appreciate it Nick!

Nick – You got it Moose… Thank you for forgiving me too…

Nick walking into Josephine's room with a piece of Mrs. Garretts apple pie behind his back

Nick – Hello sweetie pie…

Josephine – Sweetie pie? Where have you been?... you had me so worried…

Nick – A sweet piece of pie for my sweetie pie…

Josephine – Ahh... thank you...mmm that looks so good!

Nick – Just for you baby...

Josephine – Oh my goodness I hope I fit through that door when I leave here tomorrow morning, (takes a piece) mmm, so good!

Nick – Yea I dropped the 2 pie's at your folks house and I asked your mom to cut you a big piece...

Josephine – You did, ahh... that was so sweet of you... but if I don't fit into my clothes when I start back at school next week, I'm going to hold you culpable of that crime... you know that don't you?

Nick – Hey there's no law against nurturing my girl back to health, plus I don't know what culpable means... so legally I'm innocent in the first, second and third degree... (laughs)

Josephine – You are guilty as charged mister...

Nick – The only thing I'm guilty of, is being madly in love with you (kisses her)

Josephine – Now I too am culpable of that action (kisses Nick back) So where you been baby?

Nick – Oh… it's a long story…

Josephine – I'm not going anywhere, until tomorrow morning… so…

Nick – Well o.k. then… I left here this afternoon, and I stopped by the sheriff's station to sign some papers, and…

The Combs resident

Bob – (Bob here's Susan crying in the bedroom and goes to check on her. As Susan lie's face down on the bed, Bob sits next to her and rubs her back) Shhhh…it's going to be o.k. I promise…

Susan – Are baby is gone Bob… it's not going to be o.k. things will never be the same…

Bob – At the risk of sounding cliché… it will be o.k. Susan, I promise…

Susan – Your promise is not going to bring Stewart back… he was all we had, because we couldn't afford anymore kid's because we weren't financially established… now what do we have… we're still not financially established, always struggling to pay our bills and buy nice things and now what do we have to live for?

Bob – My God, Susan...

Susan – You're the one that said that we couldn't have no more kid's remember? because we need to get established financially remember?... we never did because we couldn't afford Stewart at times (Still crying as she talks)

Bob – Hey I never said we couldn't afford Stewart... you're just trying to justify his loss by being angry at me...

Susan – You use to say, we can't afford to buy him new shoes, we have bills to pay... what was that?

Bob – You know what?... I'm hurting too, but I'm not going to sit here and throw hurtful things at you for things you said in the past (gets up and storms out)

Susan – Yea do what you do best... leave! (as the front door slams shut, Susan remains crying for Stewie)

(Susan here's that Bob walked out and slammed the front door... she lays there crying, when she hears music coming from

Stew's bedroom... she slowly gets up and approaches his room and turns the bedroom light on and she is shocked to hear his radio on, but also the song that is playing...'Dry Your Eyes' by Brenda and the Tabulations. Susan sits and finishes listening to the song and smiles... she's convinced that Stewart is relaying a message to her... a message that although he cannot be seen, he is still and always will be with them)

The first full day after the tragedy comes to a close... as the night passes the next day starts the morning off with:

**Josephine leaving the hospital with Joe, Gina and Nick*

**Moose, Laura,Jimmy, Julie, Cindy, getting to School*

**The Billings Brother and others in court*

**Juan, Jesse, Sergio at work at Tompkins Farms warehouse*

**Tina's Diners in full swing*

**Paul Sr. Deborah and Andrew having breakfast at their table*

**Molly meeting with Ron Tompkins in his office*

**Jorge opening up the gas station*

**Sheriff Coleman looking at a list of boys names and tearing it up and throwing it into the garbage can*

**Mrs. McCall picking out clothes that matches Mrs. Swenson's clothes that she has picked out for Maryann including a letterman's sweater from Tommy*

**Sal and Sofia Celetti have breakfast at Tina's Diners as well As Rev. Williams*

Wednesday passes and Thursday morning has arrived

Molly Anderson's Financial Services

Molly – (Opens her front door to let Nick and Josephine in) Hello, come on in, How are you Josephine? (a quick hug) Nick...

Josephine – Oh a lot better thank you, it's so nice to see you Molly here in your business office, wow a difference...

Molly – You like?

Josephine – Oh yea compared to when I worked here, oh man this is beautiful... look at the carpet and all the new furniture, that's a womans touch for you...

Molly – Yea, dad had it a little out dated... so I had to put a woman's touch to it, you know...

Josephine – Oh it's gorgeous

Molly – Thank you...

Nick – I brought her with me because this is a big special moment in my life...

Molly – Oh sure it is, no doubt...

Nick – But I didn't think it was going to turn out to be an interior decorating conference...

Josephine – Oh stop Nick... comportarsi

Molly – What did you tell him?

Josephine – Comportarsi... that means behave

Molly – Comportarsi (behave)...Oh here comes Sal and Allen now...come on in we're in here...

(They exchange greetings introducing Allen to everyone)

Sal - Hello mia figlia (my daughter)

Josephine – Nonno (grandpa)

Molly – Wow! I got a sudden craving for Italian food (they all laugh)

Sal – Before we start here... I want for someone to take a picture of me officially handing my set of keys over to Nicky...come on son...

Nick – Here we go...

Josephine – Molly, you're going to have to take it (hands her the camera)

Molly – O.k.... (whispers to Josephine) how do you say smile in Italian

Josephine – Sorriso (smile)

Molly – O.k. sorriso, sorisso... that's not going to cut it...

Josephine – No if they say it in Italian, they won't smile Molly... How about in spanish?

Josephine – No in english only (as they all laugh)

Sal – I officially make you the new owner of the business and the 2 properties...(hands Nick the keys and documents and they hug) it's all yours son, it's all yours!

Nick – Thank you Mr. C... I actually can't thank you enough...

Sal – You can son by doing me proud...I know you can.

Molly – O.k. Allen we'll get some signatures and make some copies... then I take a you alla outa for to eata some breakfast ahh... hows that for american italian?

Josephine – That was actually pretty terrible (laughs)

Allen – I'm anglo saxon too and that was pretty bad... nowhere close Molly

Nick – Nice try though...

Sal – O.k. let's sign away here...

The High School where Moose enters the coaches office

Coach Mullen – Aye Moose good morning... what brings you here so early?

Moose – Coach... Uhh I'm just here to tell you that I'm gonna shut it down coach for the rest of the year

Coach – Shut it down... you quitting?

Moose – I'm hanging it up yea

Coach – There's only 3 games left Moose are you sure? Are you hurt or whats going on son?

Moose – My heart ain't in it coach… I can't pretend I want it you know… my heart just can't do it…

Coach – You know a year at junior college and you have some big schools looking at you too son… if you just stick it out we can finish with a good strong record you know, you're my best defensive player Moose…

Moose – I appreciate it coach…maybe if we still had a shot at the league title I'd stay and do it for Tommy…but this way too, it''ll give more playing time too for you to see what you have for next year coach.. I'm sorry, but I hope you see that I wouldn't be doing the team justice by not giving 100%...so…

Coach – O.k. Moose I understand and I apologize for seeming a little selfish… but hey you know best what's good right now (hugs Moose) I'll still give you strong recognition if schools call inquiry on big Moose Flannigan…

Moose – Thanks coach… you're the best…

Coach – And hey Moose… you and Tommy were selected all conference again and Tommy is up for all state first or second team…just thought I'd let you know that son.

(Moose smiles and walks out as Laura waits outside the coach's door)

Moose – What are doing here?

Laura – Waiting for you…

Moose – I thought we said we'd see each other in class?

Laura – Yea well I figured you might need someone to talk too, so I waited…

Moose – Well I'm glad you did…I start this Weekend for Nick at the station…

Laura – That's great Moose…just weekends?

Moose – Well I'll talk to Nick about a few hours on Tuesdays, Wednesdays and Thursdays other than that it'll be a total of 16 hours on weekends…

Laura – Wow that's good sweety…

Moose – Yea that'll be, maybe… uhh about $30.00 a week

Laura – good for you... do you plan on working there after school, I mean after we graduate?

Moose – Probably full time if Nick would have me fulltime... but I've been giving a lot of thought...I want to play football next year at JC but... I want to take carpentry classes and business classes and maybe even some drafting or architectural classes you know to build houses and room additions and stuff like that...

Laura – Yea... that's good, you look like a big burly carpenter construction guy... you know that?

Moose – I like doing things with my hands...

Laura – Yea I noticed (they both laugh)

Moose – What about you... what are you gonna do after we gratuate?

Laura – I plan on working for Molly during the summer, we already talked about it a while ago... and that business world really intrigues me...

Moose – Cool ... that is super cool. You'd make a good looking sexy business woman...

Laura – You like that huh?

Moose – Oh yea as long as it's you baby (they hug and Moose spins her around before entering into class)

The Combs residence

Susan pours Bob a cup of coffee and walks into the living room where Bob is still sleeping on the couch after a late night of drinking. Susan sits on the coffee table in front of him

Susan – Bob... Bob... here's some coffee...

Bob – (Moans a bit from a stiff neck) Uhh... why did I do that...ohhh (sits up holding his neck)

Susan – Honey... I'm sorry for last night, I'm the reason you did that, because of my big mouth and little brain...

Bob – Hay... it's understandable considering what we're going through... and if you want a divorce I can understand that too...

Susan – I don't want a divorce... I want to live the rest of my life with the father of my son... who is still with us in all reality...

Bob – You know I didn't want to tell you, but yesterday I was sitting in the office room and I heard some noise, like footsteps in

Stew's room... and I ah... figured it was you cleaning up or whatever... but I enjoyed it for quick moment because it reminded me of Stewart being in his room... but then I seen you outside talking to Mrs. Souza, so I got up to go check what was making that noise and, nothing, no one in there but his radio was on, the way he use to leave it on and we use to get upset with him, but I remembered you were in here gathering his clothes for the funeral home... then I said to myself, oh Susan left it on...

Susan – I got his clothes, but I didn't leave the radio on, I never even turned it on...

Bob – No... well I never...

Susan – Listen... last night when you left did you go into his room and turn on the radio or no?

Bob – No, I left and walked over to Jimbo's

Susan – O.k. when you left... I was still lying on the bed, right?

Bob – Right...

Susan – So I was still crying a bit, thinking how our world had just fallen apart

Bob – O.k.

Susan – Then I heard his radio playing... so I got up slowly thinking maybe you had turned it on and forgot to turn it off... so I go into his room... and all of a sudden I get this warm sense of peace on me and I sit on his bed and the radio is playing Dry Your Eyes... and I felt him in there with me and he was telling me to stop crying, that he's still here with us...

Bob – I believe he is... we just can't share this too much with a lot of people, because they will have us committed you know...

Susan – (Chuckles) Yea... so are we o.k. do you except my apology?

Bob – Of course I do (Susan moves to the couch and hugs Bob)

The Mortuary

Martha – Hello Mr. Tompkins, how are you sir?

Ron – Oh I'm just fine, how are you today?

Martha – Great!... how can I help you?

Ron – Is Russ in?

Martha – No he just left to Willow to pick up his brothers 2 hurst's for tomorrow...

Ron – Oh o.k. well I just came to drop off this check for the funerals...

Martha – Oh let me get you an invoice receipt for that Mr. Tompkins...

Ron – O.k. that's fine...

Martha – Mr. Tompkins if you don't mind me saying, I think this is wonderful and tremendous blessing to these families for your caring act, I believe you have lined yourself up for a big blessing...

Ron – Why thank you Martha... I appreciate that...

Martha – There you go, I'll put this on Mr. Grant's desk, but I'm sure he won't be back until late in the day... but I'm sure he'll see you tomorrow...

Ron – Thank you again.

(Ron Tompkins stops and views the announcement board displaying the names of Maryann Swenson, Tommy McCall, Paul Styles Jr. and Stewart R. Combs. Ron walks outside the lobby area of the funeral home and sits in a garden area and begins to weep silently... asking... why? Why? Why? With clinched fists)

The Swenson's residence

Philys – That's all she's been doing all week is laying on her bed, holding her things, crying and talking to her and Tim is just like in a trans (Philys starts to cry) and I don't know how long I can take all this without totally falling apart Todd...

Todd – I know Philys... what do you want me to do? I don't have no answers for you at this point... I know what you're saying... I keep waiting for her to come out of her bedroom, I keep waiting for her to ask me, 'Are you done with the paper Daddy?' it's driving me insane as well... what's the answer? I don't have a clue!

Philys – Are you asking a question in general or are you asking me what I think the answer is?

Todd – Tell me... what do you think the answer is?

Philys – Sell the business and sell the house and let's move away from this town!

(Todd looks empty, and Tim their 13 year old son walks in shocked over what he just heard)

Tim – What?... sell the business and the house and move away? you think that's the answer?

Todd – Hmm...maybe you're right...

Tim – No dad, that's not the answer...

Philys – That's the only answer (Philys pours herself another glass of wine)

Todd – That's not an answer either (looks at her glass of wine)

Philys – No it's not Todd I know that, but it is a temporary solution that's all it is.

Tim – Mom...

Philys – Look Tim... I know you're sentimental and all that right now... but consider something other than yourself in all this...

Todd – Philys, honey...

Philys – Consider the fact that this wretched cursed town took my daughter...you got that, your sister!... understand, I hate this town, I want out as soon as we can sell this house! (Philys goes off to her bedroom)

Todd – Tim.. son you have to realize that mom is very emotional right now...

Tim – We all are dad...

Todd – I know son, it's just that things like this take time to sort out, sometimes weeks, sometimes months and sometimes years... and we'll get through, I promise... you just have to know that whatever we decide to do it's not to hurt anyone, it's more to help... so I am asking you son to stay strong and trust me... o.k.?

Tim – (Hugs his dad) I trust you dad... is mom going to be o.k.?

Todd – Yea, but we have to help her...o.k.?

Tim – O.k. dad.

The Colletti's residence

(Gina and Josephine are preparing dinner, as Nick will dine with Josephine and her family for the first time ever)

Gina – Josie, I have always told you baby that your education is the most important asset you'll need in life... you know that...

Josephine – I know mama... I'm not saying I'm not going to finish, nor am I going to take a break... we've just talked about it many times and we both agreed that if marriage interferes with my law school then we don't get married... but if we can make a plan and stay focused on it... I can do both...

Gina – Oh so Nick doesn't mind you being away at law school?

Josephine – He doesn't mind... no, he's going to be busy with his new businesses and working a lot of hours so...

Gina – Well maybe he pay's for the rest of your law school...

Josephine – Oh he said he would... he don't have a problem doing that mama...

Gina – Hmmm... before I would have said something sarcastic, but Nick is a good young man... I guess his families past is what really scared me... but I could learn to love him too if you and papa do, after all he showed me that he really realy loves you...

Josephine – You know mama... Nick is one tough guy, he is the envy of all the guys in this town because of his ability and reputation of being a tough fighter... but when he sees you he quivers like a little boy (laughs)

Gina – Yea well he better... cause I'll still pugno le sue luci (punch his lights out)... ehh (Gina makes a fist and throws a punch and her and Josephine both laugh)

Josephine – Ahh, you are crazy mother... pazzesco mama! (crazy mother) (Josephine makes the Italian hand gesture)

Sal's Gas & Garage

Jorge – (Walks in from pumping gas, into the office area where Nick sits filling out some papers) So patron... Mr. Moose he starts Saturday?

Nick – First thing in the a.m...

Jorge – (Sits down in front of Nick) You want to open at 6 o'clock or 7 seven o'clock?

Nick – Ah, what do you think amigo... we're starting the winter month's soon... so weekend hours should be different than weekday... yea?

Jorge – It's o.k. to me... what you want?

Nick – You know what I want?

Jorge – You tell me amigo...

Nick – O.k. what I want is for you to take charge of that... you write down what hours you want to stay open, what time you want to close, just make sure Saturday and Sunday hours are different than Monday through Friday... and pencil Mr. Moose in after school Tuesdays, Wednesdays and Thursdays and all day Saturdays and Sundays, just make sure you give him 1 weekend off a month and you too and me too and whoever else you hire...just make sure not the same weekend... I want 1 more fulltime attendant that can do full service including fixing flat tires and changing them as well... o.k.? that's what I want...

Jorge – Hijole patron... can say again (laughs) just kidding...now you sound like Salvador the patron grande...

Nick – Put a sign out front or on the window that we're hiring for a service attendant, you talk to them, you know interview and you hire who you think will fit our team and start them out at $1.25 an hour after 30 day's we see how they're doing and we give them a 15 cent raise if they work out, huh?

Jorge – Oh, it's o.k. to me patron... I get it all done for you by Monday yes?

Nick – You got it Jorge

(Ron Tompkins pulls up to the pump and gets off to talk to Nick)

Ron – Hello Jorge my friend!

Jorge – Hello Mr. Ron how are you today senor?

Ron – I'm just as good as can be expected, can you filler up and check all the levels please?

Jorge – Yes for sure… Jorge says to himself 'I don't know what he mean when he say to me 'oh as to good just to be expecting', I don't know what he say hombre…

Ron – Is the owner of this establishment here?

Nick – Hey Mr. Tompkins how are you?… I'm just finishing them up for you right now… here you go…

Ron – O.k. Nick, I'll have Lynn get copies for you and I'll have one of the boys drive that gas truck down to you this afternoon before closing…

Nick – That's fine… yea because we'll be closed in the morning for the funeral, but we'll be open at least by 1 p.m. so Jorge and his family can attend and have a bite to eat at the reception before opening up...

Ron – Good, good... well I think you're going to make one heck of a solid business man Nick... I really do son...

Nick – Thank you Mr. Tompkins

Ron – Hey no more of this Mr. Tomkins stuff... you're a member of the business community now, you call me Ron...

Nick – O.k. Ron...

Ron – There you go... well I guess we'll see you at the... in the morning

Nick – Hey Ron?

Ron – Yea Nick...

Nick – Last Saturday Night... just exactly where was Juan and the boy's at?

Ron – (Chuckles) Why I ah, I don't know Nick, maybe you should ask them...

(Paul Styles Sr. pulls up to the pump and gets off to talk to Nick and crosses paths with Ron)

Paul Sr. – Ron, I've been looking for you all week…

Ron – Yea well been real busy you know…

Paul Sr. – (Extends his hand out to shake Ron's hand) I just can't thank you enough for what you did for our kids funerals and all I mean…

Ron – Hey Paul… you thanked me, that's good enough, you don't have to carry on… I did it, you thanked me and I know that you and the wife appreciate it, so let's just go with that… your welcome, I'm sorry for your loss and If I could make it up more, I would do so, we'll see you tomorrow Paul (walks away)

Paul Sr. O.k. Ron thanks…

Jorge – Fill her up Mr. Paul?

Paul Sr. – Yes sir Jorge… thank you!

Jorge – De nada Mr. Paul de nada…

Paul Sr. – Hey Nick…

Nick – Hey Mr. Styles how goes it?

Paul Sr. Oh hey it's ah... a little rough, but it's going to take some time to get use to it, but... hey life goes on you know...

Nick – I can't imagine... I can't imagine life going on without our friends... so I don't know how you and the misses and all the other parents are dealing with this whole ordeal... I really don't...

Paul Sr. – Yea Nick... I'll tell you, I guess life isn't guaranteed to anyone... I guess it's true that we have to live life expecting the unexpected... you know?

Nick – Hmm, I wish someone would have told me that when I was 4...

Paul Sr. Yea... you didn't have it so good yourself did you? But considering all that your families been through... I have to compliment you my friend, you've done well for yourself and now I hear you own this place (shakes Nicks hand) congratulations Nick...

Nick – Thank you sir... I notice you and Ron talking out there...

Paul Sr. – Yea, I was just trying to thank him... you know he paid for all 4 funeral expenses...

Nick – Yea that's what I heard, that was pretty generous of him...

Paul Sr. - Yea... I was trying to thank him and I guess he's just trying to be modest or something, but that was a real act of kindness

Nick – Or guilt...

Paul Sr. What do you mean guilt?

Nick – Ahh... I don't know... just confused I guess...

Paul Sr. Hmm... hey Nick I was going to ask you, if you happen to run across a couple of good running used cars, can you let me know... I need to pick a good dependable 2nd car for the misses and another one for Andrew to get back and forth to school and stuff...

Nick – Was Paul's car to badly damaged?

Paul Sr. – Yea unfortunately... Andrew asked if he could try to restore it little by little, but Deb wouldn't have it, she didn't want it around, you know...

Nick – Where is his car now?

Paul Sr. – It's at the house

Nick – O.k. … I'll tell you what,… Monday I have 4 cars coming in, about 10 a.m. they should be here… I'll call you or you can just stop by early afternoon, check em out… If something works for you I'll cut you a deal and you throw in Juniors car… cause I know

I can use the parts, you know…

Paul Sr. – Yea you know that car better than anybody… well that sounds gook Nick, I appreciate it…

Nick – No problem sir… tell the misses I send my condolences…

Paul Sr. – You got it…thanks (they shake again)

Nick – Hey amigo!

Jorge – Diga me (tell me)

Nick – I'm gonna cut out… go home shower up, go by some flowers and a bottle of wine…

Jorge – For me?

Nick – No amigo not this time… I'm going to dinner at Josephine's with mama and papa…

Jorge – Oh amigo… be careful that Josephine's mama no poison you patron…

Nick – (laughs) How would I know Jorge?

Jorge – You sit close to her mama… you tell her that her food looks and it smells delisioso… and you tell her, look out the window at the pretty pajaro! And you switchy the plate with her when she no look (nick laughs) and if she eat the food and she want to poison you, she fall to the floor amigo…and si no, everything is o.k. fine…

Nick – Oh man Jorge… you too much my friend… is that what you had to do with your future mother in law?

Jorge – Yes, that's how I know… because she fall to floor and died one time…

Nick – Well Jorge… if I don't make it back, the station is all yours my friend… o.k.?

Jorge – O.k. fine (Nick leaves)

Molly's office late in the work day

Laura – (Enters Molly's office, Molly is typing) Knock, knock

Molly – Oh hi Laura come on in…

Laura – Oh just in the neighborhood and thought I'd swing by and bring you a little surprise...

Molly – Really?

Laura – Yea if that's o.k. of course?

Molly – Well I guess it's o.k. what is it?

Laura – It's not what is it... it's who is it!

Lily - (Comes out from behind the wall) Hey gorgeous!

Molly – Heyyyy!... Lily! Oh my lucky stars (jumps out from behind her desk to greet Lily)

Lily – How are you Molly? (as they embrace)

Molly – Oh my goodness, what a shocker... how have you been?, you look great!

Lily – You look pretty darn good yourself girlfriend...

Molly – Oh my Lord... I'm at a loss for words... what brings you back?

Lily – Oh I just had to come when I found out about all the ones that got killed... other than little Paul, I used to baby sit all the others, Tommy, Maryann and Stewie… they were all my clients when I was in high school…

Molly – Oh that's right you were always babysitting them, I forgot all about that, all year around… you and your babysitting service 'Lily of the Town Babysitting Service' remember that?

Laura – How could I forget… she use to charge my parents for babysitting me…

Lily – She was my first paying job (they all laugh)

Molly – How tragic though huh? About those poor kids…

Lily – Oh I know, I couldn't stop crying for 3 days and Scott tells me why don't you go and spend a few day's with your family and go for the funeral, so here I am!

Molly – And where are your little ones?

Lily – With the folks… let them drive my parents crazy for a while…

Molly – Oh… I want to see them!

Laura – We'll drop them off at your house tonight (they all laugh)

Molly – Let me take you girls out for some dinner huh?

Lily – Hey, that sounds great, I'm starving...

Molly – Let lock up... give me a couple minutes...

Laura – I'm gonna pass... I have to go over to Moose's house to help him with his eulogy for tomorrow... you guys got some catching up to do...

Molly – Oh are you sure?

Laura – Yea... plus we're going to grab a burger over at Howie's...

Lily – Ohhh Howie's... I've been craving me some Howie's for years...

Molly – We can go there, that's no problem...

Lily – Or we can go to Tina's and ask for our old job's back (they laugh)

Laura – O.k. I'm out I'll see you guys later...

Molly – I'll drop her off at home when I'm done with her...

Laura – O.k. sounds good.

Lily – Gee whiz... you sound like one of my old college boyfriends (they laugh yet again)

Molly – Oh man do we have some catching up to do... tell me about Scott...

Nick rings the doorbell at Josephine's house, as he stands waiting, he holds 2 bouquets of flowers, and 2 bottles of wine and a box of fine chocolates for the family

Josephine – (Opens the door and grabs the wine) Hey baby... oh my... (Joe walks up and grabs the wine from Josephine)

Joe – Hey Nick... welcome, come in...oh wow, the good stuff (looks at the wine)

Nick – Hey baby (kisses her) hello papa Joe...(hands the chocolates to Josephine) these are for the family and these are for you (hands her a bouquet) and these are for your mom...

Josephine – Thank you sweetie, you are so sweet... mama's in the kitchen, come... (the song 'Bring It On Home' starts to play) mama, guarda chi c' e qui (look whos here)

Gina – Ahh Nicholas, welcome!

Nick – These are for you (hands her the flowers)

Gina – Oh look... che bello! (how beautiful)... thank you so much Nicky... dinner will be in a few minutes...

Joe – Look what fine wine Gina...

Gina – Oh what taste this young man has... huh?

Joe – Oh for sure.

(The Coletti's sit down for dinner with Nick... the family talks and laughs and shares a great family Italian dinner together – as the song ends)

(Josephine and Nick have a seat after dinner in the living room)

Nick – Oh... I can't believe I ate that much...

Josephine – I can't believe it either... my goodness, I thought you were just trying to win my mom's favor...

Nick – Heck I've never seen so much good food in front of me like that before...

Josephine – Well get use to it, because that's how every Sunday is around here...

Nick – Oh man I'm gonna get fat… I can see it already…

Josephine – That's o.k. baby, that's just more of you to love…

Nick – I don't wanna get fat… at least until I'm older…

Josephine – Well make room because we still have torta al cioccolato…

Nick – What the heck is tortu el ciolato?

Josephine – No silly… torta is cake al cioccolato is of the chocolate kind…

Nick – Chocolate cake? Oh man that's like my favorite…

Josephine – Just wait until you taste mama's… oh it's to die for… oopps, I shouldn't have said that…

Nick – I know what you mean baby… that kind of stuff has been happening to me more than ever this past week… I keep saying things like, knock em dead and I'd die for a piece of pie and the three stooges kill me… I mean … I don't know it's like why is that happening… I don't ever recall using phrases like that so much as I have these past 5 day's…

Josephine – It's just now more recognizable in your vocabulary... you probably always use it, it's just now more noticeable because of what just happen... we'll get through it...

Nick – Yea... I can't wait for tomorrow to end...

Josephine – I know.

Joe – O.k. here come mama's chocolate cake... make room!

Gina – Godere... godere di tutti (enjoy all)

Josephine – Enjoy everybody!

Nick – Oh I'm sure I will... how do you say I'm going to burst?

Joe – Sto per scoppiare... we all are Nicky (they all laugh) (Thursday night comes to a pleasant end)

Friday morning... 4 Hurst's pull into the high school parking lot in front of the gymnasium in the presence of seems to be the entire town of South County as well as additional family members and friends from out of town – Amazing Grace from Elvis Presley plays

6 Pal Bearers from the South County High School Football team carry Tommy's coffin off the Hurst led by Moose.

6 of Maryann's cousins carry her coffin off the 2nd Hurst.

4 classmates and 2 cousins carry Paul Jr.'s coffin off the Hurst. 6 classmates carry Stew's coffin off the hurst led by Jimmy.

All 4 coffins are placed in front of a stage in the gym, with Tommy's and Maryann's together on one side and Paul Jr.'s and Stewarts on the other side. A choir behind Rev. Williams sings in unison with Elvis Presley's version – The gym is packed. On stage along with Rev. Williams is The High School principle, The head football coach and the Mayor of South County.

Rev. Williams – I'd like to welcome everyone here this morning, on behalf of the Swenson family, the McCall family, the Styles family and the Combs family, your love and attendance is much appreciated and your thoughts and prayers for the families would be much welcomed... As this tragic event occurred, it has brought our community together, although some might say or find a negative view point, others might say it's for a positive outcome... but none the less the word of God tells us that there is a season for everything including a time to live and a time to move on to a life of eternal glory... Many question the circumstances of this event, others question God as to why it happen... I've learned over the years, that God will close the eyes of one person, to open the eyes of many others... and that time itself would reveal the purpose of the event that brought on this entire situation... We have with us here on stage... Our Mayor of South County, Tom Sanders, Our High School Principle James Tillman, the high school's football coach, baseball coach and athletic director Gary Stanfield... they will all come up and share with us some special words on behalf of our fellow students, friends, siblings, children, family member, Tommy McCall, Maryann Swenson, Paul Styles Jr. and Stewart Robert Combs, whom we pay honor this day...

Principle Tillman – These students were all very special in the eyes of every student, faculty member and member of our entire staff here at South County High School... (continues on for 5 minutes)

Coach Stanfield – Tommy was one of the best over all athlete's I ever had the privilege of coaching here in my 16 years, and Paul was an amazing, strong headed athlete with a never say quit attitude, I have witnessed in years... (talks for 8 minutes)

Mayor Sanders – At Government week this past September, Maryann expressed great interest in serving her community in the future through city council or as a county rep and it grieves me not only for her loss, but the for the loss of the others and the pain that the families are bearing, not to mention the sad effect on our entire community... I had the pleasure of awarding the South County Stars led by Stewart Combs at this years High School talent contest... that was easily won by Moose, Jimmy, Andrew and the leader of the group Stewart Combs... if you never seen it, let me just say it was nothing less than professionalism at it's finest (goes on for 5 minutes)

Jimmy – Stewie was my best friend... and he had been since we were in kinder garden... he wasn't a great athlete, but I tell myself, he could have been if he chose too... he was the type of guy, that if he put his heart in it... it would get done and get done right and good... like when he seen Jackie Wilson dance.. he said, I want to dance like that... and he did, maybe better... Stew was a smart guy with a big heart (Jimmy goes on to say something nice about Maryann, Tommy and Paul Jr.)

Moose – Tommy boy was a good friend, always encouraging... never a negative attitude... if he was in a bad mood, you'd never know it, cause he never would show that he was... him and Maryann were the envy of all relationships by other students... they were a couple that everyone knew, was meant to be... Paul, was a stand out guy, always there if you needed him, you can always count on him, I'll miss him... Stew, was a pain in the butt, but he was a pain that I loved and cared for, like a little brother (puts his head down and cries continues for another 2 minutes)

Nick – I thought I owed it to them to go with them to the Rock & Roll show... They were so excited like little kids on Christmas morning waiting to see what Santa had brought them...I was wrong... I'll forever regret the request to go to kind of watch over things... to make sure nothing gets out of line... I set up a plan, that would get us there and back and to avoid trouble, if it rose up against us... but when others had a plan to hurt and cause damage already... well, that's kind of hard to plan against that, especially if you didn't know they did... I apologize to all the families and to all those who are feeling this great loss the way I am... These were great people here, you know and ah... I wish I could, could do it all over again, meaning last weekend... My father died as to the result of this same tragedy 21 years ago... his best friend was shot and killed in front of his eyes, and there was nothing he could do about it... so he drank himself to death over it... caused pain to my mom and my brother and myself in the mean time... you see, tragedy causes pain and you don't overcome pain by adding more pain to the situation, you stop the pain and overcoming it with love... forgiveness, caring for others and bringing happiness to others lives so that you too can have happiness. So far 12 people have died in the last week over this senseless grudge, this rival vary that showed ignorance over intelligence... and now these 12 families are asking why? And 3 families, 21 years ago asked that same question... why? My deepest most heartfelt condolences to the Swenson family, the McCall family, the Styles family and the Combs... I am privileged to be called a friend of your son's and daughter, it was a great pleasure to have known them and you as well... may God bless you and everyone here.

Rev. Williams – Thank you Nick, for those most thoughtful words... The Community choir will sing a dedication to our departed.

Rev. Williams delivers a sermon on Life based on the scripture 2Cor. 5:8 that lasts 30 minutes.

(As the choir stands to sing the song 'My Prayer from the Platters begins

to play... As Rev. gives his sermon for the day and the prayer for the families and for all who attended the coffins are taken out. The next scene shows the graveside ceremony being done and soon all are back at the high school cafeteria for the reception banquet... as the song comes to an end)

Nick – (Nick sit's with Josephine and her parents and Sal and Sofia) Boy I can't wait til tomorrow morning

Gina – Why Nick, what's tomorrow morning?

Josephine – He's wanting this day to pass mama, that's all...

Joe – I second that... this as been a very long week...

Sal – You got that right Joe...

Gina – It has been a very long and sad week for all, but especially for the 4 families... oh my goodness I don't how they'll adjust...

Sofia – Fortunately they will Gina... con il tempo (with time)

Sal – Yep time is the healer of all things...

Joe – Your right there… and they'll all experience a different amount of time to heal.

(Sheriff Coleman walks up to their table)

Sheriff Coleman – Hello again… Nick, can I have one minute of your time? I promise I won't keep you…

Nick – I'm going to hold you to the one minute sheriff (Nick gets up and they walk off)

Sheriff Coleman – That was a pretty powerful message you gave today Nick… my compliments to you…

Nick – Yea well I'm sure that's not why you ask me for my time is it?

Sheriff Coleman – No… Nick somehow I feel you know more than what you're sharing with me in regards to the shootings of the Midland boys… and I'd really wish you would come clean if you have any information for me…

Nick – Your feeling like that because of the way I expressed my feelings? Just because I feel a certain way you think I have or am withholding information about 7 or 8 dead guys from Midland... your wrong sheriff... your dead wrong, excuse the term and excuse me (Nick walks back to his table)

(Los Muchachos and all their families sit at another table)

Tony – What do you think ese? (as they seen Nick talking to Sheriff Coleman)

Juan – Nothin to think about holmes...

Tony – You think it's all cool on the front line?

Juan – Simon... front line, back line and the side lines ese...

Tony – Orale pues...

Arturo – What's up holmes?

Tony - Nada ese... it's all cool...

Arturo – No se preocupe whay...

Alberto – Ghosts in the night carnal... tranquilla (relax)

Tony – That sheriff don't quit...

Sergio – He ain't gonna quit either... that's his job ese...

Alberto – That's cool ese's, because he'll be like a dog chasing his tail… and if he ever catches it… then what? He's gotta let go otherwise he ain't go nowhere with it (they all laugh)

Arturo – It's like my dog that ain't got no tail… he'll never catch it … pobrecito (poor thing) (they all laugh again)

(Bob and Susan Combs sit at the table of the Swensons, McCalls and Styles families. Ron Tompkins comes and sits with Bob and Susan)

Ron – Hey Bob, I was just getting ready to leave and I wanted to stop by and ask you a question…

Bob – Sure Ron… what is it?

Ron – Well it's probably more of a statement, but I guess there's a question in it somewhere… I'd like for you to come work for me Bob…

Susan – Oh?

Bob – In what capacity Ron?

Ron – Sales… distribution… head marketer… something!

Bob – Well... gee I ah...

Ron – Here's the thing... I know you can't be happy with what your making driving all the way to Willowood... so I'll pay you $1.00 more an hour and 20% commission on top of that... that would be almost triple of what you're making now...

(Molly and Rev. Williams walk up to the Combs)

Rev. Williams – Bob, Susan... on behalf of the other families... they wanted to bless you guys with an offering of the donations that came in today... as you may of heard by now... Ron here has picked up all the expense and costs of the funerals and therefore the other families where covered with insurance policies so they wanted you guys to have this in Stewarts honor...

Molly – Here is a check for $6575.00

Susan – Oh dear God... (shocked)

Bob – We can't thank you enough seriously... oh my goodness...

Ron – You can thank me by excepting my offer Bob...

(All the families get up to hug the Combs as they express their gratitude to everyone)

Bob – Thank you Ron... when do I start?

Ron – Well you start whenever you guys get back from your vacation... take some time off, and enjoy each other and when your ready... come on in...

Susan – We can get that second car...

Ron – Nonsense... your job comes with a company car. (Bob and Susan hug with joy and tears)

Rev. Williams – You're a good man Charlie Brown...

Ron – Ahhh... Charlie Brown?

(Nick and his table come to say goodbye to all 4 families, with hugs and handshakes and open invitations to call for whatever need they have. Others begin to do the same as the reception comes to a close)

Josephine – Now for the hard part (Josephine clutched to Nicks arm)

Nick – What do you mean?

Josephine – To begin to live without their kid and to adjust without them… boy I hope and pray we never have to experience that…

Nick – Yea that is the tough part…

Josephine – Are you o.k. Nicky?

Nick – Yea… now to get on with life and try not to look back, hoping we can put all this behind us and live a normal life…

Josephine – That be great.

Joe – We'll see you guys later… where you off too?

Nick – I think we're going to take a ride up Larkston, enjoy the town maybe have some ice cream and pie, you guys want to go with us?

Joe – I'd love too, but I have a meeting in a half hour back at work… Gina do you want to go with them?

Josephine – Come with us mama, you'll love it…

Nick – Yea , come on…

Gina – No, no I'm too tired… I'm exhausted; really… you guys go and have fun…

Nick – O.k.

Josephine – Bye...

Joe – Bye bye...

Nick – I need to swing buy and get some gas, because there is no gas stations between here and there...

Moose and Laura are driving to Laura's house

Laura – Hey since you'll be working all weekend... how about we go to the movie theatre to see that new movie... The Birds?

Moose – That's funny you say the movie theatre... I was just remembering 2 weeks ago when Stew, Jimmy, Andrew, Paul and me went to the city to see the Nutty Professor, you talk about a crazy time... we all got kicked out with about 10 minutes left of the movie for laughing to loud... can you believe it?

Laura – You know, I could...

Moose – I mean it's a comedy... your supposed to laugh, that's why they made the movie to make people laugh... and we get kicked out...

Laura – That is funny (chuckles) my sister and Molly are going to see the Birds, then after words they are going to go have a late dinner at Marshawns...

Moose – Serious?

Laura – Yea... why?

Moose – Man, Marshawns is like expensive, ain't it?

Laura – Have you ever eaten there before?

Moose – No, a little out of my budget...

Laura – Well, being you are starting work tomorrow, it's my treat for the movies and dinner at Marshawns...

Moose – Are you kidding?

Laura – No silly, I'm not, sort of a celebration, congratulations for this new relation type thing... as long as you promise me something? (as they park and kiss in Laura's driveway)

Moose – What's that?

Laura – You promise not to keep your hands of me afterwards?

Moose – Believe or not... I can do that (kissing)

Jimmy is walking home, when Julie's mom Terry asks Jimmy if he would like a ride home as they drive by

Terry – Jimmy!

Jimmy – Hi...

Terry – Can we give you a ride home?

Jimmy – No thank you... I just live 3 blocks from here...

Terry – Are you sure?

Jimmy – Yea but thank you anyways...

Terry – Julie says for you to call her later...

Jimmy – Tell her o.k.

Terry – O.k. bye...

Jimmy – Bye.

Terry – Did his parents come?

Julie – No they both work... his father works out of town and the mom works in Gorman, she's like a city official or something and his father is like a corporate lawyer, so his grandmother lives with them and his little brother and sister...

Terry – Oh wow... good income...

Julie – Yea there well to do no doubt...

Terry – Sounds like it... I got a call from Joann... and she is supposed to be coming home this weekend...

Julie – You mean coming over?

Terry – No I mean coming home... to live...

Julie – What? ... please tell me you're jesting me please!

Terry – No unfortunately I'm not... she lost her job after 2 years and she's almost broke, so she asked if she can come hang out as she puts it... with us until she gets back on her feet...

Julie – Do you remember the last time we saw her?

Terry – Yes I do... but we need to put that behind us and forgive and forget and move on hopefully still caring and loving one another...

Julie – I don't think she knows how to spell caring or loving...

Terry - Now, now you too need to do your part to welcome her and make her feel wanted...

Julie – Please.

Nick pulls into the gas station he notices the garage is still closed and someone inside attending to someone on the floor... he hears sirens off in the distance, he approaches cautiously

Nick – Stay in the car and lock it (he tells Josephine)

Josephine – Be careful baby.

Customer – Hold on they're on the way man... (Jorge on the floor moaning holding his lower abdomen)

Nick – What happen?

Customer – I pulled in to put gas and I seen this guy staggering around holding his stomach... he was yelling I shot, I shot, so I called an ambulance...

Nick – Hold amigo there coming , you're gonna be alright, don't worry... Oh man I don't believe this...

(Ambulance and 2 police cars arrive... Josephine jumps out of the car and runs to Nick)

Josephine – What happen Nick?

Nick – Someone shot Jorge...

Josephine – Oh my God (starts to cry)

Nick – (Holds Josephine as the medics attend to Jorge and place him on the gurney... the police talk to the customer)

Josephine – What is going on here Nick?
Nick – I don't know baby...

Ambulance driver 1 – Are you guys family?

Nick – No, friends...

Ambulance driver – O.k. get a hold of his family we'll need them at County Hospital... he's lost quite a bit of blood....

Nick – (Nick looks to be in shock) Hang in there Jorge... I need you amigo (Nick goes into the office area and throws an object against the wall in anger and sits in confusion holding his head down on the desk) Man I don't believe this!

Josephine – Oh baby... (hugs Nick) Sheriff

Mel – Nick, are you o.k.?

Nick – Yea I'm o.k. everything is peachy keen...

Sheriff Mel – How soon after Jorge opened up or got here did this happen?

Nick – I don't know I just pulled up before you guy's... I got to get to the hospital...

Sheriff Mel – I'll see over there...

Nick – Hey Mel?... can you stop over and tell his wife?

Sheriff Mel – I'll do that Nick...

(Nick locks up and he and Josephine leave to the hospital)

Bill and Todd converse out in the school parking lot as they leave the high school cafeteria

Bill – Wow... so when is all this suppose to happen?

Todd – I guess a.s.a.p. … we're going tomorrow to Del Ray maybe even as far as Thousand Oaks… she wants to look at houses and… who knows…

Bill – And the business… you getting someone to run it or?

Todd – No… selling it… I mean it'll take some time I know, but we'll be selling everything and clearing town…

Bill – The house shouldn't take long to sell… the business might take a bit longer unless a large corporate company buys you out…

Todd – Yea maybe… well put some feelers out there and make yourself a commission or finders fee at least…

Bill – Hey… I'll do that…

Todd – Yea Philys wants out… the sooner the better…

Bill – Are you o.k. with that Todd, I mean you're only 51, you ready to retire?

Todd – Financially I'm alright, but yea way to young… I was thinking maybe selling some used tractor rigs or cars or a combination of them…

Bill – Maybe Nick can help set you up with the cars…

Todd – That's what I was thinking… I mean I don't need to make a killing I already did that, I just need something to do more or less…

Bill – It'll all work out for you guys, give us a reason to go visit you guys on the weekends…

Todd – There you go (as they stare at the wives chatting a distance away)

The Hospital E.R. room

(Josephine walks back to Nick from the bathroom)

Josephine – I wonder why his wife isn't here… I'm wondering if Mel even went to tell her…

Nick – Yea he did… I know Mel…

Josephine – Then I bet she wasn't home…

Nick – How long we been here?

Josephine – About an hour now…

Nick – Excuse me nurse can you tell me about how much longer Jorge Reynoso will be in surgery?

Floor Nurse – Let me go check for you... you said Jorge Reynoso?

Nick – Yes...thank you so much...

Josephine – Here comes Mel and Sheriff Coleman

Nick – Oh great...

Deputy Mel – Nick, Josephine, any word on how he's doing?

Sheriff Coleman – Here we go again huh Nick?

Nick – No word yet he's still in surgery...

Josephine – Deputy, no witnesses?

Deputy Mel – Not one yet, we're still hoping...

Nick – Did you go by Jorge's?

Deputy Mel – Oh, a neighbor said I just missed her, so I went to the grocery store where they said she was going, nothing... so I drove around town and witnessed an accident , so I got caught up, then went to their house again, nothing so I came here...

Sheriff Coleman – I heard through dispatch radio and came right over...

Josephine – There's the surgeon...

Nick – How is he doc?

Surgeon – He's stable... he's lost a lot of blood, he's not out of danger, but we stop the bleeding...

Sheriff Coleman – How's his chances doctor?

Surgeon – 50/50 right now, as time goes on his chances will increase...

Nick – Oh man the last time we heard this we lost Tommy boy...

Josephine – Nick...

Surgeon – If it's any consolation... he did say for us to put him together good because he had to work tomorrow...

Josephine – Thank you doctor... can he be seen?

Surgeon – Not at the moment unless you are immediate family, but he will be out for the rest of the day, so he can get some strength back from the blood we put back in him...

Deputy Mel – Thanks doc...

Sheriff Coleman – Thank you doctor...

Nick – Alright... I need to go find Moose to tell him to find another helper for tomorrow... hey Mel look me up in the morning if you still need more info... but I need to go...

Deputy Mel – O.k. Nick see ya.

(Nick and Josephine leave the E.R. room to head to Moose's house)

Josephine – Do you think this was an attempted robbery Nick or...

Nick – I don't know... could be... could be revenge from Midland, I just don't know...

Moose's house, as Moose walks out headed towards Laura's car when Nick pulls up

Moose – What's happening Bossa Nova?

Nick – Hey Moose... hey listen Jorge was shot man...

Moose – What? when?, where?

Nick – He went to open up the station after the funeral and somebody popped him...

Moose – Ah dog gone it Nick... man what are we gonna do man, lets end this damn war already (Moose walks in a circle rubbing his head in anger)

Nick – Come on Moose!

Moose – Shoot ! (Moose walks away and circles back with his hands on his hips in discuss)

Nick – Listen... I don't need for you to throw fuel on the fire man, I need you to let this thing smoke itself out... I know it's frustrating, but we can't add to the stupidity big boy...undesrstand?

Moose – Listen to me man... let's rid of thing once and for all, lets you and me go to the city boys and tell them a rumble between their best 5 against our best 5 at the halfway point and loser go home and it's over man... like the old days Nick!

Nick – That would...

Moose – That would work, you know it will... come on Nick, these stupid cop's aren't going to end it, they don't have a clue... the only thing they know how to do is right a ticket and harass you after words... it makes sense Nick!

Nick – You're probably right man…but…

Moose – Oh I know I'm right Nick… that's how you guy's did it right… to put a stop to things or to make a point right?

Nick – (Nick takes a deep breath as Josephine looks on from the car) Let's talk more in the morning… can you get someone to help us for tomorrow?

Moose – Ah… yea let me talk to Red… I can probably get him…

Nick – O.k. let's put the help wanted sign out there tomorrow morning and you do some quick interviews and let's see if we hire someone fulltime, because more than likely Jorge will be out for a while…

Moose – O.k. Nick… In the meantime go talk to Juan, Tony and Alberto and lets end this once and for all…

Nick – (Chuckles and smiles) That's a good team (Nick shakes Moose's hand and heads back to his car)

Josephine – So what was all the drama about?

Nick – You know Moose (Starts the car and heads out)

Deputy Mike pulls Juan over on the street

Deputy – Hey Juan how are you?

Juan – Aye ese whats happening?

Deputy Mike – Oh getting to be that time of year again you know

Juan - Oh o.k. how many you need this year?

Deputy Mike – Well we got a bit more this year than last year because of all those vines from 2 years ago... so I think with 10 they ought to be able to pick and box up in what... 2 days?

Juan – For when?

Deputy Mike – Next weekend?

Juan – O.k. look, here's what we'll do... 12 workers $30. each and a bucket of grapes for each 8 hours, on Saturday and 8 hours for Sunday anything over 8 hours on Sunday is $2 an hour straight

Deputy Mike – Orale Juan... your straight up my friend... thank you (they shake hands)

Juan – De nada... anything for friends, you know that carnal...

Deputy Mike – I do...

Back at the hospital

(Nick and Josephine walk back into the E.R. room and see Sal with Jorge's wife and children)

Sal – Nicky, Josephine...

Josephine – Nonno (quick hug)

Nick – Mr. C... any word... Hi Rosa, I'm so sorry...

Rosa – I Nicky... (crying) I'm so scared for Jorge...

Nick – He's gonna be fine... he's too tough and strong for this to hurt him Rosa, you know him better than anyone else...

Josephine – Rosa... don't worry mama he's going to be fine...

Nick – Sit down here... have you talked to the doctor?

Rosa – Yes, he is stable, he sleeping right now (takes a deep breath)

Nick – Good... hey kid's, your papa is going to be o.k. you guy's keep thanking God for that o.k.? it could have been worse, but he's alright.. and God loves him too o.k.? (kids smile and agree)

Sal – Nicky – Can I talk to you?

Nick – Sure (They walk off to the side) what's up Sal?

Sal – If you know son, more than what you're sharing with me or anyone else like the sheriff's, I can understand... but you need to to let others help if possible Nicky before somebody dies again...

Nick – I'm not understanding what it is you think I'm hiding? You must have spoken with Coleman...

Sal – Well there's a reason why these guy's keep coming over here trying to hurt more people, that's why I'm asking and yes Sheriff Coleman is concerned, that's his job job...

Nick – I don't know... and I don't have nothing to share with anyone in regards to why or who or what the problem is... we are a target and we either sit here at the expense of our safety or the cops got to step in and put a stop to it or we're going to do it… (Nick expresses his anger)

Sal – What do you mean we're going to do it?… are you talking the old ways? (Nick doesn't respond, he looks away) what are you talking Nick, a good old fashion rumble… huh?

Nick – I'm not talking nothing Mr. C… but I'm worried… we could of lost Jorge today… we already lost 4 good friends… I lost my dad and my childhood cause of this foolishness, do I need to lose my life too, to try and end this?

(Josephine looks towards Nick and Sal and notices some tension)

Sal – Don't be talking this craziness Nicky… you're a business owner and future success story to the young generation and you have a beautiful bride to be you've been blessed with… don't ruin it now son…

Nick – I know Mr. C, I've been fighting all my life… it's like the only thing I know how to do better than I fix car's and sometimes fighting fixes things at least in my life it does…

Sal – I know son I already preached to you about fighting, about fighting for yourself to overcome all this past life and fighting for you future and for what's right, I'm not going to continue to harass you cause I know you're a smart young man Nicky... but you need to go through all this and grow through it son... that's the plan God has laid out for you and you can flow with it or struggle up stream with it, but it's yours to overcome regardless which direction you take... now you know you have mine and Sofia's support behind you and you have that bella giovane donna (beautiful young woman) and her family and every young and old person in this town behind you too son... don't throw it all away...

Nick – I know... thank you (Nick hugs Sal) I think you just saved more lives.

Moose at Jimmy's house

Jimmy – So you don't think they'll come back tomorrow and shoot us?

Moose – I hope not... and heck if they do we'll see Tommy boy and Stewie and them again, right?

Jimmy – Don't be a wise guy...

Moose – Why you all dolled up Red? Boy you got it working dude, seven seas, a little dab will do you (touches his hair) a gleem smile, where you headed?

Jimmy – Oh... Julie invited me over to their house tonight, so I thought I'd go over and spend some time with her and her mom and apparently her sister Joann is like headed home so...

Moose – Oh yea? How old is Joann?

Jimmy – She's 20...

Moose – Well make sure you let me know what she looks like huh? I hear she's a cooker...

Jimmy – What are you doing?

Moose – Taking Laura... well actually Laura is taking me to dinner then to the movie theatre, but Nick says to stay away from Midland, so I think we might head over to Grand Park...

Jimmy – Cool man... what time in the morning?

Moose – He opens at 7 a.m. but I'll pick you up at 6:30 to show you the ropes... later gator... (Moose heads out)

Jimmy – O.k. Moose, have a good time

Moose – I plan on it... but you make sure you don't...

Laura's front porch. Cindy and Laura talking

Laura – Yea we're just going to get out of town you know, it's like a week ago tonight when they planned the hold thing and, well Tommy and Maryann, Stewie and Paul were still alive a week ago, so I'm going to take Moose out to dinner and then to a movie and who knows I just want to keep his mind busy, he starts work tomorrow with Nick at the station...

Cindy – Oh wow, sounds like you got plans for the big guy huh?

Laura – Oh yea... you know I've always liked that goon since we were kids...

Cindy – I know... wow wee..

Laura – And all through high school... and now I find out that this guy has plans on becoming a carpenter builder guy and you know what, I want to get some business classes down and I just figured we might make a pretty good team you know...

Cindy – Hey girl that is way cool... I wonder if Moose might be able to get Eddie a job there with Nick too?

Laura – Ah you know if Eddie is cool like you say... you know Nick, that's like the major skill you'll need to have on your job application with Nick you know, if you're cool your hired (they both laugh) on a scale of 1 to 10 how cool are you? (they laugh)

Cindy – I'ma 7 and a half man... Eddie's headed in tonight and he's staying at the motel because he wants to find a job out here hopefully this weekend...

Laura – Ask Moose, here comes now...

Cindy – Yea let me run it buy him...

Moose – What are you 2 cupcakes up too?

Laura – Hey handsome (kisses Moose)

Cindy – Hey Moose... you told me you know who Eddie Hernandez is right?

Moose – Yea I know the cat...

Cindy – Well... the cat is coming in to town tonight cause he be lookin for a job tomorrow and I was wondering if...

Moose – Has he ever pumped gas before?

Cindy – As a matter a fact he's a good pumper...

Moose – What the heck does that mean?... wait don't tell me, I don't want to know (they all laugh)

Laura – What's a good pumper? (all laughing)

Cindy – I don't know, I just thought that's what you guys called someone who's pumped gas or worked a gas station before...

Moose – Oh, he's worked at a gas station before?

Cindy – Yea... he's worked a few places...

Moose – Yea, wow Nick told me to put the help wanted sign out tomorrow morning because we need to hire a couple of guy's... then Jorge goes and gets shot this afternoon by some nit wit...

Cindy – Oh my God... what?

Moose – Yea...

Cindy – Is he o.k.?

Moose – Yea he a tough guy you know... just wait til his son hears about it, he's going to be riding into town bringing hell's hounds with him and there's going to be trouble... with a capital T...

Laura – Oh yea... they use to call him little Jorge, but that wasn't his name huh? It was like Christopher or...

Cindy – Cristobal... I think...

Laura – Yea Cristobal...

Cindy – What ever happen to him any ways?

Moose – Prison time...

Cindy – What he do...

Moose – 3 to 7...

Laura – 3 to 7?

Moose – 3 to 7 years

Laura – For what?

Moose - Beating one of Tomkins foreman guy's brains in... you don't remember that?

Cindy – How old is he now?

Moose – He's like 22 or 23..I know he's out of prison because Jorge told me he wasn't like welcomed back in this town, so he's down in the San Diego area where they have family and stuff, but apparently he runs with a bad crowd of motorcycle dudes...

Laura – Oh yea, there will be trouble no doubt...

Cindy – Not for anybody here...right?

Moose – No... hope not...

Laura – Well big boy, you ready to head out?

Moose – Im'a ready teddy...

Cindy – O.k. Teddy, I'm going to send him in o.k. in the morning?

Moose – Have him show up at 8 a.m. I'll tell Nick and I think if Nick likes him he's on like King Kong...

Cindy – O.k. thanks Moose... have a good one Laura...

Laura – Oh I plan on it (laugh)

Cindy – (Cindy walking to her car yells out) Whooo hooo!

Moose – She's nuts... plain and simple...

Laura – Yea well I'm nuts for you (hug and kiss)

Back at the hospital, Nick and Josephine preparing to leave

Nick – O.k. Rosa, you call me if anything happens or if you need anything you here?

Sonia – O.k. Nick, thank you hijo…

Nick – Georgie… you the man for now huh… you watch your familia understand? … you call me if you need anything o.k.?

Georgie – O.k. Nick…

Josephine – Bye Rosa… we're praying for you all… Jorge is going to be alright… he loves you guys too much to let this stop him…

Sonia – O.k. gracias hija…

Josephine – Bye kids.

(Jorge's 2 young daughters and 16 year old son Georgie wave bye)

Nick – I gotta get you home…

Josephine – Home? Why?

Nick – You got to be exhausted…

Josephine – I don't want to go home... I want to be with you baby...

Nick – I too with you... you hungry?

Josephine – Oh yes, I'm starving...

Nick – O.k. let's pick something up and go rest at my pad...

Josephine – Now that sounds like a plan Stan...

Nick – Stan?

Moose and Laura in Laura's car driving

Moose – You really want to go way out there?

Laura – I want what you want... either way it's my treat...

Moose – You know what?

Laura – What?

Moose – My mom and my little darlings, went to Bakersfield to my aunts for the weekend and ummm...

Laura – Really?

Moose – Really … and I was wondering if ah, if ah, you ah, you know ah… humma humma humma mama…

Laura – (smacks Moose on the arm) Stop you goofy guy (laughs)

Moose – What I want is to eat and be alone with you (kisses her)

Laura – (Mmmm) Me too… let's stop at Howies and get some grub and head over to your house… hows that for humma humma?

Moose – Hey you read my mind girl… Howies then Moose's it tis…

Laura – Yes siri Bob!

(Moose and Laura pull into Howies Burgers parking lot and notice Tony and Marianna ordering at the window, then notice across the lot most of the group known as Los Muchachos were all in the parking lot feasting on burgers, fries and shakes and soda's)

Moose – What's happening amigo?

Tony – Hey… Alce grande (Big Moose)

Moose – Hey… you and the senorita out for some good ol Mexican food are ya?

Tony – Mexican … na, this the best gringo food in the state right here holmes…

Laura – (shouts from the car) Hi Marianna (waves hello)

Marianna – Oh hello Laura (waves back)

(Tony and Marianna get their food and head across the lot to the rest of their hang out friends)

Tony – Hey will check you later holmes… we're gonna go throw a scarf aye…

Moose – Later ese…

Cashier (Nadine) – Hey Moose, can I take your order?

Moose – Of course… I'll take 2 cheese burgers, 2 fries, 2 shakes, ah, 1 chocolate and 1 strawberry and 1 cherry coke…

Nadine – And what about for Laura?

Moose – Ha ha funny… there's enough comedians out of a work huh…

Nadine – That'll be $2.75…

Moose – There you go (pays her)

Michelle – And there's your change big spender... do you want it delivered or you gonna pick it up?

Moose – I'm right here... I'll pick it up...

Michelle – Order #126.

Moose (Grabs his receipt and turns to walk back to Laura's car and see's Juan and Los Muchachos) Ese Juan, what's up amigo?

Juan – Alce! ... que pasa Moose (all the Muchachos greet Moose with a Moose chant) Moooooose!

Moose - (Moose smiles and waves and raises both hands in victory) Orale Muchachos!

(Cindy and Eddie Hernandez come cruising into the burger parking lot in Eddie's 54 Chevy)

Laura – Hey did you see Cindy and Eddie just pulled in?

Moose – (Gets back into the car) Oh yea... It's been awhile since I last seen Eddie... where they at?

Laura – Back towards the back...

Moose – Oh... well well well... look it here...

Laura – Wow everybody's here

Moose – Hey Red bird...Julie!

Jimmy – I thought you were heading out?

Moose – Yea well we changed our minds... you know... You guys eating?

Julie – Nah we grubbed... we're just grabbing a shake (waves at Laura)

Laura – Hey girl... why don't we grab an outside table...

Moose - Yea sure... you guys wanna grab a seat?

Jimmy – Sure... why not...

Cindy – (Cindy and Eddie come walking up to the window) Hey this isn't Marshawns...

Laura – Yea we changed plans...

Moose – What's shaking Hernandez number 81?

Eddie – Hey what's going on Moose man (they shake hands)

Moose – You didn't go to JC?

Eddie – Nah… actually got a partial ride to Fresno St. … but still man could shake with it with grades… yet…

Moose – Oh wow… yea they came to talk to me… but the grades too you know… they told me I'd have to do a year at JC and see if I could bring em up you know…

Eddie – You gonna do it?

Moose – Ahh… I don't know… hey you guys get your order we'll grab a table come join us…

(As Moose and Laura walk to secure a table Nick and Josephine pull in and Park by Los Muchachos)

Juan – Orale Nicholas! Whats happening gato?

Nick – Juan… Los Muchachos! (Josephine waves at Gloria, Juan's girl and Marianna)

(An order taker on skates see's that Nick Pagani pulled in she hurries to get his order)

Skater – Hi Nick, Hi Josephine, 2 number 1's with chocolate shakes?

Josephine – You got it sweetie…

Skater – Coming right up?

Juan – Hijole, you come pullin in and they jump on your order like you own the joint (laughs)

Tony – They never come to take our order, even if we pull up to the order box vato…

Nick – (laughs) Don't take it personal ese… they probably think you're gonna order some tacos…

Tony – Aye don't knock it holmes, me and my old lady are thinking of opening up a taco standhere in town…

Nick – Hey we'll be your first and best customers… guarantee you that hitone…

Tony – That's o.k. with me man…

(5 newer cars go driving past the burger joint, 1 rev's up the engine… Los Muchachos notice along with several other patrons) Juan – Did you see that Nick?

Nick – I heard it… who was it?

Sergio – There was 5 car's ese…

Arturo – That's the third time they past aye…

Nick – City boy's?

Arturo – Got to be... expensive caruchas...

Tony – Let's block em off...

Nick – No...

Juan – What are you thinking holmes?

Nick – Someone shot Jorge today after the funeral there at the station...

Juan – What? Obviously he's o.k. right, otherwise you wouldn't be here right?

Nick – He's gonna be fine... but...

Tony – It might be these vato's Nick let's cut em off and find out...

Nick – Yea it might be... and these vatos might still have the guns Tony... then what?

Sergio – Well we'll find out... here they come...

Juan – Pongase trucha...

(Nick steps out of his truck as the 5 cars come pulling in with an average of 5 guys per car)

Nick – Jesse make your way to Howie and have him call the sheriff's office now...

Jessie – Gotcha Nick (Jessie runs to Howie)

(Moose notices the potential situation and stands up to look on) Here we go, come on Eddie, it's a nice time to meet Nick...

Eddie - Right behind you big man (Jimmy follows)

Laura – Man these guy's might be the ones that shot Jorge... Be careful Moose!

(The 5 cars stop right in the middle of the driveway, one rev's it up again, then they all shut off their engines... a guy in the first car gets off followed by all the others.. This guy is known as the Animal, his name Big Jim Antinello, 6'4 270lbs. of rock solid muscle... He was a star football player at Midland Central High and went on to a major college to play football but was unable to play after 3 season due to a major knee injury 4 years ago)

Big Jim – Who's who?

Nick – Who's asking?

Big Jim – I'm asking... the guy right in front of you...

Nick – I'm Nick (Nick walks towards him)

Big Jim – Well Nick, I'm big Jim, did you or any of you're compadres here have anything to do with killing our friends, family members?

Nick – No... nobody here... but I do know that your dead friends did in fact kill our dead friends...

Big Jim – You know that for a fact Nick... were you there?

Nick – Yea... I was Jim and you're dead friends almost killed me and my fiancée and 2 friends who riding with me and happen to kill the guy that your friends, perhaps family jumped in the bathroom and beat him pretty bad at the show...

Juan – What are you here to do, lynch us or shoot us?

Big Jim – To tell you the truth... we're here to do what the cops refuse to do, investigate this problem here between our two towns...

Moose – You're damn cops are dirty...

Jimmy – They are the reason why everybody's dead big Jim...

Nick – All right cool it...

Big Jim – We're looking for answers...that's all...

Juan – Why you come here with an attitude ese?

One of the other guy's – No one's talking to you ese...

Tony – A you know what (starts to go towards the other guy)

Arturo – Calmate...

Nick – Be cool Tony... it's alright...

Big Jim – (Tells his own guy) Do you remember what I said?

Other guy – Sorry...

Big Jim – Don't mind him... he's a little upset cause one of his closest cousins died last weekend in that shooting...

Moose – We buried 4 of our closest friends today all in one funeral and then today my employee was shot at my station, so excuse me if we seem a little defensive Mr. Jim...

Big Jim – All 4... wow... I guess out of the 7 that died they buried 2 today and 2 more scheduled for tomorrow the rest next week and 1 guy died last night... so that's 8 with one still critical condition...

Nick – Look man... no one won anything from this... like I said one of my workers was shot today at my station, we don't who and we're not accusing you or anyone else, but we too need answers...

Big Jim – Is he dead?

Nick – No he's gonna be o.k....

Big Jim – No, I think if anyone was brave enough or stupid enough to have done that, sure wouldn't be cruising back up in here tonight you know...

Nick – Yea well, when revenge becomes a priority, people tend not to think right.

(2 sheriff car's with 4 deputy's pull in behind the visitors)

Deputy Mike – Good evening gentlemen...

Los Muchachos – Good evening Deputy Michaelson (All laugh)

Nick – Deputy...

Deputy Mike – Is everything o.k. here or should I call for backup?

Big Jim – I think everything is stable, don't you think Nick?

Nick – I'd say so...

Deputy Mel – Hey Nick, the grandson of that old man is being processed out right now, for lack of evidence and they captured a guy in Larkston robbing a gas station attendant, that fits the profile of Jorge's shooter...

Moose – Cool man...

Nick – That's very cool...

Big Jim – Is that guy that's being released Dan's brother?

Deputy Mike – Yea... Donald Mills...

Big Jim – Is that good news for you guys or bad news?

Deputy Mike – Nick here didn't want to press charges on the grandfather, after he tried running Nick over... then Nick didn't want to press charges on the kid because he wants to try and put an end to all this mess between South County and Midland... so it's good news to us...

Big Jim – The Mill's are related to me...

Nick – You know I'm no lawyer and I know all this might be considered hear say but, I think those dirt bag brother's Frank and Fred Billings not only put all your guys up to their dirty deeds to what they did and then somehow some way killed them off to hide any witnesses of the event... that's just my opinion...

Deputy Mike – That's what it's starting to look like...

Deputy Mel – We have 8 investigators on this case working non- stop and we cannot find anything that doesn't lead to the Billings brothers setting this entire tragedy up... but we'll keep looking...

Big Jim – Huh... I never realized and I don't think anyone else did either about those Billings having set everything up and killing off any and all witnesses... makes sense as evil as they were...

2nd other guy – What started all this mess anyway? Hasn't this fight been going on like forever?

Nick – 21 years... My father's best friend Steve Bennett and Phillip Billings got into a fight outside of a dance at the college in

1942, according to a couple of witnesses that were there all said the same story, so I had to take it as the truth...It was a fair fight they said and pretty even when Billings pulled out a switch blade, so my dad distracted him, when Billings turned his head Steve shoved him to get away, Billings fell and hit his head on a car bumper... the crowd was still as they check on Billings, then out of the dark a shot fired hitting Steve in the back and everybody scattered but my dad, he drove them both to the hospital, only to have them tell him they both had died immediately... things were never the same since... that went for my dad too.

Big Jim – What happen to your dad?

Nick – Drank himself to death... couldn't handle the whole ordeal... you know.

Big Jim – (Big Jim walks up to Nick. Everybody stands alert and ready for anything) I'm really sorry for your family and for this whole entire mess (shakes Nicks hand and hugs him, then turns and makes an announcement) The only reason why we came over here was to find some type of closure for our friends families, My name is Jim Antinello also known as Big Jim a.k.a The Animal... we can't get no answers from our police department so we thought we'd take matters into our own hands and take a chance and come get some answers. I am studying Law Enforcement classes at the academy and I am about 6 months away from graduation... we weren't looking for trouble just answers and I think Nick here and the sheriffs have given us what we came for and as far as I'm concerned this fued or rivalry is over, done... finished.

(As the crowd surrounded the entire parking lot area where this potential confrontation was taking place, everyone cheered and applauded Big Jim as Nick and Big Jim hugged again and everyone began to shake hands and cheer with delight as if they had just won the world series)

Nick – (Nick and Josephine hug and kiss as Nick gets up on the tailgate of his truck) Hey can I have your attention please... hey look this is probably a week to late, but Tommy boy and company are probably why this all took place... and now it's because of them and the boys from midland who lost their lives looking down on us right now...Howie I hope you have enough, but in celebration of our new found friends Soda's or shakes on me for everyone here... That includes you guys Mikey! (jumps down from his truck)

(Everyone becomes relaxed and feeling good about this truce that was just declared by the Midland City boy's. Groups break off, shaking hands and sparking up conversation... Los Muchachos begin to talk to some of the guy's about their custom cars, Moose and Big Jim greet each other and begin talking about football and Tommy boy... while everyone else goes back to what they were doing prior to the arrival of the city boys.)

(Nick sits on his tailgate of the truck and Josephine leans against him)

Josephine – Man look at this... peace between the small town and the big city... amazing...

Nick – Yea... do you somehow get the feeling that Tommy boy, Maryann, Stew and Paul and maybe some of those other cats had anything to do with this?

Jospehine – Maybe... but with all the prayers that have been going on this past week, I'm going to give God the credit...

Nick – For sure...

Deputy Mike – Well looks like our work is done here...

Deputy Mel – Can you believe it Nick?

Nick – Just another thing that'll take some time to sink in...

Deputy Mike – Well let's just hope the big man over there will go back to Midland and get it all straightened out with the rest of them...

Nick – I don't think anyone is going to object to anything he says or wants to do... do you?

Deputy Mel – Nooo way... that is one Large man (they all laugh)

Deputy Mike - Well let's get our shakes and get back to work...

(This night has a certain peace that lingers in the entire town and has not only brought peace, but unity and new beginnings for many)

Julie – So Jimmy... what do you think of all this?

Jimmy – Well at least they didn't bring the beast out in me again to have to lay another bomb on them (Cindy, Eddie, Julie all laugh)

Eddie – So Jimmy, Cindy tells me you're going to be mayor of this town one day huh?

Jimmy – That's right, by the time I'm 24, I'll be mayor of this small town and then we'll grow it together to a big town…

Eddie – So you really into politics huh?

Jimmy – Yea I am, as a matter of fact I'm planning on going to Dallas Texas in a few weeks to see President Kennedy…

Eddie – Cool man…

Cindy – That's really cool…

Julie – Yea… maybe I'll sneek away with you… (Over across the parking lot)

Marianna – Hey baby, maybe know we can go to the city to shop…

Tony – Orale… lets make sure the coast is clear baby… I'd hate to be the ones to find out that not everybody over there know's, that we all smoked the peace pipe… sabes?

Marianna – Oh that's true…

Jesse – A Juan… I'm going to walk over to Tina's, Katey is buying me dinner and we're going to tell her parents that we're going steady…

Juan _ Anda menso... I'll start planning your funeral first thing in the morning (They all laugh)

Jesse – Ah cut it out... Later gators...

Tony – Hey Jesse make sure her dad don't put no veneno in you sopa mijo (they all laugh)

Marianna – Povrecito... don't tell him that...

Gloria – Deharlo... you guys are going to scare him...

Juan – He's too much in love to be scared...

Alberto – Yea , senor cupid got him right in the heart aye...

Arturo – Right in the nalgas ese ... que heart (still laughing)

The Combs residence

(Bob and Susan sitting on the couch drinking coffee)

Bob – What a day huh?

Susan – I'll say... has our world changed or what?

Bob – Well as our son would have said… or What!

Susan – First we lose Stewart, then we bury him, but financially it don't cost us anything, then you get a job that pays you 3 times more, a company car and over $6000. to catch up and get ahead on life… wow!

Bob – We didn't lose Stewart Susan… he's still here with us in spirit, I can feel him and he'll always be here with us…

Susan – Your right,I know he is too, I'm sorry for saying that…

Bob – You know what… you're still young, I'm still young… we can have that little brother or little sister Stew has always wanted us to have… what do you think?

Susan – Are you serious? I was going to eventually talk to you about that, but I thought you'd…

Bob – Hey, let's not think for each other, let's just get away for a week or so and start working on our new addition (kissing)

Susan – I'd like that.

What everybody is doing at the moment

(Andrew and Kathy are watching t.v. at the Styles resident, while Paula Sr. and Debbie entertaining family in the kitchen)

(Connie sits with friends at Tina's Diners as Jessie walks in and is greeted by Katie)

(The McCalls at home sharing pictures of Tommy with family as they drink coffee and enjoy desert)

(Joe and Gina entertain Sal and Sofia)

(The Swenson's sit with family members at the dinner table)

(Sheriff Coleman and his wife are out to dinner with Detectives Mitchell and Carson and their wives)

(Rev. Williams is visiting with a his daughter and her family) (Molly and Lily are having dinner at Marshawns)

(Terry answers the door to find Joann has come home as they embrace)

(Ron Tomkins sits in his truck across the street from Howies Burgers, staring at the crowd in the parking lot... he opens the Midland City newspaper and reads 2 obituaries that will take place tomorrow, of the 2 boys that jumped his son Raymond and smiles knowing these 2 boys have been paid back for their crime, in his eyes)

(Jorge is being comforted by his wife and 3 children as he lay's awake being fed jello by his wife... and in the dark parking lot of the hospital a roar in the distance approaches rapidly... and into the parking arrives a thunderous motorcycle... Jorge's oldest son Cristobal)

www.ingramcontent.com/pod-product-compliance
Lightning Source LLC
Chambersburg PA
CBHW020328030826
48979CB00021B/476

* 9 7 8 1 9 6 2 3 6 6 5 7 1 *